JUDY MURRAY is a former Scottish international tennis player and has 64 national titles to her name. In 1995, she became the Scottish National Coach. Judy is a powerful voice in the battle for equality of opportunity for women in sport and was awarded an OBE for services to tennis, women in sport and charity. Alongside her tennis and coaching achievements, Judy was a contestant on *Strictly Come Dancing* in 2014 and a Costa Book Award judge in 2021, and she made her debut at the Edinburgh Fringe in 2022. Her memoir, *Knowing the Score*, was a *Sunday Times* bestseller and nominated for Sports Book of the Year. Her debut novel, *The Wild Card*, was released in 2023. *Game, Set & Murder* is her second novel.

Also by Judy Murray

The Wild Card
Knowing the Score

GAME, SET & MURDER

Judy Murray

ORION

First published in Great Britain in 2025 by Orion Fiction,
an imprint of The Orion Publishing Group Ltd.
Carmelite House, 50 Victoria Embankment
London EC4Y 0DZ

An Hachette UK Company

The authorised representative in the EEA is Hachette Ireland,
8 Castlecourt Centre, Dublin 15, D15 XTP3, Ireland (email: info@hbgi.ie)

1 3 5 7 9 10 8 6 4 2

A CIP catalogue record for this book is
available from the British Library.

ISBN (Hardback) 9781 3987 1138 9
ISBN (Ebook) 9781 3987 1141 9
ISBN (Audio) 9781 3987 1142 6

Typeset at The Spartan Press Ltd,
Lymington, Hants

Printed and bound in Great Britain by Clays Ltd,
Elcograf S.p.A.

MIX
Paper | Supporting
responsible forestry
FSC
www.fsc.org
FSC® C104740

www.orionbooks.co.uk

GAME, SET
& MURDER

Prologue

ELEANOR

The grass will turn soon, thought Eleanor as she walked from the pavilion to the clubhouse. Give it a week and the courts will be looking somewhat less than perfect.

The gentle *pt-pt-pt* of the sprinklers had been the soundtrack to the last couple of months at the Royal Oaks Tennis and Country Club. But summer was at its height and the grass had been used so heavily over the last few sun-dappled weeks that there was only so much that they could achieve without a decent downpour. Still, it was a good job they'd got the league matches played before the perfect green of the courts gave way to scruffy tinges of beige and brown.

As Eleanor tucked her long grey hair behind her ears, she felt a sense of immense satisfaction at the way the season had gone so far. It really had been splendid, and now a win for the ladies' team to top it all off. She brimmed with pride as she approached the white-washed steps to the clubhouse, ready for another day of making sure that every single second at the Royal Oaks ran as smoothly as her members expected.

She heard a stranger's voice.

''Scuse me, ma'am?'

A well-built young man was approaching her from his van, his hair in a neat, twisted bun at the back of his head. It was the sort she'd seen on some of the professional footballers who regularly frequented the club. His hands were upturned in front of him, and on them was balanced a large cardboard box.

'Yes?'

'A delivery for the club ...'

'May I ask who it's addressed to?' she said with a polite smile, glancing at his baggy grey tracksuit bottoms. Hopefully it was just a bulk order of protein powder or something similar she could redirect towards the gym block.

'Doesn't say, just got the club's name on it.'

Eleanor leaned forward to peer at the label on the lid of the box. He was quite right.

'And the invoice?' she asked.

He balanced the box on one hand as he unfolded the invoice taped to the side.

'Ah, order ref says, "Congratulations ladies, and enjoy the tea party."'

'No name?'

'No name.'

Still, it must be someone who knows about the event, and the club, Eleanor figured.

'Follow me, I'll sign for it at the desk myself,' she told him, leading the way up the steps and into the clubhouse. 'Let's get it out of the sun, shall we?'

But the courier wasn't listening, apparently immune to her brisk charm and efficiency. Instead, he was gazing at the club's interior. It was undeniably impressive, from the depth of the carpets to the uniquely expensive smell of the dressing and steam rooms just a little further down the corridor.

Behind Eleanor was a wall almost entirely covered by annual team photos of the winners of various leagues and tournaments. Precise configurations of players, knees neatly together, smiling at the camera with their silverware lined up before them; row after row, until the lower rows turned to faded seventies Kodachrome, then eventually black-and-white images. Smile after smile looked out, grinning proudly. Decades' worth of achievement by what Eleanor liked to call the Royal Oaks Family. And all on display for each and every visitor who passed reception to admire.

'So, I presume it's a cake?' said Eleanor as she gently pulled the box across the front desk towards her, noticing as she did that the driver's T-shirt had 'Cake-issimo' looping across it in gaudy pink italics.

'Sometimes it's buns.' He shrugged. 'I just deliver the boxes, ma'am, I don't know what they've put inside.'

She watched as his eyes were drawn to the members' noticeboard, with its tapestry of announcements of social events: book club (an iconic cricket player's biography), a history talk (the evolution of the marathon), an upcoming theatre trip to the West End (*Dear England*). Eleanor was pleased; she'd rearranged the noticeboard just last week – at least someone had noticed.

'Will there be a note inside saying who it's from?' she asked.

'No idea,' he replied, a hint of irritation in his voice now.

A young woman walked past in navy leggings and a boxy puffer jacket, holding hands with two tiny children in immaculate tennis whites. *How young do these people start?*

'Everyone's bringing one, you see – a cake – for the celebratory tea this afternoon. I don't want them to get muddled,' Eleanor continued. She lifted the cardboard lid from the box until she could see inside, then let out a gasp of delight.

'Oh, it's for our championship team!' she exclaimed. The man looked blankly back at her. 'Our Ladies Team won the Southeast District League last week. We're so proud of them.'

Eleanor beamed as she looked down at the cake, then pushed it towards the surly man so he could peer down at it too. Inside was a neat sponge rectangle covered in green fondant icing, with immaculately piped white lines denoting a tennis court. On one side of the tiny latticed-sugar net stood four marzipan players, a couple of whom had their hands raised in victory, while the middle two held tiny tennis rackets.

There they all were: Kristin and Vanessa, the Chappell sisters, at either end of the group; then Hailey and Beatriz (or Bibi, as she was often called) between them. Younger sister Kristin was identifiable by the brown plait of neatly folded marzipan down her back, while her older sister Vanessa's shoulder length black locks had probably been an easier task for the cake's creator. Hailey's mini-me figurine was perhaps the most recognisable, complete with a mass of blonde curls and her trademark sweatband; then Bibi, whose marzipan hair was in a high ponytail, and at her ears were two tiny dots of yellow icing. *Such attention to detail*, Eleanor thought – Bibi always wore those familiar gold earrings, even when playing.

'Cute,' said the delivery driver. 'Right, well, if you're happy to accept the package, I just need a signature, ma'am.' He held out a plastic device for Eleanor to sign.

'Oh, and there's their trophy!' Eleanor continued, spotting a small marzipan trophy, delicately balanced on the 'grass' in front of the figurines. The champions.

'A signature, please, ma'am,' the man huffed.

'Oh, right, yes, of course,' she said, scribbling a signature onto the screen of the device and handing it back to him. 'Well, what a lovely touch. I'm sure we'll find out who ordered the cake in due course. Thank you for dropping it off.'

'Enjoy your party,' the man replied, his smile not reaching his eyes, before he headed back through the door and into his delivery van. Eleanor winced as he accelerated out of the drive of the Royal Oaks, the wheels of his van screeching.

★

Five hours later, Eleanor hurried back to the front lawn outside the clubhouse to stare up at the moody-looking sky. The day had been a whirlwind of preparations for the celebrations that afternoon and now the weather was threating to ruin everything.

A whoop went up in the distance and Eleanor saw that the victorious ladies team were having their commemorative photographs taken. As was tradition, four chairs had been lined up in front of the one-hundred-year-old clock tower that stood between the original grass show courts.

A future classic for the ladies' dressing room, thought Eleanor with a smile as she watched Vanessa, Kristin, Hailey and Bibi toss their tennis caps into the air in jubilation. She was so proud of those women: the way they carried themselves with such good-natured confidence, the way they wore their victory so lightly, the way they all had *so much* on their plates and yet never hesitated to give *so much* back to the club.

She watched the four women as they made their way back towards the clubhouse past the ornamental lake, waving at her as they did. Vanessa slung her arm around her sister Kristin, giving her back a congratulatory rub as they walked. Eleanor smiled to herself as she watched them: they really did look just like their tiny cake caricatures.

Kristin's plait was neat, chestnut brown hair scraped back off her face, while Vanessa was the spitting image of a young Posh Spice. Even Hailey's sweatband was the same colour as its tiny marzipan replica. *Someone had taken a great deal of care over that cake*, she thought.

Kristin's son, seven-year-old Freddie, scampered towards his mum for a hug, grabbing her leg as she stooped a little to run a hand through his unruly hair. Hailey stepped slightly away from the group to walk up the ramp alongside her husband's wheelchair as he reached the steps. He seemed brighter than last time Eleanor had seen him, but still very frail. And finally, Bibi, turning heads as she passed, despite the best efforts of the grounds staff. The men, especially the younger ones, were so indiscreet with their gawping. Eleanor had had a word once but to no avail. Bibi didn't seem to mind, and the men didn't seem to be able to help themselves, they were all besotted by her. *How glorious it must be to exude such effortless glamour*, thought Eleanor as she turned to the terrace to make sure everything was ready for their arrival.

She glanced up at the sky. Surely the rain would hold off for a few more hours?

All afternoon, she had kept a careful eye on preparations for the celebration, making sure that everything was in just the right spot on the terrace to catch the late-afternoon sun going down over the ornamental lake. All the cakes were laid out with labels on a large trestle table, each one written in Eleanor's neat cursive. She'd placed the mystery tennis-court cake right in the very centre of the table. It was quite the showstopper. Eleanor hoped that either its owner made themselves known or, even better, people simply assumed she'd organised it for the women herself.

She frowned as Jeremy Hale, Kristin's husband and the ladies' team coach, emerged from the French windows of the club-house and sauntered over to the goodies on the tea tables. He was well-known for his sweet tooth and she watched as he ran a sly finger along the edge of an immaculately iced red velvet cupcake. Eleanor knew they were Vanessa's offering for the event: she had pretended to bake them, but they were clearly from the fancy patisserie in Sunningdale. His tongue flicked out towards his finger, reptilian, as he licked the glistening ganache. He popped his finger in his mouth, smacking his lips, oblivious to whether anyone had seen him.

Ugh. The man thought he owned the place, she thought as he swigged from his ever-present club-branded water bottle.

Eleanor made a note to discreetly remove the tampered-with cupcake before someone else had to eat it. Before she could get close enough to make her presence known, Jeremy was nudging the corner off one of Hailey's special brownies, a fat crumb falling onto his chin, almost obscured by his dark stubble. She felt as if she could hear the spit as he pressed his lips together before opening them in a wide grin. There was chocolate between his bottom teeth despite him now running that tongue across them all. For heaven's sake, she'd have to check all the tables again at this rate.

Eleanor strode back across the lawn and up the steps of the clubhouse onto the terrace in the hope that nothing else would end up with clumsy fingerprints on it. She heard clapping from inside, which meant that the women had entered the restaurant, and was relieved to see that Jeremy was finally stepping away from the tables to join the start of the celebrations.

For a moment, she let herself imagine being part of that close-knit group. What it would be like to have the champagne corks pop *for* her, rather than being the person who laid the bottles out in their ice buckets. But she'd never been any good at tennis, she reminded herself. Being a part of the Royal Oaks Club, its success and its wonderful atmosphere would have to be enough. And despite the administrative nature of her title, she was no small part.

The sun suddenly disappeared behind a cloud and Eleanor's mood curdled. The heavy stillness of the day had been replaced by a brisk, ominous breeze. She shivered in her light summer dress, and watched the skin on her arm prickle as the hair rose against the breeze. The starched tablecloths were flapping wildly, napkins whipped up off the tables and into the air, name cards for the cakes pirouetting alongside them, up and across the lawn.

The best laid plans, she thought.

Then she snapped into action, snatching up the showstopper cake as the first fat raindrops fell from the sky. She called out to Jessie, her most reliable summer worker, who looked up from where she was pouring the champagne into slim flutes and darted straight out onto the terrace.

'Quick,' she said, 'We need to bring the cakes in before the tea is ruined!'

A few more waiting staff ran out after Jessie, their white starched aprons fluttering, and began wrestling all the carefully arranged platters of sandwiches and scones inside.

A flash of lightning, followed by an immediate crack of thunder, made Eleanor jump. A few of the women shrieked and more of the guests ran out to help. Eleanor noticed that Kristin was one of the first, her sister Vanessa with her, piling up plates and even gathering up the tablecloths beneath them.

Her husband, Jeremy, poked his head outside the French windows, a slim green bottle of beer in his hand. He took a swig, grinning at the kerfuffle, then wiped his mouth crudely with the back of his hand and headed back inside.

'Oh, Eleanor, all your hard work!' Kristin said, as she rushed past, five champagne flutes clutched precariously in one hand. 'I'm afraid I've no idea what goes where,' she confessed with a smile as she plonked the glasses onto a hastily rearranged table. 'I couldn't leave it to you to sort out, could I?'

'Don't worry, ladies,' said Eleanor with a smile. She had hoped that by this stage of the party she might have been invited to have a glass herself, or even be offered one of the cakes. Those moments when she stepped away from the rest of the staff and felt almost like one of the family were always ones she treasured. 'You go and enjoy the fun!'

And so they did, while Eleanor kept an eye on proceedings. The room filled with cheerful chattering, everyone tucked into the platters of teatime treats, and the French windows misted up with condensation.

A clinking of glasses broke through the noise and the room quickly hushed itself into silence. Eleanor paused with the other members to watch as Vanessa, Kristin, Hailey and Bibi were ushered up to the front to be presented with their freshly polished silver trophy.

Together, they raised it aloft and the crowd broke out into cheers. Eleanor gave a small whoop, before snatching a glance around her, immediately blushing at her own exuberance.

'Of course, we couldn't have done it without our superstar coach!' said Hailey, glass aloft and looking out into the faces in front of her.

'Jeremy, where are you? Come and accept some praise!' followed Beatriz, one side of her deep-red mouth curled in a smile.

Eleanor watched Kristin's eyes scan the room looking for her husband. Everyone was twisting round, searching for Jeremy's familiar brown hair. *It wasn't like him to miss out on a moment of glory*, Eleanor thought.

The sudden grim scrape of a chair being dragged across the room's expensive parquet floor pierced the momentary quiet. A second later came a strangely sinister thud. A shriek rang out, and the murmuring in the room dropped to a deadly silence as the crowd broke away from the back tables.

Eleanor clutched her chest as she saw Jeremy writhing on the floor, his eyes bulging, gasping for air. He'd clearly dropped a large slice of sponge cake as he'd fallen, and she watched as he

9

rolled into it, the crumbs crushed into his otherwise immaculate suit. She gasped. It was the cake that had been delivered earlier; she could see the green icing even though she was standing several metres away. A horrible gurgling sound came from his throat as his pristine white trainers kicked out beneath him. His head rolled back and, in a flash, his entire body went suddenly from struggling to limp. A spine-chilling scream cut through the air and Eleanor realised it was Kristin, who had collapsed to her knees at the sight of her husband's lifeless body.

'Oh my God,' Eleanor heard someone whisper at the back. 'He's dead.'

Six weeks before...

Chapter 1

KRISTIN

Kristin walked into the en-suite bathroom, stumbling slightly as her arms stretched behind her, struggling to reach the tiny zip on her expensive dress.

'Darling, could you give me a hand with this?'

Jeremy didn't answer, his gaze fixed on his own image in the bathroom mirror. Even as his wife appeared behind him in the reflection, her silk bias-cut dress shimmering as it caught the overhead lights, he kept his focus on the bow tie he was tightening.

He was an undeniably good-looking man. Chocolate-brown eyes, full, almost petulant lips, and a tan that looked expensive – one that suggested destination holidays or outdoor sports, not building sites or farmers' yards. A flicker of a smile crossed his face. Yes, he looked good tonight.

Satisfied, he looked beyond his reflection.

'Wow,' he said, as he noticed his wife's outfit. 'Someone's put in the effort this evening.'

It was true. Kristin *had* put in the effort. She'd made sure her hair, usually scraped back in a plait while she was working, playing tennis or parenting, had had a bouncy blow dry. At her sister Vanessa's insistence, she'd had her nails done at the club nail bar – a proper gel manicure that not even grating cheese over her son, Freddie's, pesto pasta would ruin. She'd also had a spray tan, covering up so many of the freckles that sprinkled her chest and arms, rendering her skin a consistent bronze, glowing beneath her golden gown.

Kristin smiled back warmly, pleased at what sounded unusually like a compliment, though she couldn't help but notice that it was the effort Jeremy had mentioned, rather than *her*. *He never seemed to praise her when she put effort into anything else*, she thought. The way she ensured that their home was always spotless, his shirts crisp and ironed. How she carefully checked every ingredient list when shopping for the family, ensuring that their home was seed- and nut-free. A rule that she'd put into place at the Royal Oaks Club, too, ever since Jeremy joined. The vats of homemade soups, pasta sauce and bone broth she kept in the freezer. It all seemed to be filed under standard rather than praiseworthy.

She caught herself as soon as she'd made contact with this speck of a grumble. Why be picky? He *had* noticed tonight, hadn't he? Noticed that she looked great? He was probably just a bit clumsy at expressing it.

Jeremy turned and took her face in his warm hands. She could smell the toothpaste on his breath and feel the callus where the base of his thumb had long ago blistered from holding a tennis racket day in, day out. As he held her face and leaned in to kiss her, she was sure to do what she always did in these moments, and buckled her knees a little so as to ensure their faces were equal height. He did get very sensitive when she was in heels, after all. *Let's keep everything sweet*, she reminded herself, *it's so early on such a special night*.

'You look like a winner,' he said softly, even stepping back to admire her a second time. 'The codgers downstairs aren't going to know what to do with themselves. Some of that lot are probably as old as the club itself. They might not all make it to the toasts with you looking like that.'

As he said it, he let go of her face and walked back into the bedroom, giving her bottom a gentle pat as he passed.

The zip she had asked for help with remained open.

Kristin opened her mouth to repeat her request, but Jeremy was already heading out of the flat's front door and downstairs into the club. The family apartment was only small, nestled in the mock-Tudor beams above the Royal Oaks' Clubhouse, and Jeremy was gone before she could speak.

'Yooohooo!' came Eleanor's voice on the threshold of the flat. 'Jeremy let me in,' she explained as she peered into the living room.

'Hi, Eleanor, lovely to see you. And thank you so much for stepping in to babysit Freddie tonight. Our regular girl says she's ill but I'm sure she just has a hot date,' said Kristin with a smile.

'Not at all, Kristin. And might I say, you look absolutely gorgeous.'

'Bless you, Eleanor, thank you – although I can't manage to do it up by myself, would you mind zipping it up?'

'Oh, of course!' Eleanor zipped up the last few inches, before pausing to admire her boss.

'One hundred years, eh? What a thing. I hope you have a wonderful evening. If anyone deserves to enjoy the centenary celebrations, it's you and your family. You've transformed the place in the last twenty years. Unrecognisable from when I was a girl. It's absolutely right that you're here for the centenary. And I know how much work you've put into it.'

Eleanor was correct. They had put months of work into the celebrations, culminating in tonight's gala dinner. Yes, it was a centenary, but it also felt like a celebration of the Chappell family's two decades at the club, and all they had achieved.

Kristin's parents, Edward and Tamara, had taken it on when she and her sister were teenagers, and had turned it from a small home-counties tennis club to the sort of luxury facility that it was today. But they hadn't just made it a venue that could appropriately serve the elite sportsmen and monied second wives who lived in the recently built mansions around the club, they had also managed to keep its feeling of being a family club. Somewhere for the stay-at-home mums who wanted something to do with their organically fed preschoolers once they had exhausted the local nature walks between the idyllic Hampshire villages that lay alongside the M3 corridor back into London.

Yes, tennis had remained central to the club – after all, it was how her parents had met back in the eighties – but when they'd finally turned their back on full-time coaching and scraped together enough to buy their dream business, they had had their work cut out. To say the very least.

When Edward and Tamara bought the Royal Oaks, they'd sunk their life savings into the project and were determined to make it work. They had taken one look at the fusty old club-house, the dank flat above the main building and the stealthy creep of mildew in the 'luxury' shower rooms, and realised that it was going to take some serious savvy – and investment – to get things back into profit. But they'd done it, and they were rightly proud of it.

It was getting too much for them now though, and all these decades later, Kristin and Vanessa were gently guiding their parents to look beyond the game itself and towards what else the club could offer. They weren't officially running the place, but their discreet hands so very close to the tiller meant that Royal Oaks was inching ever further towards the wellness world of year-round ice baths, a café menu of functional mushroom supplements and regularly scheduled vitamin injections. And what a success it was proving to be.

To the guests, the Chappells represented the very best of British – multiple generations of a family business that had both stayed true to its values and moved into the future with class. An inspiration to the members and the community. It had been nearly ten years since Kristin had followed in the footsteps of her mother, and married Jeremy 'Jez' Hale, a man who seemed made in her father's image: one of the club's leading coaches. He had proposed within weeks and with barely enough time to plan a wedding, she had relocated from a not-entirely-successful attempt at being a spinning instructor in London and the two of them had moved into the apartment above the clubhouse to start their own family. It had seemed as if the next generation of the Royal Oaks was assured, and when little Freddie was born, his cherubic cheeks swiftly appearing on the club's website and marketing material, along with plans to open a soft play area, the Royal Oaks' march forward into further greatness seemed guaranteed.

So, yes, Kristin had worked hard for tonight, in all sorts of ways and over a very long time. She wanted it to be perfect. For her parents, for Jeremy and – although she'd never admit it – for herself.

She opened her mouth to thank Eleanor for her kind words when Jez's voice boomed up from the stairs.

'Quite right, Eleanor, Kristin has worked damn hard on tonight. And now she has the temerity to be heading downstairs with a better tan than me, goddammit!'

Kristin blushed; she hadn't realised he was still there, listening in on their conversation.

'Well, Mr Hale, you both look splendid. I just hope you take a moment to toast to your success,' Eleanor replied, *rather diplomatically*, Kristin thought.

'Indeed, indeed.' Jeremy's voice faded as the noise of his feet on the stairs restarted.

Kristin gave Eleanor a wave and darted out of the flat to catch her husband up. As she ran her hand along the solid oak of the banister, she wondered how many times she'd done it before. She had moved into Royal Oaks as a young teenager, when her parents had taken charge nearly thirty years ago. This apartment had been her home back then too, although she'd been sharing a room with her sister in those days, not her husband. It had looked very different under her parents, who had been so proud of the enormous floral sofas, the pastel borders stencilled around each room, the wooden farmhouse-style kitchen.

Back then, the flat – which was more of a maisonette, but no one could really bear to use that word – had undeniably been a haven of cosiness. Somewhere Kristin had spent hours prone on those sofas, feet up, watching MTV, motionless with exhaustion after a Saturday of training in the sun. Her older sister Vanessa was away on the Tour, already something of a big deal in the tennis world, and her parents were busy for long hours with the club and its guests – so Kristin had had hours at a time when she was left with both the flat and sometimes the whole club to herself, spending countless afternoons getting to know the building and its grounds, finding all the best hiding spots, shortcuts and discreet corners for an occasional kiss with a fellow teenager.

But a decade or so later, 'Home Counties hell', was how Jeremy had described the flat, a mere ten minutes after Edward and Tamara had made their generous offer that the newlyweds might want to take it over. 'We'd have to rip out the kitchen, burn all the chintz and tart the place up a bit,' he'd said to Kristin with a conspiratorial wink.

So of course, the flat was 'seen to' as soon after the wedding as they could afford it, even if it had meant that Kristin had gone back to work a little sooner into her maternity leave with Freddie than she'd wanted to. Walls were whitened, windows were widened and white goods were replaced. Kristin had never been quite sure if it had been a compliment when her sister had chuckled that the new units looked like 'the Camerons at Number Ten', but she blushed with pride anyway.

The whole plan had seemed so thrilling back then. Getting rid of every cupboard she'd slammed after a teenage argument with her parents. Ripping out the carpet she had sat and cried on when Vanessa had told her she wasn't going to make it back for her eighteenth birthday. Installing pristine kitchen surfaces in a white as gleaming as her tennis skirts – then feeling the cool, hard granite press against the small of her back as Jeremy leaned against her hips, kissing her hard when he came in from the court. Losing matches still did that to him; he needed instant gratification. Some sort of positive reinforcement, as soon as he walked up those stairs.

With a sudden thump, her hand hit the final newel post, which brought her back to the moment. They were downstairs. Time to make the shift from private to public that she had made so many times, and head into the clubhouse. Work mode. Yes, it was a celebration, but it was one that had to run perfectly. There was just too much riding on it.

Chapter 2

BIBI

The room was already noisy by the time Bibi and her husband, Garrett, made it to the bar. She knew she looked good. Even if she couldn't always rely on Garrett, her looks were something that had never let her down. Tonight, she was in a red minidress, her hair in a high ponytail, leaving her toned back and lats exposed. She knew the muscles would be rippling and flexing as she leaned to kiss hello to people on her way across the room. The gaze of almost every man she passed turned to follow her as she sashayed towards the bar, but she knew that the most effective way to respond was to pretend she hadn't noticed. Kristin had asked her once if she had any idea, if she *ever* noticed that she was that gorgeous, and she'd wanted to laugh and say, 'Of course I do. It's my life's work.' But she applied the same rule that she did for the men, and pretended she had no idea what Kristin was talking about.

So many old faces were here tonight, she thought, *but where were her* actual *friends?*

Kristin didn't seem to be here yet, which was a little unlike her. *Perhaps she was nervous,* thought Bibi. She knew her friend didn't like to show it, but how could she not be after the effort she'd put into this event. God, heading down those stairs must be like being backstage before walking out to greet your audience. Urgh, she was glad the days of that sort of, well, more *professional* hosting were behind her.

And there they were, Jeremy and Kristin, walking through the room towards them. Jez was one step ahead of course, his broad hands clasped in front of him like a smug politician, opening them wide to embrace an older club member and his well-maintained third wife. Bibi knew she was one of his most regular clients.

Don't even think about butting in, Bibi, she said to herself. *It's none of your business.*

The client's face lit up as she leaned in to kiss Jeremy, while Kristin lingered a few steps behind him, seemingly scanning the room to check that everything was running smoothly. She smiled to herself as she watched her friend. Jeez, she needed to relax, the entire room could almost see the nervous energy radiating from her. Or was it just because she knew Kristin so well that she was noticing it?

Either way, it seemed written all over her face that this was a big night, and one that needed to go perfectly. All four of the women had known for months that these centenary celebrations meant the world to Edward and Tamara Chappell, and that Kristin had done her very best to think of everything, planning this event with meticulous attention to detail. It had been in the club's calendar for over a year and Bibi had heard of little else for the last couple of months. No one was saying it out loud – least of all Bibi who wanted as little as possible to do with the family politics clearly going on behind the scenes – but it had long been implied, or at least understood, that after tonight the club would become Kristin and Jeremy's. That it would be *their* time to take the Royal Oaks' legacy forward with pride.

You can do it, K, Bibi thought to herself, trying to catch Kristin's eye to will her on. She was following Jeremy through the room, waving to the guests as she did so.

She smiled as she saw Kristin spot Grace, one of the school mums, among the crowd. 'You made it!' Kristin said, excitedly, hugging the glamorous, slender brunette. Earlier in the week Bibi and Kristin had earmarked Grace as someone who would really get the party going. Grace was clearly being effusive in her praise, her arms flailing wildly, statement bangles threatening to knock a tray of drinks clean out of a server's hands.

'Thank you! Not hard to make this room look spectacular...' Kristin seemed to be shrugging as she replied with a tight smile. Bibi despaired at her friend's inability to take a compliment. Perhaps she should get her a shot, loosen her up a bit... Hmm, tequila? Maybe she could just lob one in her champagne as she passed.

Then, just as her *Project Relax, Kristin* strategies were threatening to get risky, Bibi saw with delight that one of the elder members of the club, an old friend of Tamara's, was closing in to embrace Kristin's arm, their heads close together in the hubbub of the room. And at last, Bibi saw Kristin mouthing 'thank you' over and again with a broad smile – finally accepting some praise for a job well done.

It was all very well that the room was warming up so nicely, but it was threatening to stop Kristin from ever reaching her friend across the throng of partygoers. And where were the others? Sure, Hailey often ran late. Something about Justin not being able to sustain being at big parties that long, and fair enough. But surely Vanessa was around here somewhere – this was her family's *fiesta* after all?

Bibi scanned the room once again, painfully aware that she was craning her neck away from her husband and that he would lose his patience with her if she carried on doing it. Mercifully, this time Kristin was smiling back at her. Now half wedged behind a pillar, slightly hemmed in by some old biddy's walking frame, but there she was, grinning at last. Perhaps it was because Jeremy had peeled away from her and was making a beeline for the bar himself. Or perhaps that was too unkind a thought, Bibi reminded herself.

'Spec-tac-u-lar,' she mouthed at Kristin from the bar. She had edged slightly away from Garrett now and was waving an arm frantically up and down to indicate that it was Kristin's outfit she was referring to, not just the party. After all, it was under Bibi's advice that Kristin bought the silk gown, something that both knew she would never usually consider. Wow, that woman had taken a lot of persuading – even to get her to a headspace where she *deserved* to look good, where she *could* look good, rather than feeling like she should just be *seen* to make an effort.

But tonight had long felt like the sort of occasion that was as much about the potential for change as it was a celebration of the past, and when Bibi had sent her a WhatsApp link to the dress with 'For the centenary. I've reserved it at the boutique in the village. GO', Kristin had surrendered to the purchase with uncharacteristic ease, even if Bibi suspected she had still made sure to hide the shopping bags from Jeremy.

And just as she thought of Jeremy, there he was, leaning in over Garrett to say hello. He smelled woody, although she couldn't work out if it was his aftershave or whatever product he seemed to have slicked through his hair. Either way, the smell as he leaned forward was undeniably great. She leaned in to kiss him hello, the red gloss of her lips leaving an imprint on his carefully trimmed stubble. She felt his hand on her hip through the lightweight fabric of her dress.

'Oh, Jez, I've messed you up!' she said, licking her thumb and rubbing it on the gleam of lipstick she'd left across his face.

'Don't worry about it, Beatriz,' he said with an impish grin. Jeremy had never called her Bibi, like everyone else. He did the same with his own thumb, rubbing away at his cheek. As he did, she noticed that he was wearing a new watch, his shirt sleeve slightly tucked back just as Garrett often wore his. She took a breath and turned to Kristin, but was interrupted by Vanessa, who had suddenly popped up behind them all.

'Bloody hell, Krissie, I think you've actually pulled it off.'

Vanessa grasped her sister round her slender waist and winked at Bibi.

'Thanks, sis,' replied Kristin, embracing her sister back. 'And look at you!'

Vanessa stepped back and gave her sister a twirl while the men made a silly show of admiring her. She was wearing a black tuxedo, shot through with silver thread, and a pair of vertiginous silver heels. As ever, her sexiness lay in her refusal to perform 'ladylike' for those in the club – and her life – who might have preferred to see her in something rather more traditional. Beatriz thought to herself that the men would never have broken into that chorus of 'oohs' and 'aahs' for any of the rest of them. Far too risky to be passing comment on each other's wives like that. But Vanessa, seemingly forever single, appeared to command a different sort of respect among them. She knew they wouldn't dare overstep a line with her.

'What do you reckon?' she asked as she pirouetted unashamedly. 'Will Colonel Redburn approve?' Vanessa gave a cheeky wave to a doddery gentleman dressed in his old military uniform who looked as if he might have been a club member since Churchill's time.

'Oh, don't be daft,' replied Kristin. 'Everyone loves you whatever you do.' And it was true. Vanessa's skill on court, combined with her breezy charisma, somehow made people admire her no matter how much disdain she showed for the rest of the tennis establishment. It had been the case the day the Chappells had taken over the club, and it remained the case today.

'Well, nearly everyone ...'

'Ha, ha. Now come and help me check on these auction items before dinner. I'm terrified something is going to get nicked. People have been so generous!'

'Oh, give it a rest, you haven't even necked any bubbles yet.' Vanessa grabbed three glasses of champagne from a passing tray and handed them in turn to her sister and to Bibi. 'Now get some of that down you and relax.'

Chapter 3

VANESSA

Vanessa clinked glasses with Kristin and Bibi as a waiter in a pristine dinner jacket disappeared with the tray of champagne through the crowd in front of them. The room was heaving now, beads of sweat starting to gather on a few top lips as the laughter got louder with every sip.

She watched Kristin look out across the guests, holding the cool condensation of the champagne glass to her cheek. She so rarely drank that they had flushed easily, but as she stood there with her glass, Vanessa could see her relax a little. It was going fine. Perhaps her shoulders might lower an inch or two now. Perhaps she might even breathe using more than just the top half of her lungs.

'Darling, it's a roaring success, as we knew it would be,' said Bibi, to Kristin. 'I'm so pleased you bought the gown; you look like a goddess.'

'Yeah, and you look like crap, as per,' replied Vanessa, with a conspiratorial smirk.

'So rude. And especially when I'm wearing my most discreet dress, to fit in with you Brits...' Bibi pursed her red lips together, a glint in her eye.

'If this is you doing "English rose" I don't think any of us would survive you doing bombshell, babe.'

Bibi cackled and threw her head back, attracting a few looks from older club members standing nearby. *Maybe there was some fun to be had if Bibi was in the party mood,* Vanessa thought. Her gestures were characteristically loud, her gold bangles clinking. Bibi looked like a house plant in a sunny corner, turning her leaves to get the most light. Vanessa couldn't help noticing Jeremy staring, unashamedly, as Bibi twirled around.

She glanced at Kristin, to see if she'd clocked her husband's gaze, but she seemed distracted, her eyes darting around the room.

'You all right, sis?' she asked.

'Oh, I'm fine. I should really go and check on the entertainment, they're meant to be arriving soon. I haven't said hello to Mum and Dad yet, either.'

'I didn't know they'd arrived,' she said. 'Where are they?'

Kristin pointed over her shoulder and Vanessa turned to see her father roaring with laugher, his face in silhouette against the early evening sun. He was holding their mother's hand, the picture of marital bliss.

'Can't Jeremy check on the entertainment? Look at him, it's like it's *his* party.'

'Well... it's to celebrate all of us, Vee, you know that,' Kristin replied, a flicker of annoyance flashing across her face.

'I know, I know, it is kind of his party. But you know what I mean. It's you who did all the work, sis. He's just been swanking around in his short shorts while you've done all the hard yards.'

She wanted to say more, about how he'd be just another washed-up coach trying to make a bit on the side with a pro shop if it wasn't for her sister and her family. But she hadn't had *quite* enough to drink yet. Yet.

'Oh, Vanessa, take it easy, he's not that bad.'

Vanessa shot her sister her most charming smile. *Take it easy, Vanessa*, she reminded herself.

'I know he's not *that* bad. And I know it's strange me raising this with you, when you're married to him. But for a minute, let's just pretend you're not – and you're just my boss. Because he has been a *bit* bad, hasn't he? He's dropping hints left, right and centre that Mum and Dad will be retiring soon, and he'll be in charge of the club, that everyone should watch their step ...'

Vanessa noticed Bibi, uncharacteristically tactful, raise her eyebrows and pretend to notice a loose thread on her dress, as if she couldn't hear the conversation between the two sisters.

'Don't exaggerate. He's excited, and he's just been trying to make sure everyone's on board with the celebrations—'

'On board with the new management more like,' said Vanessa as she waved her glass between Kristin and Jeremy, indicating the change in hands that they all knew was coming. 'All I'm saying is that perhaps he should back off on the Lord of the Manor stuff with the staff a little. If he can.'

'As your boss, I have listened to your concerns and I will address them,' replied Kristin with a wry smile. 'As your sister, I want you to know that he just wants what's best for the family. OK?' Kristin stared directly at her sister and Vanessa recognised the ice in her eyes.

It was time to back away from any further hint of a sisterly squabble. Kristin had long known that Vanessa wasn't her husband's number-one fan, but somehow Vanessa fluffed it whenever she tried to explain why. Each time, Kristin would shoot her that 'earnest listening' face and Vanessa's arguments would slip away like sand between her fingers. Or she'd be met with this, the glacial stare that meant *not now*. Anyway, message received. No more Jeremy chat.

'Well, you know I want what's best for you.' She shrugged and downed the rest of her fizz.

'I do know that, Vee. Now, you and Bibi get a top-up of that champagne before Colonel Redburn drinks it all, and I'll make sure that we have some music to keep us entertained after dinner!'

Vanessa watched Kristin weave her way through the club members towards the reception, hugging their parents as she passed them. Her father was clearly beaming with pride, and she was glad Kristin was getting the accolades she deserved for an evening planned and received so well. It meant so much to her, just as her father's attention always had. As for Vanessa, she'd long ago realised that one competition it wasn't worth taking part in was the one for her father's attention. Kristin really was the apple of his eye, if only she could relax enough to see it.

'Come on, Vee, let's do as your sister says, and top ourselves up,' Bibi said, nudging her in the ribs.

Vanessa laughed, grateful for her friend by her side. 'Well, someone's got to, I suppose. I doubt Kristin will even finish her glass! You know, I think she actually enjoys the mild-mannered martyr act,' said Vanessa with an excessive eye roll. She knew she was going a little far, but Bibi knew them both, didn't she? She'd know there was truth in what she was saying.

'You are a wicked sister, I'm saying nothing,' Bibi replied with a wink. 'Unless she's sat me next to some old bore at dinner. She wouldn't, would she?'

'Of course not. You're near *me*, and some of the more bear-able parents from the school crowd. He's more of a player than she is but they're both a laugh – we won't have to stick to polite tennis chat.'

'Praise be!' replied Bibi, her hands raised in mock prayer, before she swooped on a passing waiter to take two more glasses of fizz.

'And hopefully Hailey will be close by, too. Where is that woman? Is she *ever* on time?'

Chapter 4

HAILEY

Better late than never, Hailey thought as she stepped inside the Royal Oaks club, pulling her sequinned gown just above her stiletto heel so she didn't trip. She'd come a little late on purpose, so that her husband Justin's wheelchair wouldn't get caught in the melee of guests as they arrived. She'd had a couple of years to master tactics like this, and her judgement was usually spot on. But tonight, she had arrived at the same time as the entertainment – Chris Couzens and his band who were performing, much to Kristin's delight. She had hoped she and Justin would be able to slip into the function room without too many people noticing that it was nearly eight o'clock, but here they were, caught in a criss-cross of caterers, musicians and now Kristin herself.

'Hailey!' she heard a familiar voice call out, and she turned to see her friend dashing down the hallway, beaming.

'Sorry, Kris,' she said, grimacing, 'typical last-minute crisis with this case I'm currently heading up.' Sometimes having a high-flying legal career was *very* useful if you just wanted an extra half an hour soaking in the bath.

'Oh, don't worry at all,' her friend exclaimed, squeezing her into a hug. 'I think the band's only just got here, you haven't missed anything.'

'Yes, I saw Chris and his crew unloading,' Hailey replied, gesturing back over her shoulder. Kristin's eyes widened, excitedly.

'Will you come with me to greet them?' she asked, as Justin nodded that he was fine heading into the main room alone, mouthing the word 'STARVING!' at them with a grin.

Chris was a suave thirty-something who had first found fame as a mediocre contestant on a reality show, but had recently exploded on TikTok, ten years older, but with far better hair, and a slick line in swing classics. His chiselled jaw, recent light smattering of crow's feet and impressive collection of velvet dinner jackets meant he was sure to go down well with the ladies in the room – and his regular appearance on sports quiz shows over the years meant none of the men in the room were likely to be too threatened either.

'Not nervous, are you, Kris?' Hailey poked her friend lightly.

Kristin's cheeks reddened. 'He's just so …'

'Young!' Hailey said, laughing. 'Come on, we can wait by the doors.'

Hailey knew that Kristin was more than a little giddy at the thought of meeting Chris himself. The two women headed over to the glass doors in the reception and watched as the band unloaded various instruments and luggage hangers from a minibus, while still able to hear the rumble of the room behind them.

At the bar only a couple of metres away, Jeremy's familiar public-school burr caught her ear. As it did, she realised she had instinctively turned her gaze to her friend. Why did she feel so protective of her? Hailey found herself wondering. She's a grown woman.

She watched as Kristin snatched a glance behind her, so Hailey snatched a look too. Now she saw that the body language between Jeremy and Bibi's husband Garrett was significantly less relaxed than that of the rest of the room. Sure, Garrett was still languidly leaning against the bar, in his usual way. An Irishman with a past that everyone seemed interested in, but no one seemed keen to ask him about, he managed to maintain his high frequency on the local grapevine by being one of the few men in the Home Counties who could genuinely be described as roguish, while treading a fine balance between looking utterly charmed and utterly bored at most events. His and Bibi's parties were legendary, but the jury was out on what he *really* thought about anyone else's.

From where Kristin and Hailey were silently watching him, his eyes were uncharacteristically intent, glinting at Jeremy who seemed to be doing all the talking. Garrett was a man of few words at the best of times, but this evening he appeared to be all but silent. Jeremy meanwhile was flushed, almost babbling. Hailey strained to separate the chatter around her, keen to grasp whatever snippets of this conversation she could that had left her friend's husband with the vein on his left temple so unusually raised. She could see the band unpacking microphone stands from their van through the windows at the far end of the atrium, but moved closer to the bar instead, trying to look purposeful so that none of the other guests would stop her.

'Yeah, mate, it'll be with you shortly—' she heard Jeremy say.

Garrett was nodding slowly, his blinks long, his eyelashes longer. He almost looked sleepy.

'Just a cash-flow thing at the moment, you know how things can get.'

Kristin snuck another look now, slower this time. *So as not to catch their attention?* Hailey wondered. It must be something to do with the pro shop that Jeremy was running at the club, she told herself. What else *could* it be? Kristin had mentioned to Hailey that she knew – as did her father – that Jeremy was desperate to get more involved, but Edward still felt he needed more business experience. Jeremy had apparently found this mortifying, but a compromise had been reached where the pro shop had become his, and he seemed to have accepted it as his empire. Kristin seemed to think that everything was going wonderfully there. 'How hard could it be to shift rackets and tennis kit from an ex-pro to a captive audience of enthusiasts?' she had said to Hailey. But Hailey wasn't married to the man, and had found it considerably easier than Kristin to imagine Jeremy making a mess of it. As she caught snippets of their conversation now, her doubts seemed valid.

'Things will move fast once we're in charge of this place though ... selling off a bit of land ... restructuring here and there ... You know the drill ...'

Hailey slowly turned her gaze back to Kristin, imagining her stomach would be tightening at the casual use of 'once we're in charge'. She knew Jeremy was longing to play a bigger part in the club – everyone bloody did – but had Vanessa's recent mutterings while they'd been taking a post-match sauna last week been right after all? That he saw the deal as a sure thing, the transition a mere formality. Garrett raised an eyebrow but didn't seem to reply. Instead, he turned away from Jeremy, lifted his crystal scotch glass, immediately catching the barman's eye. As he did so, he tapped the glass's edge, indicating that he'd like another single malt. Irish whiskey was all Hailey had ever seen him drink, and the staff here all knew which one was his regular. When she first found out, Hailey had thought it charming that he'd taken the time to get to know the bar staff, but now, as he had turned and left Jeremy hanging, it looked a lot more like power play. He was a nice enough guy, and she adored Bibi, who was a good friend, someone who had never judged or patronised her and Justin while they'd been through some grim times. She had been a discreet confidante, cheery and dependable on court, yet enough fun to share a bottle of Picpoul and some gossip with when the need arose. But in spite of all this, a surge of protectiveness welled up in Hailey at this glimpse of him seeming to toy with Kristin's husband.

Chris Couzens and his band were now standing in reception, ready to keep the guests entertained during the meal. Kristin clearly couldn't leave them any longer and stepped away from her momentary earwigging to attend to the musicians, welcoming them to Royal Oaks as she had done a thousand times for a thousand other events. Hailey smiled to herself. That's who Kristin was: the person who made things run smoothly. If only Hailey could be convinced that her pal was as good at feeling the same way inside as she knew she appeared to everyone else.

Either way, as the evening progressed, it seemed to Hailey that it was all going far better than either the senior Chappells or any of the extended family could have anticipated. She knew they'd been talking about tonight for years. Both sisters had been devastated when Edward's ill health had meant that the family couldn't really celebrate his and Tamara's big wedding anniversary. When Vanessa of all people had realised the centenary was coming up, the family had decided to make it the Big One. To have a huge celebration of the club and all it had achieved in the years since the Chappells had taken over. Then, as Edward's health had had its ups and downs and talk of the next generation taking over had increased, the unspoken meaning of the evening – perhaps a discreet passing of the baton – had started to intensify. Which, in turn, she knew had fuelled Kristin's desire to manage the evening perfectly, for her parents to have a night to remember, and for Jeremy's ambition to be kept under control.

The meal was perfect. The chefs had surpassed themselves with four courses, all allergy-free, of course. Even by Hailey's sophisticated Central London business lunch standards. There had been none of the grim spinach and feta parcel followed by a rubbery chicken breast and some depressed-looking Lollo Rosso nonsense. She had been highly flattered when Kristin had asked specifically for *her* help researching healthy but delicious food and the two of them had spent three happy days that spring preparing for a healthy but innovative menu.

They had come up with something spectacular. First, there were warm chunks of local sourdough with generous bowls of both extra-virgin olive oil and gleaming dollops of smoked charcoal butter. Then, a starter of exotic – but healthy – mushrooms cooked in multiple ways including fried enoki, a small porcelain ladle of tremella soup, and slivers of lion's mane steaks with chimichurri, followed by miso salmon with golden dashi broth and finally a plate of local cheese and crackers. Then, just as guests had thought there might not be a pudding, starting to cross the room to chat at different tables, shimmying to the band, or just walking to the bar to ease the tension against their cummerbund, the pièce de résistance arrived: satsuma and popping candy ice cream, banoffee tart, canelé Bordelais and lemon crème fraîche, with a lychee macaron.

There were gasps of delight around the room as the traditionalists and fashionable health-fad followers alike tasted course after course. Barely a soul noticed that – as ever – there were no nuts near any of the dishes and not a single one had even entered the kitchen. As the guests ooh-ed and aaah-ed over their final treat, Hailey had caught Kristin's eye across the room and raised a glass and a clenched fist at her. Those training sessions they had sacrificed in order to spend time on getting that menu perfect had not been wasted.

The drinks had flowed generously throughout. Kristin had arranged for a carefully-selected handful of long-standing members to share their memories of the club over the years and Kristin and Vanessa had stood up together to talk about their idyllic childhood at the club and how they hoped that it would provide the same sense of community to families for generations to come. To top it off, Edward and Tamara Chappell had delivered a pitch-perfect speech as the final glass of champagne for each guest was delivered to their seat.

As Hailey sat listening to these speeches she had one hand on the table, her enormous eternity ring sparkling against her champagne glass as the candlelight hit it, and the other clasped in Justin's resting softly in his lap. She looked around the room and felt blessed to have made such good friends here. Her competitive edge and commitment to professionalism meant that she didn't make friends easily and had never been the type to have a gaggle of female 'besties'. Even the word made her want to brush her teeth with wire wool. Her hen night had been dinner at Noble Rot with an old university friend and her future sister-in-law. But a passion for tennis that she, the sisters and Bibi shared had taken some of the pressure out of the 'girlie' dinners or weekends away that would otherwise have been gossip only. There had been training advice, match strategy and a shared commitment to the win that had forged a bond far deeper than she had ever imagined she'd have made this far into her life. On her wedding day, she had been perfectly happy with the idea that it would be her and Justin from now on, but a decade later she found herself treasuring these women and the role they played in her life. And she hoped they felt the same way.

Hailey watched Kristin, beaming with pride at her dad's speech, but trying to ease her gold heels off one by one, rubbing at the balls of her feet under the table. She knew Kristin only wore shoes like that once in a blue moon — partly because of Jeremy's sensitivity about her height, but also because she was almost always in sports kit. She imagined the dull ache she must be feeling after standing for so long, leather pinching at her while she smiled politely, making sure everyone else was comfortable first. Her heart was surely hammering from the pressure of putting on the sort of show that she knew her parents had dreamed of and now, as Kristin sat back in her chair, Hailey hoped that at last she might feel the pressure start to trickle away a little.

She had hoped too soon though, as Jeremy was on his feet moments later. He was grinning innanely, ready for his own big moment: the charity auction. Months ago he told Kristin and his in-laws that if they let him compère the event, he was confident he'd bring in a fortune for the local charities the club supported. And to their surprise, it turned out he wasn't wrong.

Jeremy had introduced each item with the sort of 'effortless' schmooze that looked practised to those closest to him, particularly those who had heard him rehearsing in the bathroom mirror in the evenings, but seemed to go down a storm with the rest of the room. He had researched quips and anecdotes about both the prizes' donors and those who he suspected would be most likely to be bidding on them — even if a few of them flew perilously close to the wind.

But for the most part, he won the crowd over with his lines about 'dashing Irishman Garrett O'Brien' and his 'urgent need for a new racket so that one day he might have a chance of beating his wife', or 'clubhouse favourite, Hailey De Vere', whose 'county-famous herb garden and poly-tunnels house delicacies that we're all dying to sample after dinner'. It was only his jibes about Kristin herself that failed to cause quite the same ripples of faux-scandalised laugher.

'She thinks she runs the place!' Jeremy had said at one point, microphone and notes waved for emphasis before he winked at the seated guests. 'But we'll soon see about that, eh.'

Kristin had tried to laugh along, and perhaps it was just the exhaustion kicking in, but it looked to Hailey like she didn't really get the joke. She *did* run the place, or at least she had been since her dad's diagnosis of multiple sclerosis. Perhaps Jeremy hadn't meant it to sound as if he were undermining her, but she doubted it. Hailey felt her own hackles rise, a burst of cortisol as she felt wronged on her friend's behalf. Worst of all, she knew it would never be worth mentioning that sly dig to Kristin; she already knew what her response would be.

'Oh, he was so nervous, of course it was the joke about me that didn't land because he trusts me.'

'These things happen, it's not personal.'

'You're taking it too seriously, of course it wasn't a dig at me.'

When Hailey looked at the flicker of anxiety on Edward Chappell's face, she suspected that she wasn't the only one who had heard these well-rehearsed excuses, or indeed noticed that they were coming a little more often these days. She'd say nothing, she told herself. For now, anyway.

And the moment passed quickly enough, the entire room buoyed by the sight of the night's tally jumping higher and higher with every bid. Cafetières of coffee and steaming pots of fresh mint tea arrived on the tables, alongside teeny tiny tennis-ball-shaped petit fours, and when at last the final item was auctioned and the total revealed, there was no question that the mood in the room was overwhelmingly positive.

Applause rippled through the room and Jeremy sat down flushed with pride and self-importance. Even Vanessa seemed charmed by his performance, tipping him a thumbs-up from her end of the table. Hailey chuckled to herself when it became obvious that the moment was over all too quickly for Jeremy: he couldn't hide his slight crestfallenness as the auction was immediately followed by the appearance of Chris Couzens and his band, who took no time at all to prove themselves the perfect summer crooning experience.

Chris had sung the first few numbers while guests were still seated, but now that they were getting restless, finishing off their coffee and chocolates, he was serenading guests as they passed the band, making the ladies blush and some of the men start to look a little worried. As people began to get up, tables were discreetly pushed back, and the parquet of the clubhouse dining room became the perfect dance floor.

Edward Chappell was looking tired now, but was determined to have at least one dance with each of his daughters. Vanessa trotted him around the room, her heels flashing silver as she went, while his head tipped back with laughter at the way they were making up steps and hoping not to trip.

Then, slower now, he took to the floor with Kristin.

Hailey watched as Kristin checked that her dad was OK with still being on his feet and felt for her – it was tough watching someone you love deteriorate. She glanced across to Justin, who was holding court from his wheelchair, looking as dapper as ever in a bespoke dinner jacket, his signet ring glinting as he held his glass.

Lucky Kristin that that person was her father, and not her husband.

She smiled at something her dad said as they clasped each other, making their way delicately around the dancefloor. God, how lucky she was to have this many years' worth of happy memories with him. And how fortunate to have the club, a place she'd associate with him long after he was gone. His stamp and his footprints were everywhere.

'This really is a special place,' said Justin, resting his head on Hailey's shoulder. 'We are lucky to have it.'

'You're so right, darling,' replied Hailey. 'I wish we could freeze this moment and that everything could be just like tonight, forever.'

Chapter 5

KRISTIN

Kristin woke with a start to see her son's face only an inch from hers.

'Mummy, how long until morning?'

Her first thought was that it seemed only minutes since her head had hit the pillow. Her second was that the balls of her feet were still aching from last night. She leaned over to look at her bedside clock. It was four and a half hours since she had made it to bed, having waved off the last of the guests and somewhat rashly invited her parents over for a bacon sandwich first thing.

'Oh, darling, it's a while yet,' she muttered, hoping against hope that Freddie might somehow decide to head back to bed. Or even, one day, choose his father to wake up first.

'But... it's *day* outside...' Freddie was right. Sunlight was streaming through the small gap in her curtains, the early summer sun already high. She shuffled over to make space for him, her back hitting the warm, heavy weight of Jeremy who remained, as ever, sound asleep.

She tried to breathe deeply, soothing Freddie in the hopes that he'd fall back asleep, or at least doze. Maybe until six-thirty, she told herself, wrapping an arm around him, her other hand stroking his soft pale hair. She closed her own eyes and replayed key scenes from the evening in her mind – her pride for her parents, her joy at watching her sister and friends having fun, her thrill at seeing how incredibly glamorous everyone had looked, the music, the food, and the strange comment Jeremy had made during the auction.

Had it been an ill-judged joke, or was Vanessa right, and he really was beyond desperate to take over the running of the club? She'd always thought that playing and coaching was his lifeblood – he'd been such a fabulous player, coming up through the ranks with Vanessa, two young teenagers as part of the national squad travelling around the country and beyond. He'd seemed impossibly cool, glamorous even, back then. He was tall, much more wiry than he seemed today, but he'd had that same easy charm. Always wearing a baseball cap backwards, flipped to the front only if he was at the sunny end of the court. The soft fuzz of the hair on his legs and forearms had entranced the gawky thirteen-year-old Kristin when she got up close to him. So manly. And anyway, in those days she had mostly just admired him from afar, hanging out with Vanessa and the rest of the squad. Years ahead of her.

Back then she had never dared confess to her sister that she had a crush on Jeremy. It had seemed an unreal proposition that she would ever get to speak more than a couple of sentences to him. He was headed to the top, after all. And he had everything he needed to make it. Wealthy parents who provided all the opportunities he needed. The good looks and good manners that made dealing with press and potential sponsors and agents, a breeze while Vanessa was finding that side of the business fraught and full of anxiety. And he had the talent. Tennis just seemed to come easy to him.

In hindsight perhaps it had come a little too easy. Perhaps if he'd found the game more challenging, he might have trained harder when the going had started to become a little tougher.

And perhaps if he had trained harder, he wouldn't have found himself left behind by the time he was in his early twenties.

He *had* become a brilliant coach, though. His good-natured ability to chat to anyone and everyone – about almost anything – meant that he'd turned into the kind of guy who could charm the bigwigs at prestigious clubs with the same confidence with which he could persuade nervous kids that tennis was the game for them, and that it was all worth it. And when he returned to the Royal Oaks for a top coaching role and met Kristin all over again, she had finally had the chance to fall for him all over again, only this time as a young woman and one able to hold her own.

And they'd been happy for a while, hadn't they? Didn't he love playing, and coaching, and even running the pro shop? Or had Vanessa been right? Was he just biding his time with her to gain control of the club? Some days it felt as if the magic was just fingertip-distance away, one glance from those chocolate-brown eyes and she'd be a lovestruck teenager all over again. Others, it felt like life was admin, and she was never going to get it right.

Kristin pushed these thoughts, checklists and spreadsheets to the back of her mind, twirling Freddie's soft curls between her fingers. Why would she immediately start worrying about something else? Only hours after she'd got through the last big stressful event in her life. For once, the path ahead was looking clear, positive, exciting even. She should leave this here.

Convinced, she tapped Fred – who was very obviously still wide awake, with no intention of being otherwise – on the shoulder and whispered, 'Come on, let's go and get some breakfast.' He needed no persuasion and the two of them padded quietly out of the bedroom and towards the kitchen.

Kristin filled the coffee maker with fresh water and slotted a pod into it, while pulling a packet of flour out of the cupboard above it.

'Pancakes?'

His face lit up and once they'd made a great stack of them, topped with a smidgen of butter and a dollop of jam, they settled into the squishy sofa in the living room for more episodes of *Bluey* than were normally allowed.

Just as Freddie was starting to wriggle away from the TV, Mrs Chappell texted to double check that they were on for breakfast, and if so that they'd be about half an hour. Kristin replied that they were looking forward to it, before hopping into the shower, asking Freddie to dress himself while she was in the bathroom, and finally emerging feeling somewhat less bleary.

When the bell for the flat buzzed, Jeremy was still sound asleep. Kristin welcomed her parents in, no longer caring about the noise, and put on some fresh coffee. Freddie appeared, dressed only in a pair of dinosaur pants and a light blue T-shirt, keen to show his grandparents his most recent LEGO creations, while the adults chatted about how the night had gone. There was high-fiving around the vast sum raised by the auction, Kristin and her mother dissected some of the most spectacular gowns – and the most awful – and how they'd been access-orised, while her dad flopped on to the battered leather sofa in the kitchen bay window announcing that 'parties are more tiring than tournaments. Although in tennis terms, that was a perfect three-set victory. It started with a bang, built momentum steadily, and finished in style.'

'Ah, thank you dad. It was worth all the effort,' replied Kristin. 'I'm quite relieved that Vee has flat-out refused a party for her fortieth. Did I tell you she's making us all go axe-throwing?'

'Dear God! We never could contain that girl!' replied Tamara.

'Just promise me you won't want anything quite as full on for your retirement party, OK?' said Kristin as she plonked a bottle of ketchup and a bottle of brown sauce on the kitchen table. For a second, she'd shocked herself that she'd said the great unmentionable 'r' word out loud. In the corner of the room, she saw Jeremy hovering at the door. His hair, normally so glossy, was matted as if he'd been asleep for a week. He rubbed his eyes like a baby, before smiling at the room.

'Oh, jeez, we're straight on to planning the next party, are we?' he groaned, reaching into a cupboard for a box of eggs.

'Don't worry, that won't be happening anytime soon...' replied Edward, as he brushed a crumb off his knee and crossed his leg.

'Really?' asked Kristin, trying not to sound too surprised.

'God, yes,' he continued. 'When I first got the diagnosis, I thought that after this centenary business we'd be done, but your mother and I have been talking about it and I'm feeling better than ever. We've got a few years left in us yet.'

There was a crash as the box of eggs fell and smashed onto the floor and Jeremy swore loudly.

'Daddy, you said a bad word,' came Freddie's small, shocked voice. Kristin feared it might not be the last.

Now ...

Chapter 6

ELEANOR

Eleanor stood by the window of the clubhouse and looked around the dining room, wondering where to start. The blue of the ambulance lights flickered against the glass. The room suddenly felt very quiet. Tables and chairs had been pushed back to make space for the paramedics, leaving crumbs, cutlery and those damn cake labels scattered on the floor. An upturned coffee cup lay askew in its saucer, its contents overflowing onto the table and slowly tap-tap-tapping onto the floor. Next to the brown puddle was a mobile phone, a sticky thumb print on its dark screen.

Fifteen minutes ago, the room had been packed with people. Bibi screaming in horror, her blood-red nails against her mouth in shock as Jeremy lay unconscious on the floor. Kristin ashen, silent, seemingly paralysed by the rush of action in the room. Vanessa, stepped up to put a protective arm around her, telling her she was sure it was all going to be fine; the professionals were here now. And Hailey, confidently standing at the door to the clubhouse, directing the ambulance crew to where Jeremy lay as if it were her home.

Eleanor couldn't help but feel that in those crucial minutes she had failed Royal Oaks, failed the Chappells, failed herself. For so long she had prided herself on being the calm and

49

competent first port of call for anyone arriving at the club, but at the merest hint of a crisis she had provided nothing. Instead, she had stood rooted to the spot, as Hailey was forced to take control of the room. But the sight of Jeremy against the wooden floor, barely visible behind the legs of those leaning over him, had left her frozen. As the cries for help from the women had turned into the sharp, specific instructions of the ambulance crew, she could only watch as Jeremy's body, as slack as the heaps of tennis netting piled up on the outside courts over winter, was lifted onto the stretcher.

Eleanor had peered out of the dark windows as Kristin climbed into the ambulance with her husband, her face white, her hands shaking. Edward Chappell put his arm around his wife, Tamara, and as the ambulance drove away, blue lights flashing, but no sirens, they turned to head back to the clubhouse. Vanessa had already taken an inconsolable Freddie, the poor thing, upstairs to the family's flat.

Eleanor turned away from the glass; she didn't want anyone to think she was one of those awful window twitchers. She could hear the police in the room next door and an icy shiver ran down her spine. *It was all her fault.* Should she tell them that she was the one who let the cake in? Jeremy Hale had died because she had failed to check the ingredients, the way Kristin had always instructed her to, because of his allergies. *But then,* she suddenly thought, *she'd also have to admit that she didn't know who sent it.* She gasped. Could someone have sent the cake on purpose? Surely this wasn't a *murder*?

'Excuse, me, Madam?'

Eleanor jumped. She hadn't heard anyone come into the room. She turned and saw that the voice belonged to a policeman who looked barely old enough to be out of short trousers.

His cap was in his hands, held in front of his waist as he waited for a response.

'Yes?' she asked, automatically going to smile, but then stopping herself. This wasn't the time to start grinning in a welcoming manner.

'I'm going to need you to leave the room, please, madam. Just while we try to work out what's gone on here.'

'Oh, yes, of course, officer,' she blustered. Her heart seemed to be leaping up out of her chest and beating in her throat. She tried to swallow but her mouth was too dry.

'Nothing to worry about. Just standard procedure. But we've been asked to find whatever it was that Mr Hale was eating when he had his reaction.'

'It was a piece of cake, sir. I saw it in his hand. I'd laid out all the cakes earlier in the day, so I can tell you which one it is. I'm the General Manager, you see,' she said, breathlessly.

'A piece of cake? Well, if you can show me which one, that would be very helpful madam. I understand the hospital needs to know what was in the cake as soon as possible.'

'He's... He's still alive?' Eleanor asked, shocked.

'Madam, if you could point out the cake, please, this is important.'

'Sorry, officer, of course. She walked over to the table, her legs trembling slightly, the police officer one step behind her. Eleanor wondered if he could hear her heart pounding. She pointed at the beautiful green cake, now with a large slice missing. 'It's this one, definitely.'

'Righto,' he said, firmly.

'I'm so sorry,' she gulped. 'I should have checked that it was nut free. It completely slipped my mind.'

He raised his eyebrows. 'That was the problem then, was it? Some sort of nut allergy?'

'It must have been. He was so allergic. The entire club, the whole menu – it's all nut free. Everyone knows.'

'And this cake seems to have slipped in, does it?'

Eleanor nodded, her eyes shining with tears.

'Well, we'll get this to the hospital as fast as we can then, so they can work out exactly what we're dealing with here.' The policeman was stooping down with an evidence bag covering his hand. He scooped up the marzipan figurine with the deftness of a seasoned dog walker, and nodded in the direction of the main cake, 'Don't touch that, I'll have a colleague come in and collect it.'

Eleanor nodded again; she just wanted to go home.

'And where did it come from, the cake?' continued the policeman.

'I don't know,' Eleanor stuttered. 'It just arrived this morning. From a bakery I hadn't heard of. But it had figures of all the ladies on it, very detailed; I just assumed that it was from someone who knew them. It's been such a busy day, you see, we were meant to have the party outside, and then it started raining so we had to come inside, and I think in all the chaos I just forgot to check about whether it contained nuts. It's my fault…' she tailed off.

But the policeman was no longer looking at Eleanor. His gaze had strayed to behind her, where Edward Chappell was now at the doorway, having headed down from Kristin and Jeremy's flat. He looked exhausted.

'Eleanor, could I have a word?'

The policeman stepped forward. 'We are just collecting whatever it was that Mr Hale seems to have ingested, Mr…?'

'Chappell,' replied Edward, holding out his hand. 'Mr Hale's father-in-law.'

Eleanor noticed Edward's hand was shaking.

'Good to meet you, sir,' replied the police officer. 'Now then, we need to get this back to the hospital as soon as possible. I understand that Mr Hale has a nut allergy?'

'Yes, yes, he does. But we've just spoken to Kristin, our daughter. She's at the hospital. I'm afraid the urgency to establish the contents of the cake has now passed somewhat. Mr Hale was declared dead a few minutes ago.'

Eleanor couldn't prevent a small whimper escaping. She had never liked the man, but surely Jeremy didn't deserve to *die*? And it was her fault!

Five weeks before ...

Chapter 7

VANESSA

The axe hit the target with a satisfying thud. Out of the corner of her eye, Vanessa noticed her sister jump at the sound. *She was so jittery these days*, she thought. Next to her, Hailey gasped, and Vanessa raised her hand to her brow to see how accurate her throw had been.

Squinting into the sun, she could just about see the axe still juddering, off to the right of the bullseye. Good, but room for improvement. A lot more fun than a spa day to celebrate her birthday.

'Nice one, Vee!' cried Bibi beside her, her gold bangles jangling on her wrist as she clapped excitedly.

'Well, ladies, the bar, or rather the *axe*, has been set,' Vanessa replied, with a little bow. 'Christ, that feels good.'

'Doesn't it just?' replied the instructor with a twinkle in her eye. *He must be almost half my age*, Vanessa thought.

AXEL'S AXES was written on his khaki gilet in bright yellow lettering, which was rather confusing, given he'd told the four women that his name was Dave. He stepped forward to retrieve Vanessa's axe from the target, Bibi blowing a wolf whistle that only the two of them could hear, as his biceps strained to remove the axe from the thick straw padding.

Vanessa turned to look at her sister, who was neat as ever in a pair of slim-cut jeans and a still-pristine Breton top, her eyes also fixed on the silhouette of the instructor.

'Pretty hot today, isn't it, Kiki?' she called out. Kristin blinked furiously, her cheeks reddening. 'Go on, it's your turn, show us how it's done.'

'I'm worried my axe won't even make it as far as the target,' said Kristin as she approached the throwing area.

'Oh, don't make us laugh, Kristin,' Bibi said. 'Your overheads on the tennis court are the stuff of legend. This is basically the same action!' She laughed huskily. When Vanessa first met Bibi, she had assumed that laugh was something she put on when in men's company, an affectation to enhance her already overwhelming charisma. But as she had grown to know and love her, she'd realised that it was just her laugh. That Bibi really was one of those women who was intrinsically sexy.

'You can do it, babe!' cheered Hailey.

'Oh, sod it,' said Kristin, taking a deep breath and stepping up to the rack. The giggles that had been there a minute ago gave way to a genuinely anxious look. The blades were glinting in the sunlight.

'Don't overthink it, sis,' said Vanessa. She wanted her smiling, carefree sister back. The one she remembered growing up, the one who these days only made the rarest of appearance on the odd girly lunch, when she could be persuaded to slip away for a shared bottle of white wine and some gossip about the most irritating club members.

'For once, I'm not here to win – it's just a nice break to be away from the club for a bit, isn't it?' Kristin's voice faded in the second half of the sentence as she realised she didn't want her sister to think the day was more about escaping work than celebrating her 40th.

Vanessa walked up to Kristin and put her arm around her, so they were looking at the rack of axes together. She felt Kristin's shoulder drop a little as she relaxed against her. For a minute she thought she was going to lean in and rest her head against her shoulder, as she had done when they'd been young girls, sitting at the side of a court watching their mum play.

'Go on,' she said softly, and Kristin edged forwards to pick one.

'You'll be fine,' said the instructor, placing his hand over Kristin's to position her grip correctly on the axe. Vanessa chuckled softly as her sister's cheeks deepened to an almost burgundy hue.

A split second later she hurled it at the target with all her might. Even the air it passed through seemed to hum with the force of her throw. Kristin's hands flew to her mouth in shock as she realised her own strength. A tree rustled as even the nearby birds seemed to take flight at the thwack of the blade on wood.

'Bloody hell, sis. What do you do when you're actually angry?'

'Haha, well, I hope you never have to find out.'

You've got me wrong, sis, Vanessa longed to say. *I'd love to see you angry for once.*

And she really would have loved to see it. But she stopped herself from saying so out loud. Maybe she should stop judging her sister by her own standards. Maybe Kristin genuinely enjoyed the straitjacket of non-stop obligations and domestic routines that she seemed to wear. Including taking it upon herself to organise Vanessa's birthday, which originally had been a surprise spa day at a nearby hotel. Vanessa's worst nightmare.

Thankfully, she'd got wind of the idea – Bibi whispered the secret plans to her after practice a few weeks ago – and she'd told Kristin in no uncertain terms that she'd be taking her fortieth birthday planning into her own hands. Not that she wasn't grateful, of course.

And so, Vanessa had messaged Hailey, Bibi and Kristin on their WhatsApp group, *Their Royal Highnesses* (Hailey's idea, a terrible play on Royal Oaks, but somehow it had stuck), that wandering around all day in a white fluffy robe, then being forced to drink hot water brewed with lemongrass – or seaweed – was her idea of hell. Instead, they were going axe-throwing, and then for a boozy picnic in the sunshine if the weather held up.

She had other friends, but none formed as perfect a group as these four, who she played tennis with week in, week out, come rain or shine.

Most of the friends she'd been close to in her twenties and thirties had slowly spread across the country, falling prey to marriage and babies. Friendships had faded as playdates and school runs had become those women's main source of socialising, and Vanessa was honest enough to admit that she simply wasn't interested in hanging out at baby showers or school fetes.

She'd lost touch with the girls she'd shared everything with as a twenty-something on the women's tennis tour, but continued to follow the careers of those who still spent their lives on the road, either as coaches or players and sometimes as wives, but that wasn't for Vanessa either.

Once she had settled back into a role at Royal Oaks a few years ago, she had found herself closer to her sister than ever before. Even if she disliked Jeremy, she adored their son, Freddie, and relished any opportunity to look after him for a few hours. She was well aware that over the last seven years Jeremy and Kristin rarely had a 'date night' when she was roped in to look after Freddie.

Once Vanessa returned to Royal Oaks, it was through Kristin and the club that she had got to know the indomitable Bibi (always Bibi, never Beatriz) and then Hailey who she had a particular fondness for. The four women, 'Their Royal Highnesses' worked as a friendship group because they had a shared goal in the tennis team, but also because they were each so different.

Kristin's more reserved, gentle nature was balanced by Bibi's boisterous, playful personality, and Hailey's fierce yet friendly lawyerly interrogations across the dinner table even managed to break through Vanessa's carefully constructed walls that she'd built up over the years. And even though Hailey had been dealing with a lot of late, herself and her husband Justin in the process of coming to terms with his motor-neurone diagnosis, there was rarely a post-match dinner when Bibi didn't have all of them in hysterics or when Hailey's wry Texan charm quickly put a stop to the sisters' occasional bickering.

Today, however, the sisters seemed more at peace than ever. No digs about Jeremy. No snipes about the club. It felt like a golden day. The sun was shining, even if it wasn't *that* warm, and Vanessa was delighted to be with the three women she cherished most in the world. Even Kristin was cheerier than she had been for weeks.

'I couldn't have wished for a more perfect day with you all,' declared Vanessa from her perch on a tree stump behind the axe rack, feeling quite sentimental. 'Thank you, ladies, for bending to my wishes. And for switching your tennis rackets for axes today, I know it's not a normal birthday request. Now, who's up next? Don't play nice just because I'm turning forty, I'm not over the hill yet,' she cackled.

'Oh, you think we're playing nice?' said Hailey, grinning widely and standing up from her tree stump. 'The first throw was just a warm-up, I'm ready to play for real now.'

Chapter 8

HAILEY

Holding the axe in her hand, Hailey turned her face to the sun and breathed in through her nostrils, out through her mouth, just as she did first thing every morning, while she sipped on her black coffee, laced with two scoops of grass-fed collagen. She'd read somewhere that just ten minutes of sunlight on your face before you start your day improves your overall health.

'How lovely to have the time for these little rituals,' Kristin had once said without thinking, and even Vanessa had whipped her head round, shocked. But Hailey knew that she hadn't meant the comment cruelly. She knew that she was lucky to have time for these moments, but it was undeniably these little rituals that usually kept her going.

She inhaled deeply, with the intention of someone who really, truly *cared* about breathing. She wouldn't be rushed for her turn at the axe-throwing any more than she would be in the mornings or even in court. She *insisted* on the time, and she wondered if Kristin had ever considered doing the same for herself. Or maybe it was that Jeremy never gave her the opportunity. She frowned. She'd never been able to understand how lovely Kristin had ended up married to such a self-obsessed narcissist.

And so, picturing Jeremy's smug face, she raised her arm and hurled the axe at the target with the force of a Viking queen, letting out an animal-like roar, which would have been familiar to anyone who had faced her formidable first serve.

The target juddered, hit squarely in its centre, and the women cheered.

'Bloody hell, Hailey, I wouldn't want to cross you in the woods!'

Vanessa was clapping, her hands above her head in awe.

'You wouldn't have a thing to fear if you bore me no ill intent,' replied Hailey, poker-faced. Her Texan twang sounded particularly pronounced in the dappled English countryside. She smiled at the group, coyly using her little finger to hook a couple of stray blonde curls back behind her ear.

It was late morning now, and the sun was high. It had been a brutal start for Hailey – the sun rising earlier and earlier each day meant that Justin's pain woke him earlier too. A trickle of sweat hit her eye, the salt making them sting even more than they already were. She eased her back round to the sun and stretched her shoulders as if she were trying to let the warmth release a little tension.

She was only just turning away from the target when she found herself scanning the group to work out when her next turn would be. That animalistic roar had felt good. She had let go of something that no amount of wild water swimming or reformer Pilates had yet enabled her to. And it wasn't just the lingering resentment towards Jeremy, she was just so *angry* about everything at the moment. It was so unfair, Justin's diagnosis. Why *him*? They had so many things they wanted to do, so many dreams they'd never get to chase together.

Over the last two years, the minute she left her office in her chauffeured car, she'd have her iPhone out, scanning the internet for more information on Justin's condition, contacting specialists all over the world, and reading wellness advice on how to keep the two of them optimised at all times. She marvelled at how this word she had so rarely used two years ago now dominated so much of her headspace. If she wasn't optimising her sleep, she was optimising Justin's physical strength; if she wasn't optimising his treatment regime she was optimising her nutrition. It was all in pursuit of optimising their time left together, but lately she had started to wake up in the morning feeling sick to the gills at the prospect of another day's optimising. So, the sight of these grown women indulging Vanessa in her renegade birthday plan felt more healing than any amount of Lion's Mane supplements ever could.

Bibi leaped up. 'My turn! Stand back, chicas, I'm going in and this time it's personal.'

'When isn't it, Beebs?' replied Vanessa with a smile. 'Getting in the zone with anyone in mind?'

'You know it...' Bibi, who carried herself as if coiled with energy about to spring at any minute, seemed particularly spry as she grabbed her axe and bounded towards the marker.

'Aieeee!' she yelled, as the weapon left her hands. It was not a good hit, but the groan of satisfaction she let out suggested that her goal had been more personal animalistic than competitive. 'I pictured Garrett's face on the target,' she giggled. 'He spilled his coffee on my brand-new white wool rug this morning.'

The women burst out laughing and Bibi smirked, before sitting back down alongside them. Hailey smiled; clearly she and Bibi had a similar approach to this axe-throwing.

'All right, birthday girl, you're up next,' Hailey called to her friend.

She beat a mini drum roll on her thighs as Vanessa stood, shrugging off her leather jacket and pulling at her grey T-shirt to smooth it over her hips. Then, she stretched dramatically, and to the amusement of her friends, kissed both biceps, picked up her axe and strode to the spot marked on the ground for them to throw from.

The sun momentarily slid behind the only wisp of cloud in the sky, covering the target in shade, and the group fell silent. Hailey could see Vanessa's characteristic look of total concentration on her face, her eyes narrowed, her lips pursed. It was the same look as when she was lining up for one of her show-stopping volleys. She was going in for the kill.

Unflinching, she dipped her head to peek over the top of her sunglasses and lobbed the axe with all she had, her right lats rippling against the tight fabric of her top. Bullseye.

She spun on her heel, one eyebrow raised, but clearly very pleased, as the three of them jumped up and cheered, applauding her epic shot.

'Wow, Vee,' Kristin said. 'Who did you picture on that target?'

Hailey had no doubt whatsoever who Vanessa had been picturing. If it wasn't the same as her, and Vanessa wasn't picturing Jeremy's puffy, red face on that bullseye, she'd eat her tennis racket.

Vanessa winked back at her sister. 'That's a secret I'll never tell, but didn't I say this would be more fun than getting your toenails painted...?'

'I confess, I doubted you, too,' said Bibi, 'but damn, you were right. This feels... like therapy.'

'Just like therapy,' Hailey said, chiming in. 'Just what I needed, honestly. I might need to get a few axes to take home and add this to my morning routine.'

'Me too,' agreed Kristin, smiling. Then she turned to face Hailey, the smile replaced with a look of concern. 'How is everything at home at the moment, Hailes? I didn't get a chance to ask you at the party last week – but Justin looked well?'

'Oh, he's doing OK,' she said. 'We're lucky in so many ways, but you know, it's still tough.'

Hailey didn't find it easy to talk about how she was really feeling, but with these women she knew she could drop her guard a little. Most of the time, where her husband Justin and her professional life were concerned, she was a rigid façade of inscrutability. Partly because she knew her highly respected legal career depended on opponents knowing as little as possible about any weaknesses, and partly because she knew she didn't have limitless time left with Justin – and she didn't want him to spend a second of it worrying about her.

'For both of you,' said Vanessa, holding out the axe for Kristin, who was up next.

'Yeah, for both of us. He hates becoming less mobile. And I hate feeling him slip away. But like I say, we're lucky. We have each other. We have the garden. And the blessings that the garden brings.'

It was only a couple of years since Justin's diagnosis, and already they had made the very best of every single day since they'd received the news. But managing the pain, the sadness, the fear – and of course the increasing level of disability – took its toll. Hailey prided herself on not being the sort of woman that others would ever feel sorry for though, and she had set about creating the very best version of their personal tragedy with a vision and single-mindedness that most around her found inspiring.

Justin was, after all, a once-formidable man: top of his year at Oxford where he had met a youthful Hailey, before becoming a leader in both business and philanthropy. Of course, he didn't need to be such a high achiever in either of these fields, given that his family had long owned vast swathes of the West Highlands, and he had inherited his own stunning home and grounds in Hampshire. These days, he cut a very different figure, as his degenerative disease advanced and affected his mobility and his mood. Then there was the relative indignity of being a man who entire boardrooms once stood up to greet but who now had to be wheeled into the room.

His wheelchair was the very best that money could buy, imported from a specialist in Boston, where Hailey regularly travelled to meet with consultants, attending seminars and lectures on the very latest treatments and even studying holistic remedies.

'Aaah, yes, the *blessings*,' Bibi said, looking slyly towards the instructor, who thankfully seemed to have given up on trying to teach the women and was now fully-focused on typing away on his phone. 'How are they going? Good harvest this time of year?'

Bibi was referring to the discreet crop of hydroponically grown medicinal marijuana that Hailey oversaw in her beautiful grounds, for the management of Justin's chronic pain. There was also a wooden-walled mushroom hut, elegantly disguised as one of the groundsmen's sheds, where she grew a variety of fungi for both micro-dosing and what she liked to refer to matter-of-factly as 'basic cognitive functions'.

The illegal nature of this enterprise went undiscussed by the women. This was in part because of their sympathy for Hailey and her husband's predicament but was also a mark of respect for the woman and the knowledge that she had accrued – both legal and illegal.

None of the women ever cast judgement on her way of managing the illness, and Hailey had long appreciated it. She had hoped to keep the entire enterprise secret, but after a particularly taxing week, Hailey and Beatriz had been enjoying a simple kitchen supper at hers (lobster, imported from St Ives that morning), when she had offered her some 'herbal' tea with pudding. Minds had been blown, respect had increased, and the secret had been kept as tight as a drum.

The fact that Hailey was the legal expert among them was of course an added incentive to all four of them to keep their lips sealed where her extra-curricular medicating was concerned. Despite her Houston upbringing, Hailey had graduated from Oxford University in the late nineties (having already breezed through law school in the US), before going on to play a key role as a government legal advisor early in the Blair years. Now she was a formidable and exceptionally well-connected KC at a Central London chambers, as well as dabbling in consultancy work from time to time. If anyone could outfox His Majesty's Finest, it was going to be Hailey – particularly as a healthy portion of the men who came across her professionally only registered blonde curls and a Texan drawl, as if somehow, they were indicators of a less than razor sharp mind. What fools they were. No one asked to speak to her boss twice.

Bibi liked to joke about the 'harvest', but she was far from a stranger to its produce. Not that the Chappell sisters knew that. Just as there were some things that the sisters kept between themselves, there were also some confidences that Hailey and Beatriz kept to themselves and would never share. They had, after all, been playing together as a doubles team for a few years before the friendship with the Chappell sisters had really taken off, and anyway, wasn't it more chic to sometimes keep a discreet secret to a smaller audience?

'My little farm is doing very well,' Hailey said softly to her friend. 'Let me know if you ever need any herbs.'

Bibi smiled back at her and none of the girl gang spoke – the Chappell sisters because they had not heard Hailey's last comment, and Bibi because she knew now was not the time. And all of them were mindful of the instructor, who was still present, despite seeming more interested in Instagram than any of the women's conversation. Perhaps a few seasons of blocking out hen-night chat had rendered him immune to eavesdropping. Or, judging by the look on his face, he'd lined up a hot date for that evening. *The hen parties must be ripe for the picking*, Bibi thought.

It was Vanessa who spoke next. 'And how is Justin doing?'

'As sharp as the day I met him,' explained Hailey. 'Still running things. Honestly, I pity anyone who thinks they can take advantage of him just because of this wretched condition.'

There was an edge to her voice as she said this. She shocked herself when she noticed how vulnerable she sounded. But she was glad to have kept her voice from cracking, as it very occasionally did when she let her emotions get the better of her. Still, none of the women seemed to have noticed. In fact, they were looking totally unconcerned.

Perhaps, she wondered, *this was because none of her three friends were quite sure what the 'things' that he ran actually were.* Yes, he had family money, but he was also very evidently a titan of business – the sort of man who political ministers would call for an opinion before a keynote speech. The sort of person that shadow ministers would beg for approval when elections came round. She had once overheard Vanessa joking to Kristin that he was an arms dealer, but she had made sure that neither of them knew that she'd overheard it, or what the truth might be. They simply didn't know, and Hailey trusted that even if they pondered about it in their own time, they weren't going to start fishing when he had so little time left. So, the four of them continued to dance delicately away from the topic, whenever it threatened to come up. Some things are best left unsaid, and as far as Hailey was concerned, most things were.

'It's so cruel,' said Kristin. 'It's not even as if he's elderly – he should have so much ahead of him.'

'Yes...' Hailey's voice was now almost inaudible. 'But he doesn't. And yet... the time he has had has been filled with love, success, joy.'

'Too true,' said Vanessa, standing up with a slap of her thighs. 'A lesson to us all, to make the most of what we have, that's for sure.'

'Hark at the birthday girl. Don't tell me you're getting senti-mental in your old age,' said Bibi.

'Never! I'm just mindful that we don't know what's round the corner and we only live once. I'd like to have lived even a year of my life with the purpose and drive that Justin displays.'

Hailey watched Vanessa, seemingly impressed by her convic-tion. Where had this sincerity come from? It really was unlike her. Was it a sort of contemplativeness born of a milestone birthday reflection? Or did she have something else on her mind?

'Speaking of which...' said Bibi. '...when's lunch? I'm just about ready for a cocktail.'

'You have ten minutes left in the session,' said their instructor, who seemed to have finally broken away from his phone and remembered that he was meant to be teaching a session.

The slightly sombre mood that had fallen across the group since the mention of Justin was lingering, despite Bibi's talk of cocktails. Kristin stepped up to take her throw, then each of them hurled the axes in turn, as the instructor applauded their efforts despite being baffled by their collective lack of direction.

GAME, SET & MURDER

The trees shivered slightly as a breeze ran through the woods. But the sun had climbed even higher in the sky, and by the time their ninety minutes was up, they were more than ready to sit in the shade with a drink. Or two.

As they left the axe-throwing facility, Kristin Google-mapped the directions to where they were heading, and the group set off together.

Hailey noticed Vanessa slide an arm through her sister's as they all fell into step beside each other.

'So, has Jez got his head around the fact that he's not going to be taking over the kingdom anytime soon?' asked Vanessa.

'Wait, what?' asked Hailey, instantly curious.

'Dad broke the news the morning after the party,' Vanessa explained, struggling to hide her delight. 'He's feeling as fit as a fiddle and he's not ready to retire *anytime* soon!'

'No way!' Bibi squealed. 'Jeremy's been saying to Garrett for weeks now that he'll be taking over the helm by the end of the year!'

Kristin grimaced. 'I know, he's fuming.'

'Was it really such a huge surprise?' Hailey asked. 'I mean, we had kind of assumed it was coming up, but it was only Jeremy who seemed to have taken it as read.'

'Typical Jez,' Vanessa said. 'Always expecting things to just land in his lap.'

'Vee, come on. It was a little presumptive, yes, but honestly, I can't say I blame him...'

'No one's talking about blame.'

'You don't *need* to when your face is doing all the work for you,' Kristin snapped as her sister.

'Ladies, ladies,' Bibi interjected. 'Let's not get into this today, shall we?'

Vanessa's voice softened, 'I just want to make sure you're okay, Kiki. I know how he can be ...'

'We'll be fine. Can you just leave it alone?'

Hailey watched the words fly between the sisters like a never-ending baseline rally, unsure whether she should interrupt the play.

'I'm not talking about *you plural* – I want to know that *you're* OK. You, Kristin.'

'It's not easy, you know what he's like ...'

Hailey raised an eyebrow, and they stayed silent. Behind closed doors, Bibi, Hailey and Vanessa had a *lot* to say about Jeremy Hale from their days back on the tennis circuit, but they knew that Kristin wouldn't want to hear it.

The trouble was, Hailey wasn't sure Kristin *did* see the Jeremy they all saw. And she wasn't sure she ever would.

Chapter 9

VANESSA

'I do,' said Vanessa to her sister, gently now, as the women continued walking, joining a farm track that Kristin checked against the instructions on her phone. The maize in the field adjacent towered above, letting flickers of sunlight in as they followed the path. 'You *know* I know what he's like. That's why I'm asking. Remember, at one time I knew him very well indeed. And I just want you to be happy.'

Vanessa had been on the junior tennis circuit with Jeremy back when the two of them had been teenagers. While Kristin was still at primary school, idolising them both largely from afar, Vanessa had all but grown up with Jez, watching his ascent from up-and-coming junior tennis champ to potential superstar with agents and sponsors starting to circle. And then she'd seen it all vanish just as quickly. A couple of seasons of squandered chances, of putting partying ahead of training and choosing to believe his own hype over deference to sponsors and potential managers. Surely it hadn't just been as simple as that, though? She had often wished that she'd known the whole story, as his professional career had seemed to be guaranteed one minute, then suddenly, it was all over.

To this day, she didn't know what happened. Not for sure. There had been no injury, just some gossip about his attitude, and his arrogance, then a string of losses. At the time, Vanessa had just assumed he had grown too complacent, enjoying being a bit of a heart throb on tour while having the safety net of returning to the teenage Kristin's adoring gaze if a tournament didn't go to plan. Then, once he had left the Tour altogether, she had started to notice the odd raised eyebrow, hushed conversations and passing comments. Nowhere near enough to build up a proper picture of what had happened, but enough to suggest that there was a lot more to it.

She recalled the woman she'd met at a corporate lunch at Queen's once, who had found out that Vanessa's sister was married to Jeremy, only to blanch before asking in a whisper if she was OK. Then, as she'd left, she'd handed over her card saying – eyes darting – that she should keep it in case Kristin ever wanted 'to talk'. At the time, Vanessa had assumed she was a woman her brother-in-law had cheated on. Then, a couple of years later, someone had casually asked if the Jeremy Hale her sister was married to was 'the Jez who'd broken that Italian player's jaw' once. After that, she had checked in on her sister a little more. No harm asking, she'd told herself.

The truth was, she felt guilty for not having Jez directly or shown more interest at the time. In all honesty, she hadn't cared to ask what the truth was, because back then she and Jez had been good mates. He was someone she would confide in about the pressure she felt from her parents, because he suffered from that too. It was tough being so young and away from home for so many weeks of the year while also being subjected to the third degree from afar. They shared confidences about off-court dalliances and even helped each other out with potential dates – although this was something she had never told Kristin about and knew she never would. In those days, Vanessa had found his tendency towards bravado or nonchalance almost

74

endearing. He took her teasing well and gave as good as he got. But then when things petered out for him, she found Jeremy started to avoid her. He would pass her at the club as if they'd never shared a drink, let alone a five-hour flight discussing who they'd consider sleeping with on the US team. He turned his gaze entirely towards her sister, who asked fewer questions and made fewer smart-ass quips. Kristin was older now, able to be taken seriously as a girlfriend. And it wasn't long before she stepped in as full-time balm for his self-esteem, and Vanessa was no longer required.

Within what seemed like months Kristin had transformed from the quiet little sister that no one really noticed around the club and courts, to the girlfriend of one of the most lusted-after young men on the GB tennis scene. Once a wall flower, watching everything and saying very little, now she blossomed as if basking under the warmth of Jeremy's attention. He began his successful coaching business, based largely out of Royal Oaks, and the couple became a regular part of the day-to-day set-up at the club. When Vanessa returned from the Tour herself a year or two later, she was just in time to see him make a showy proposal at dinner one New Year's Eve. A few years after that they started a family; it seemed as if he too had healed, the light of her sister's sunny temperament chasing away whatever secrets his past had held.

'All couples go through difficult patches…' continued Kristin, who was clearly not going to be strong-armed into a more in-depth conversation by her sister. 'He just gets so angry sometimes.'

Vanessa was shocked to hear Kristin admit this about Jeremy. Her sister was loyal to everyone she knew, someone who followed the rules of friendship with an adherence that bordered on frustrating at times. (Why didn't she want to gossip as much as Vanessa did, especially when they lived somewhere with *so much* gossip?!) Her marriage had long been an impenetrable fortress, something she protected above all else. Vanessa paused, no longer walking, keen to keep her sister talking without interruption from the others.

'I just want you to feel safe in your own home,' she said, plainly, a hand lightly on her sister's forearm. It seemed daft that she had even thought this, much less said it out loud. But she had seen too many women married to once-sporty egocentric men become the focus of their aggression.

'Oh, Vee, don't be daft. Of course I'm safe. God, you're so dramatic. He's got a temper, he's not *violent*.'

For a second, Vanessa thought she'd gone too far. Only she realised that she had never mentioned violence. So why was Kristin bringing it up. *She couldn't mess this conversation up now,* she thought as she determined to tread cautiously.

They turned off the track that they'd been following, and headed into the glade where lunch was going to be served, beside the River Meon.

Vanessa double-checked the map still in Kristin's hand, suspecting that this might be a far-flung part of Hailey's extensive estate, such was its almost invisibly maintained rustic beauty. No point in asking, she figured. Hailey wouldn't have okayed it if she wasn't happy with it, and she'd probably never say either way. That woman really was as generous as she was allergic to being thanked for it. In the distance, a willow tree was growing at the riverbank, elegantly dipping into the water.

Slightly to its left, a few hired staff (she suspected Bibi was behind that) were preparing the lunch beneath a temporary gazebo. A young man in a stylish denim apron was turning steaks on a griddle, while a blonde female colleague was arranging thick slices of juicy tomato and oozing burrata onto four plates before drizzling them with olive oil from a terracotta bottle. In front of the makeshift cookery station there were a couple of white cotton broderie anglaise parasols creating some much-needed respite from the heat of the day. Blankets and cotton throws were arranged on the grass, as well as over a couple of hay bales, which were doubling as side tables and benches.

From the other side of the field, the sisters watched as Bibi walked ahead, approaching the temporary serving station first, before turning with what looked like a jug of Pimm's in one hand, making a thumbs-up signal at them with the other. Vanessa smiled and waved back.

'Sorry, I'm sorry, Kris. I just remember what he used to be like when we were kids, if he didn't win a match, or something didn't go his way.'

'He was a *teenager*, Vee. God, none of us act the way *we* were when we were teenagers!'

'You're right. I guess I just want to check that you're following your dreams, not just Jeremy's – or Mum and Dad's.'

'I want this, Vee. But when Mum and Dad are ready. I love the club, I love knowing we can stay there even if we're not taking over. It's so good for Freddie that's all, and it's *home*. But Jez is just getting a bit impatient, that's all.'

'How so?'

Across the field, Hailey was now walking towards Beatriz, to help carry the drinks back over.

'Nothing too bad, don't get yourself in a state. He's a good man, he just wants to succeed, to fulfill his potential, to make me and Fred proud of him. He wants to provide, to be a provider...'

'Yes, he's ambitious...'

The sight of Jez, twenty years ago, hurling his racket across a court and injuring a ball boy's eye sprung to mind. Violence, threats, money … he would do anything to get what he wanted; she had heard people say that about him. There had always been talk about his 'I'll get a win one way or another' attitude at the height of his career; was that what he was doing now? Hoping to catch a ride to the top?

'…He's definitely always been one of those "whatever it takes" guys …'

'Not *anything*, obviously.'

'Obviously, it's just a turn of phrase,' Vanessa countered, quickly. But as a memory of Jez yelling in an umpire's face, flecks of spittle hitting his forehead as the man blinked in shock, came to Vanessa, she wondered if it really was. She couldn't press it any further now though, the others were nearly back with them.

'If it's just about him being cantankerous then I will say no more.' To her surprise, Kristin stopped in her tracks, holding on to Vanessa's arms and preventing her from walking towards Hailey and Beatriz.

'I think he's worried about money,' she whispered, her eyes wide. 'Investments.'

'What investments? Tennis coaches don't invest.'

'Well, he has. He wanted to bring something to the club, to give it, you know, a boost. Modernise it a bit. And he's being very guarded about it, but I've got a feeling that it's not all been plain sailing.'

Kristin was almost babbling now, something she'd done since they were little girls when she was feeling anxious.

'Back when his dad died, I think he thought that a chunk of money was a sure thing. And now his mum spends like it's water. I don't know, maybe he'd been depending on it and now he frets. Like I say, he has strong boundaries about discussing this sort of thing. But I wish he would include me, so I could help really. Maybe I've entirely got the wrong end of the stick. You know how I can overthink things!'

Vanessa nodded intently, noting with interest that Jeremy's use of the word 'boundaries' was very similar to most people's use of the word 'secrets'. But there was no way she was going to say a thing if it meant interrupting this flow of admissions from her usually cagey sister.

'Yes, it's probably that,' continued Kristin. 'You know what it's like when we're at the Oaks, it's hard to have a proper conversation without someone or other walking in and interrupting. I didn't see it as such a bad thing, Mum and Dad wanting to stay on, now I'm just worried it's, well, a bit of a final straw... type... situation.'

Her voice was petering out as she lost her nerve, realising how much she'd said.

'But the club isn't going to save him financially – it's not like he can sell it or anything.'

'Of course, of course. And I *do* want to run it once Mum and Dad actually retire. I just didn't see it as such a bad thing if they stay on a bit. I want Dad to be OK, of course I do. But he insists he is, so, I was thinking let's make the best of it, you know? Jez and I have always talked about travel. Maybe a summer in Europe or a term home-schooling Freddie while we go somewhere, see the world. But now... Well, now he says he's seen the world already.'

'Trust me, it wasn't *the world* he was looking at while we were on tour,' says Vanessa, trying to lighten the mood, but immediately fearing she'd gone too far.

'Oh, stop it,' said Kristin, smiling now. But in the harsh light of the midday sun, Kristin looked older, a little tired even. Vanessa started to wonder if she had kicked a hornet's nest here. She had been worried Jeremy was being unbearable to live with, but not *this* reckless.

Kristin sighed. They had reached the parasols now, within earshot of the others, and everything seemed less resolved than ever.

The scene before them was stunning. And as Kristin raised a glass and mouthed 'Thank you' to Hailey, Vanessa got her answer. *Look at that food*, she thought, *of* course *this was Hailey's doing*. Private land, private caterer, private handsome waiter… And now, as a starchy-shirted waiter seemed to appear from a small SUV to stand by the barbecue, waiting for meat to be placed onto the plates, Hailey walked over to have a word with him. The boss indeed.

Beatriz was reclining, her face towards the sun, as if soaking in its light and heat. Her skin was dark year-round, the sort of complexion that only ever glowed, rather than looking ruddy or flustered as Kristin's so often did after too much sun, too much wine, too much emotion. Without opening her eyes, Bibi gestured towards the jug of Pimm's, muttering, 'Please, I am already one-deep.'

Vanessa filled her glass for her, then looked up at the waiter who was indicating that the food was ready. In front of the barbecue was a buffet table groaning under the weight of salads, dishes of bearnaise sauce and a bottle of what looked like priceless olive oil. As they stepped up to collect their steaks, Vanessa noticed Hailey was standing with her back to the group, on the phone, head tilted into the device discreetly. As the sisters approached, Vanessa could just about make out her mutterings.

'Yes, yes, they're here now. Of course I'll do my best,' before turning to face them with an inscrutable smile. 'Happy Birthday, darling Vanessa. You deserve nothing but love and joy.'

Vanessa smiled, and the four of them clinked glasses with their customary 'Chin Chin'. What a perfect day.

But somewhere in the pit of her stomach, Vanessa felt queasy, unable to explain even to herself why she didn't like the sound of what Hailey had just been talking about. But there wasn't time to dwell on it. She threw her arms in the air, then around the women. The four of them embraced, glasses aloft, voices happy. A breeze rustled through the willow tree.

Lunch, let's just focus on lunch, each of the women thought to themselves.

And so they did. Beatriz, dishing the gossip on her new masseur who she swore looked like Jonathan Bailey. Hailey, laughing along at the jokes while remaining watchful, her owl-like eyes following each speaker as the group took turns with confessions of embarrassing moments at massage and beauty appointments. Vanessa, relaxed now, buzzing at the almost ribald sharing of such confidences. And even Kristin seemed to forget about whatever had been bothering her back at the club and lay on the grass, chatting until the last of the picnic had been cleared away, and the Pimm's was all gone.

The road was dusty with heat as Vanessa was being driven home half an hour later, Hailey having of course arranged cars for all three of them. Vanessa watched the sun glowing over the dip of the South Downs as she sped home and smiled to herself at what a happy birthday she had had after all. There had been times in the last few months when she had had moments of queasiness at the thought of herself, single at forty, planning a huge party alone. She relished her single status, but never liked discussing it with well-meaning strangers, the sort who revealed far too much about themselves when they expressed anxiety over whether she had a 'man in her life' yet. Today had avoided all that. She had felt relaxed, cherished even. As the four of them had held their glasses together, the sun glinting through the amber of their drinks, she had known she didn't want to be anywhere else. She'd do anything for these three women. *Whatever it takes.* Perhaps she was more like Jeremy than she realised.

Now ...

Chapter 10

ELEANOR

Eleanor hadn't slept at all the night that Jeremy died. She'd watched as the soft dawn light had broken through her floral curtains and spilled across her bed covers. She'd listened as the quiet of the night had been interrupted by the morning chorus of local wildlife and then the sound of a few car engines being started up, the first commuters of the day on their way. She'd gone back over the previous day again and again, the intricate details of the cake, and every time she felt wracked with a deep guilt at how she'd let it in to the celebratory tea without checking the ingredients. What had that delivery guy looked like? She remembered his hair, his neat stubble, but could she remember his face? And what was the name of the cake brand he had had on his T-shirt? Cake something or other? She was sure it was Italian. It all felt like a blur now, like it was weeks ago. She couldn't honestly say that she liked Jeremy Hale, but she wasn't sure he deserved to *die*.

Finally, her alarm clock rang out as the hands ticked onto the little number seven and she shifted herself to sit up in bed, slightly relieved that the night was over. A new day.

An hour later Eleanor walked into the Royal Oaks, like she did every other day – right on time. There was a stillness in the air and a police cordon around the main function rooms. She spent the first twenty minutes tidying her office – it looked like the police had rifled through a few of her papers because they were slightly askew, her cup with its 'My Little Cup of Postitivi-tea' slogan on it (a present from last Christmas's office Secret Santa) no longer sitting on its coaster. She was relieved that they hadn't found anything of interest, but it didn't lift the heavy cloud of guilt still sitting on her shoulders.

Edward Chappell had sent an email the previous evening saying that the Royal Oaks was closed for the rest of the week to clients, but Eleanor wanted to feel busy. She sat down at her computer and waited as it whirred into action, then she started replying to emails and responding to queries as she would every other morning. The blue of the office screen was stinging her tired eyes, but someone needed to reply to the countless emails asking what had happened at the Centenary Celebration – and a few who'd climbed further up the gossip chain asking if Jeremy was OK. Her heart was in her throat as she typed out messages thanking them for their enquiry and saying that the club would be in touch soon.

Making herself a cup of tea in the clubhouse kitchen, Eleanor didn't notice when the police car discreetly pulled up to the side of the main entrance. Or when the same duo of policemen from the previous night quietly got out of the car and walked round past the main entrance to the outside door to Kristin and Jeremy's flat.

After pouring herself a glass of cool water from the tap, Eleanor took a sip, rested the glass on the stainless-steel work bench and opened the fridge. Inside were the remaining cakes from the day before, neat plates of cupcakes, brownies and millionaire's shortbread, each under a tight cling-film dome. She could tell on sight that there were a few of each missing – taken by the police for testing, presumably. At least with these ones, she knew who had made them. She could put a face to each and every plate. Unlike the one she had idiotically let on site. *Still*, she thought, *better to be safe than sorry*. She heaved the tray out of the fridge and deposited the rest into the bin.

At the back of the fridge she could see some mozzarella, and when she scanned the lower shelves she could see bits and pieces of veg in there, wilting a little but with some life still left in them. On the side was a cardboard catering tray of eggs. They'd surely be wasted if left in here for the week while the club was shut.

Slowly, she reached for a stainless-steel mixing bowl, cracking a few eggs into it, then some chopped-up veg, a few ripped slivers of basil and finally some salt and pepper. She dragged a muffin tin from a high shelf and poured a little of the mixture into each hole before dotting some torn mozzarella onto the top of each one. She knew these omelette muffins were a favourite of Freddie's, and she was pretty sure Kristin wasn't going to be up to making something like this, so when she pulled them out of the oven half an hour later, she hoped they'd make things a little easier, for the next couple of mornings at least.

The elasticated sides of her soft canvas shoes stretched slightly as she timidly climbed the stairs up to the flat. Once she was at the front door, she knocked only very softly before calling out to say it was her, just popping in with something for Fred. She heard adult voices in the living room, which sounded like the Chappells, and a moment later Kristin appeared at the door.

'Oh, hello, Eleanor,' she said. She looked surprisingly put together, her hair neatly pulled back in a French plait, and even a touch of mascara on her lashes. But the dark circles beneath her eyes told another story. 'Thanks for popping by, it's very kind of you.' She sounded exhausted, poor thing.

'Hello there, Mrs H,' said Eleanor, using the informal nickname she'd long called Kristin. 'I've brought Freddie a little treat.'

'Thank you, Eleanor, I'm sure he'll love them. Do you want to take them through to him? I'd offer you a cup of tea, but the police are here ... we're just chatting with them ... I'd better get back.'

Eleanor wasn't sure what she had been expecting. Tears? Rage? Shock? But this polite ghost at the door was most disconcerting. 'Of course, you do that. Shall I keep an eye on Freddie for you?'

'Would you? That would be very kind ...'

Eleanor stepped cautiously into the flat, turning away from the sitting room and into the kitchen. She reached for a side plate from the cupboard where she had got a hundred plates for Freddie over the years, before easing one of the breakfast muffins out of the tray. She grabbed a paper napkin from the drawer and headed to find Freddie, knocking gently on the door to his room.

No answer. She pushed the door gingerly and peered her head round it first.

Freddie was on his bed – wearing not school uniform but a *Minecraft* T-shirt and a pair of tracksuit bottoms. He was staring intently at a tablet, stabbing away at the screen while zombie noises grumbled from the device. She realised with horror that she didn't even know if he'd been told about his father yet. The thought winded her, leaving her breathless with panic at the prospect of putting her foot in it.

'I made these this morning and they'll just go to waste downstairs, what with the club shut, so I thought I would bring them up to you as you're off school ...'

He didn't look up, but mumbled, 'Thanks, Eleanor ...'

'May I?' She indicated towards the bed, but he ignored her, so she sat on its edge cautiously, before looking over towards him.

'And how are you doing, my dear? I was so sorry to hear—' She stopped abruptly. *Shut up, Eleanor*, she thought. *Stop blundering in.* Her back felt cold when she realised what she had potentially nearly done.

He shrugged, apparently unfazed. 'Fine, I guess.'

'OK … good.'

'Daddy's dead, though. I heard Aunty Vee say she wished he was dead a week ago to Mummy and now he's gone.'

Eleanor's eyes widened. What had this child heard? What had gone on here? Her body froze, the roots of her hair feeling icy with panic as she felt deeply that this was something she should never have been told. Maybe she'd misunderstood, she told herself. That must be it. Freddie was staring ahead at his screen, apparently unaffected by his admission.

'Oh,' replied Eleanor. Her mouth had made the shape, but she wasn't sure she had made any sound at all. 'I'm so very sorry to hear that.'

She leaned in to ruffle his hair, but he ignored her.

'It's OK, he was a bully.' Then, as if he'd said nothing at all, he looked at her and smiled. 'Can I get a glass of milk with these?'

Four weeks before...

Chapter 11

HAILEY

The squeak of plimsolls on the gymnasium floor at New Beeches School made Hailey wince. *How had they not found a way to prevent it?* she wondered. It was a long time since she'd been at school, and it hadn't even been in this country. With all the resources that these British private schools had, surely they could have come up with something quieter by now. Honestly, it was like shrieking feet whenever one of the kids leapt or skidded for a ball. At least it was relatively cool in here, away from the sun.

Hailey's eyes darted from side to side so Kristin – who was only across the room – wouldn't see her discomfort, but she was having a moment of panic that one of these kids was going to touch her, wiping muddy fingers on her immaculate outfit. She was not in sports kit, unlike Vanessa who was standing next to her, or some of the other volunteers, most of whom were school mums. Instead, she was wearing her usual mix of taupe and biscuit-coloured sports-adjacent clothing. A pair of stretchy capri pants with a wide stripe in some sort of technical fabric running up the sides. A gilet whose zip alone looked pricier than any jewellery Kristin owned, and a pair of pale orange leather Hogans that Vanessa had once unashamedly told her always made her think of a horse's hooves.

Hailey pressed her lips together to stop herself smiling at her memory of the moment: Kristin's gasp of horror at her sister's cheek, and Bibi's uncontainable giggles at all three of them. *Anyway, maybe they did look like hooves*, she thought, but they'd cost her hundreds and she didn't want someone's jam sandwich dropped on them.

'Aunty Veeeee!' shrieked an excited voice that seemed extraordinarily loud for such a small person. 'Will you be umpiring my match?'

Hailey looked up to see Freddie charging towards her and Vanessa from the other side of the pickleball court. Hailey had a sudden pang of affection for the little guy, immaculate in his stiff cotton sports shorts and logo-ed school polo shirt. Next to him was his buddy Sid, who was flashing the classic seven-year-old's smile: three teeth missing and two new ones, comically too large for his mouth.

Hailey looked at her clipboard and the impeccable list of today's players and matches. Neat lines and an almost minute-by-minute schedule. Just as she'd planned it. If anyone other than Freddie had asked who was umpiring, she'd have been livid; after all, each of the adults involved had a crisp copy of the day's timetable, and every match's umpire, neatly laminated. But this was sweet Freddie, whose innocent nature she was currently very invested in, as her suspicions about his father's temper were starting to grow.

'Yes, sweetie, she is,' said Hailey, ushering him and his friend over to their court as she wandered across the gymnasium with them. On the far side of the school hall was a clutch of girls the same age, in the same uniform, only with more elaborate hairstyles. Multiple ponytails, neat plaits reaching around the sides of their heads, even space buns with navy-blue ribbons tied around them.

'Oh, good! Grandma's here too,' Freddie said, although Hailey couldn't help but think he sounded a little anxious at the idea. *Fair enough*, she thought, Jeremy's mother, Petunia Hale, was an intimidating woman.

Behind them came the sound of the headmistress clapping her hands as she walked in with the original Mrs Hale herself: Jeremy's mum, and chair of the board of governors at New Beeches.

The kids in the hall stopped talking and the whole room turned to look at Petunia Hale as she strode into the room like a queen surveying her kingdom.

Petunia was only a decade or so older than Hailey, and undeniably formidable. She had long been a single woman, but was far from what anyone would call a spinster. Instead, she gave the distinct impression that she was a lady who had no one to worry about but herself. Her skin glowed with the sort of expensive foundation that Hailey knew cost almost the same as a year's Botox. Petunia's creamy blonde hair must have gone grey years ago, but it almost glittered in the sunlight and no doubt required hours in the salon each month to ensure it looked so immaculate. She was wearing a tailored pair of (clearly designer) white trousers, a crisp white polo shirt and a tennis-style cropped jacket with mint-green trim. Yet, despite her prickly appearance, the woman had a real charm and warmth. Hailey recognised a woman who wore seriousness as a sort of armour, determined to be respected in a world full of men who assumed their place at the table was granted while she had had to fight for hers. And whenever Hailey spotted these women, she found herself drawn to them.

Hailey knew that Jeremy's father, Peter, had passed away just before Kristin and Jeremy's engagement, but his mother still wore both her wedding ring and a dazzling eternity ring. Hailey and Vanessa often joked that the jewellery must have been the only thing worth sticking around for with Mr Hale senior – apparently he had been a cantankerous man, a ruddy-faced bully who fought Jeremy's corner regardless of whether or not he ever deserved it. Kristin had once commented that Petunia seemed to find a real spring in her step in the years *after* her husband's death.

Hailey wasn't sure where Mr Hale's wealth came from – *something to do with car sales*, she thought. The few times Vanessa mentioned playing with Jeremy at a young age, she'd said that Mr Hale senior always came across as a bit of a wide boy, forever knowing the 'right' people, always there to tip the waiter or ball boy a crisp £20 note. There was no doubt he had been as proud of his bulging wallet as he was ashamed that it was full of 'new money', so Vanessa had told her that he had spent whatever was needed to get Jeremy, the apple of his eye and the Hales' only child, the very best in his nascent tennis career. Because tennis clubs, he had swiftly realised, were a top-tier place for networking and burnishing reputations. And the better Jez did, the more contacts he would have access to.

So, when Peter had died suddenly of a heart condition, Jeremy had been devastated. Petunia, on the other hand … well, Petunia had surprised everyone: after an appropriate amount of time, she had, well, she'd blossomed. Instead of being at a loss for what to do with her days, as Jeremy (and the Chappells, although they would never have admitted it) had assumed she might, she found herself with a better social life than ever. Unencumbered by having to please her husband, or even keep herself in shape for him, she spent her time at midday cinema screenings with a bag of popcorn on her lap, or buying a new, leopard-print-heavy wardrobe, or taking a series of classes on how to read Tarot. She still played tennis and was an active member of the nearby Cavendish Lane club, even if she'd taken a gentle slide down the rankings over the years. Hailey knew that the Chappells had offered Petunia a free lifetime membership to Royal Oaks, but she gathered the generous gift hadn't gone down too well, with the words 'don't need their charity' being hissed by Petunia on more than one occasion.

These days, Petunia continued to profess both that she still *adored* tennis, and that her time was better served 'giving back' to the community, which was why she was on the board of so many local schools. And this was how her latest fad had resulted in the 'Pickleball Superslam', a fun doubles event for kids, with equipment provided by Royal Oaks and the tournament sponsored by an enthusiastic local entrepreneur. Oliver Rudolph who was something of a silver fox. A recent widower who had just sold his successful birthday party supplies company, he was gaining a reputation among the older ladies of the local tennis circuit not just for his considerable wealth, but also for his muscular, tanned legs – the legacy of fifty years spent on the court, year-round, a feat that he had achieved by being a member of *both* Royal Oaks and the prestigious La Manga resort in Spain. A busy man indeed.

A few weeks earlier, Bibi had mentioned casually on their WhatsApp group *Her Royal Highnesses* that she'd spotted Petunia on a couple of afternoon drives in Oliver Rudolph's chic metallic blue Alfa Romeo Spider. Vanessa had joked that perhaps Petunia might want to do a little more than ride in the handsome sixty-year-old's car. A few rather naughty messages had followed, but it had got Hailey thinking – maybe *Petunia* would be her way into convincing Jeremy to setting up pickleball courts at Royal Oaks.

She was reluctant to admit it, but Hailey wasn't actually an enormous fan of pickleball. What she *was* a huge fan of was the opportunity to play a sport that so many of her American clients adored right here on her doorstep. The game was huge with so many of her older but extraordinarily wealthy clients, and she knew that being able to host them at Royal Oaks would be an enormous business advantage for her. She adored tennis, but that was what she did with her scant down time. The thought of taking some Texan billionaires to a sun-dappled pickleball court then for a cream tea in the Royal Oaks clubhouse as they cut a deal while enjoying the view of the ornamental lake was hugely attractive to Hailey. But not everyone had quite seen it that way.

Hailey had raised the idea of introducing pickleball at Royal Oaks months ago with Kristin and Jeremy, with little success. It was of course Jeremy who had been the real obstruction. He had opposed it at every turn. His first argument: did they really want to turn the club into little more than a well-appointed childcare facility? (Kids, too, enjoyed the sport.) His second: it was naff, it made the place seem like 'an unserious clown show for bloody amateurs'. And his third: the rat-a-tat-tat of the plastic ball on the solid wooden bats was infuriating, when heard from the nearby tennis courts or worse, from the clubhouse. He muttered darkly about tales of tennis courts being lost to pickleball in the States and managed to convince Edward and Tamara (who were quite open to Hailey's proposal) that it would be a terrible financial investment.

In the end, Hailey had outsmarted him. She'd taken Petunia Hale for a Champagne Afternoon Tea, knowing full well the woman wouldn't be able to resist. As Petunia finished her fourth glass of the finest French fizz, her cheeks flushed and a few crumbs from her last mouthful of scone still resting on her ample chest, Hailey had kicked into action.

'It's massive in America,' Hailey had told her with confidence, as she topped up Petunia's empty glass. 'It would be a really smart addition to the club. It's inclusive, hugely sociable and a great revenue generator. It's absolutely exploded across the pond.'

'Well, dear, it does sound an awful lot of fun.'

'I knew you'd understand it, Petunia,' Hailey had replied, leaning in to serve her final ace, the icing on the cake that she hoped would tip Petunia over the edge. 'And you know what, I spoke to the Royal Oaks about introducing it, but sometimes I worry that the Chappells can be a little stuck in their ways.' She paused, knowing how much Petunia enjoyed being reassured that she was higher on the pecking order than her son's in-laws. 'Provincial, almost,' she continued. 'What I need is to speak to a true businesswoman about it. What do you think? Can you suggest anyone?'

Hailey stayed silent, holding her nerve. She peered inquisitively over the top of her tortoiseshell reading glasses that she wore for effect only.

Petunia's eyes glittered.

'Consider it done, my dear. I'll talk to my son tomorrow.'

Game, set and match, Hailey thought.

Within a week Petunia had told Jeremy that she wanted to get involved with pickleball, and a few days later, his protestations about the sport had abated. Hailey's sunny charm with Edward Chappell, alongside her absolute insistence that getting more children playing pickleball was the perfect way to get more adults playing tennis was a win for everyone and sealed the deal. Jeremy was left fuming, grumbling that all the admin of setting up new pickleball courts at Royal Oaks would be left to him (*Kristin, more like*, Hailey had thought), but quietly everyone else now seemed to think it sounded like a great idea.

A week later a deal had been struck for a pickleball tournament to be held at New Beeches Prep School. It was the perfect place to start their new venture, as Petunia had been head of the governors ever since Freddie joined at four years old. Everyone was happy: the kids were buzzing with the new school activity, the school was delighted by the generous donation of equipment from Royal Oaks, and Petunia was thrilled to be spending more time with dishy Oliver Rudolph.

It was only Jeremy who was left with an uncanny sense that he had been outmanoeuvred by all the women in his life. Which, to be honest, he had.

So, this was how Hailey came to be in the gymnasium of a school where she had no children, with three generations of the Chappell family, about to introduce a woman who had started off as a useful ally and had quickly become a rather good friend.

First, she took a moment. She looked around her, smiling gently, ever mindful not to excessively crumple her face while trying to extend the time between aesthetician's appointments. She took a breath, using the box-breathing technique that had proved so successful for her before some of her biggest cases: in for four seconds, hold for four seconds, out for four seconds, hold for four seconds. She felt the blood settle, her heart rate controlled. She looked around the room one last time and stepped forward, lifting the microphone to her lips.

'Ladies and gentlemen, staff and pupils,' she began, a warm smile across her lips, if not quite reaching the corner of her eyes. She knew her Texan glamour would be satisfyingly highlighted by this most Home Counties of settings. Sometimes, in Central London, where it could come across as brash or showy, she tried to tone it down a little. But here, in what Justin sometimes referred to as 'the provinces', she found that the glossiness could do her a favour. Her nails were Barolo-coloured gels, and she knew they'd flash through her curls as she ran a hand above her ear to push the hair off her face.

'I am thrilled to be here today alongside my dear friend and your loyal governor, Mrs Petunia Hale. I'm sure none of you need any introduction to this wonderful woman but, please, let me take this chance to say a huge thank you – on behalf of all of us – to her for her role in spearheading the introduction of pickleball at New Beeches. We do so hope you're going to have fun!'

The assembled adults clapped politely, everyone in Hailey's thrall. She looked around the room at the children standing about, fiddling with their paddle bats, clearly wondering when this much-mentioned fun might begin again. Vanessa was at the back of the hall looking as if she were thinking much the same.

'...I'm now going to hand you over to the magnificent Mrs Hale...'

Kristin's head jerked up reflexively at the mention of a 'Mrs Hale', before she realised Hailey was referring to her mother-in-law. Hailey watched as her eyes darted, wondering why she seemed so wound up. *The woman was coiled as tight as a spring lately*, thought Hailey. She'd have to get her some gummies. Or something from the 'veg patch'.

'...to blow the whistle on the semifinals of today's pickleball doubles, the last matches before this afternoon's finals. Good luck, one and all!'

Petunia stepped forward, motioning with her hands for her audience to stop the applause. 'Too kind, too kind...'

The applause continued, but Hailey noticed Vanessa roll her eyes at Kristin, who stifled a snigger before politely joining in the clapping for her mother-in-law. She couldn't help feeling that the sisters were being a little unfair; as she had got to know

Petunia over the last few weeks, she had realised that she was nothing like her miserable son.

Hailey stepped back as she watched Petunia Hale say a few words of welcome to the crowd gathered in the hall. Then the sound of children chattering and the clatter of bats and balls filled the air, as the adults led their charges to the relevant areas of the court.

Then, as a hushed silence descended and the coins were tossed to decide on who would serve first, she noticed Jeremy Hale appear at the door of the sports hall. Better late than never, she supposed, as he waved at Freddie, then strode over to the headmistress, a great beaming smile on his face. *How did all these women fall for his charms?* she thought as the headmistress blushed a deep scarlet and almost dropped to a curtsey. With any luck, he'd be too busy flirting with all the other school mums and she wouldn't have to talk to him today.

Chapter 12

KRISTIN

Kristin, too, had noticed her husband's gregarious entrance into the sports hall, *and* the headmistress's flustered response. He hadn't even acknowledged her yet, but she was relieved he had at least waved at Freddie – she knew how anxious Jeremy's attendance at his matches made him.

Embarrassed by her own husband ignoring her, something she was sure wouldn't go unnoticed by Vee, she decided to take matters into her own hands and walked across to join him on the other side of the hall. On spotting her, he made an immediate change of gear and greeted her like a long-lost lover in front of the headmistress, pulling her in for a kiss and holding her tightly against his side.

Together, they looked over at their son, who was nervously walking onto the court. 'Good luck, mate,' Jeremy shouted, his voice echoing loudly in the sports hall, despite all the chattering students. 'Hale and hearty make a winner!'

Kristin cringed internally at this little saying the two of them now seemed to have going. When she first heard it, she had made the error of congratulating Freddie on the motto, figuring that it was a take on one of his *Phoenix* comics or even one of the joke books that they had given him in his stocking that

Christmas. But it was Petunia who'd told her where the saying had really come from.

'That was Peter's saying, you know. He used to yell it at Jeremy across the court for *years...*' she had whispered conspiratorially.

Knowing where the motto came from had instantly given it a heavier, darker weight in Kristin's mind; a pressure she didn't want Freddie burdened with. She certainly did not want him suffering under the same weight of expectation that Jeremy had experienced with his own father.

She looked over at Jeremy, his eyes fixed on Freddie from the side of the court as his first match started. Her husband's cheeks were already flushed in anticipation, as he squatted forward, hands on his thighs watching intently. He was wearing a pair of jeans, his brown brogues peeking out underneath them. Kristin remembered queasily the meme she had once seen online, featuring an image of men dressed similarly to watch the Boat Race. He was repeatedly pulling down on the battered blue baseball cap he was wearing. It was an old habit; she remembered how he used to do the same when watching her matches, but it was a while since he'd been to see her compete. How ironic that she was playing so well this summer, when he'd yet to win a match for the men's team. If they continued their winning streak, Kristin and the girls were starting to think that the ladies might just have a chance of winning the league. As the temperature in the sports hall rose, Jeremy took off his Royal Oaks fleece and tied it round his waist. The twin-oak logo flapped at his hip as he paced along the side of the court. And of course, his ever-present water bottle was in his hand, condensation dripping from the logo onto the sticky sports-hall flooring.

Kristin wondered if he was wearing the branded fleece on purpose, some sort of dig because the pickleball event was being held here at the school. Then again, she could be reading too much into it. After all, he lived and breathed the club in a way that even she could see was over the top. Vanessa, who actually worked there half the week coaching the junior squads, only wore branded clothing when she was on official time, but Jeremy was rarely seen without it. Possessive was the word Vanessa had used about his devotion to the logo, but Kristin had corrected her, preferring the more diplomatic use of 'loyal'.

Now, as she literally stood on the sidelines, she felt very much like a bit player. Everyone else appeared to be having fun, and she seemed to have been largely excluded. She knew it was silly, childish even, but she did feel a little unnerved that Hailey had become such good friends with Petunia who was after all her mother-in-law. She wasn't daft, she could tell that as Hailey was a bit older than her, she might have had more than she imagined in common with Petunia. But it just felt off. You were supposed to be able to bitch and moan to your mates about your in-laws, weren't you? And if Hailey and Petunia were now sharing lunches – and confidences – that was going to feel like it was bordering on betrayal. Maybe she had just been too busy, too self-involved with everything else going on? She barely had time for herself, never mind anyone else.

Woman, get a grip, she told herself. *It's not always all about you. Be a better friend and you might find yourself more included . . .*

Her train of thought was interrupted by a roar from Jeremy as Freddie had apparently hit a great shot. Kristin almost jumped out of her skin and could see from the stolen glances between some of the other parents that those around her weren't enjoying the show he was putting on. He jumped in the air, fist pumping with obvious glee as Freddie grinned at his parents from the court.

But then, only a few moments later, another winning shot by Freddie was ruled out by the umpire – Vanessa.

'Oh, come ON!' he yelled at his sister-in-law.

Vanessa glanced over at Jeremy, her eyes raging. She raised her hands to silence him. The decision was made. They were moving on.

'Are you blind?' he said, still louder than anyone else in the hall, making Kristin cringe. A half smile formed on his lips as if to suggest he was joking but Kristin knew he was deadly serious. Kristin's eyes darted from her sister to her husband, her face reddening with embarrassment, the familiar knots in her stomach tightening once again.

To Kristin's relief, Vanessa completely ignored Jeremy, gently encouraging the boys to play on. They looked so little on the court, their first proper tournament. The grin had disappeared from Freddie's face, and he was starting to look at her with increasing anxiety. She smiled encouragingly back at him, giving him a double thumbs-up, and he seemed to perk up a bit.

Freddie loved pickleball, not because he was particularly competitive, but mainly due to the fact that his two best school friends were in his coaching group. He also loved his paddle bat. It was luminous green with a black lightning bolt and handle, and the plastic whiffle ball made rat-a-tat noise that Freddie found as amusing as his father found it infuriating.

Kristin knew that Freddie had been looking forward to today – he much preferred playing doubles to singles, partly because he could never remember the score and partly because he and Sid were good mates who were no longer in the same class at school. They'd been so excited about playing together. *Play*, she found herself whispering under her breath. That's what it should be … The format of the rather grandly named Superslam was Round Robin: They got three matches within their group of four teams and made lots of new friends. Each match was first to 11 points and lasted around ten minutes. This was quite enough for a bunch of seven- to nine-year-olds' attention spans and seemed to be working perfectly. The boys were having a blast, as was most of the emerging New Beeches pickleball family. If only certain parents could see it as just a bit of fun too …

As the match continued, Jeremy largely ignored Kristin, becoming ever more frantic as he followed Freddie's progress. He couldn't resist giving tips from the sidelines.

'Get ready, Freddie.'

'Move your feet.'

'Hit it higher.'

Couldn't he see he was confusing the child … not to mention making a spectacle of himself. He was also giving his mother the brush off as she paraded round the match courts.

God, she hoped he wasn't holding a grudge because she'd gone over his head in organising the pickleball tournament. It was all meant to be a bit of fun, and a learning experience for the kids, not a mother-and-son feud over a simple game of bat and ball, the introduction of a new sport. She had no idea why he'd been so violently opposed to pickleball, and she wasn't sure why Petunia had defied him with such glee. It had started to feel as if Jeremy's once quite private disdain for his mother was starting to implode, especially since she had become so noticeably independent in recent years.

Kristin had long since learned not to comment on their relationship and had instead focused on maintaining a healthy bond with Petunia herself. Her lesson had well and truly been learned when she had been pregnant with Freddie and had encouraged Petunia to take the trip of a lifetime, even if it had meant missing the baby's birth. It was a cruise she knew her mother-in-law had dreamed of taking since she was a young girl reading endless Scandinavian stories about adventures under the Northern Lights. Jeremy had been livid about the timing, but Kristin had pointed out that she couldn't have known they were pregnant until they'd told her. Then, she had made a comment about how Petunia 'couldn't be expected to grieve forever', which had gone down *far* from well, resulting in nearly ten days of silence from Jeremy. He had pointedly told her that *he* was still grieving, choosing to emphasise that point by failing to attend Kristin's twenty-week scan.

At the time, Kristin had been stunned by the no-show, sitting in the airless, blue-walled waiting room with one eye on the clock, and the other eye kept checking on the door, unable to believe that Jeremy really wasn't going to appear at any minute. He did not, and for the rest of her pregnancy Kristin found it hard to look at the scans of her beloved baby, each and every one of the black-and-white images reminding her not of Jeremy's failure to attend, but of her own mistake in speaking her mind, and how dangerous that had felt. She shook herself, forcing her focus back to today, to the match, to her son.

That afternoon, not a soul would have known that Jeremy had resisted the encroachment of pickleball into his life with the fervour that he had. His little performance continued, as he rocked back on his heels, cheering, and clapping with his hands spread wide as if to echo as far as possible. Other children were now glancing round anxiously at the noise, and Freddie really did start to seem unnerved, despite doing his best to respond well to his dad's 'support', by forcing a smile through wobbly teeth.

Freddie and Sid had made it through to the knockout stage, where they came unstuck against a pair of nine-year-olds with longer limbs and a lot more experience. At the moment of defeat, Jeremy threw his hands into the air, vehemently shaking his head, his lips set in a thin line. His disappointment was obvious to everyone and he was clearly oblivious to the other three lads on the court being gently ushered away by their parents. Perhaps he thought this was tough love, Kristin tried to tell herself. But as she saw Freddie's face dissolve into tears, she ran to him, ignoring Jeremy's protestations that he'd deal with this. She had seen more than her fair share of junior competitions end in tears over the years, but this was next-level. Petunia joined her as she stooped, wiping the tears from Freddie's cheeks. Kristin could feel that her own cheeks were scarlet with shame as she reassured her son that he had done nothing at all to upset Daddy.

'Honestly, Freddie, your dad has never known the meaning of "fun and games",' said Petunia. 'You played brilliantly today, we're very proud of you.' She glanced over her shoulder in scorn as Jeremy stormed out of the hall. Freddie mustered a small smile and clung to his mum.

Next, Vanessa appeared, fresh from her umpiring stint. 'Come on, lads,' she said. 'You two did an awesome job against two such big boys. They were taller than you and it was only really because they could reach further for some of the shots that they managed to beat you. You did so well!' She rubbed Freddie's back, and he smiled up at her. 'Let's go and find an ice cream outside. I don't care if we haven't even had lunch yet. Ice cream is good for your forehand.' She winked at Kristin and the group headed towards the sunshine, where a local Mr Whippy van had been invited onto the school grounds and was serving a queue of happy and exhausted children.

Freddie and Sid rejoined their friends amid much congratu-lating and commiserating and the adults followed, crossing the athletics track towards a marquee where a feast had been laid out for all the players, parents and volunteers. Children, familiar with the school property, were starting to line up neatly, while parents were trying in vain to persuade their little ones that the ice cream should come after some food.

Those at the front of the queue were loading their plates with egg and cress sandwiches, shiny red apples, slices of orange and fistfuls of crisps. The adults among them took longer, chatting as the line moved slowly forward, hands hovering over cream cheese and cucumber brioches and chicken tikka wraps. There were small bowls of olives and hummus alongside various crudités, which almost everyone struggled to load neatly onto their plates while maintaining polite conversation.

Just as they were nearing their place at the front, Bibi snuck up behind the Chappell sisters in the queue, squeezing their waists, her face between theirs. Kristin didn't even bother to act surprised that she was well over two hours late for an event she had promised to help out at.

'Looks like a success for Hailey, does it not? The kids are lapping up this new sport as much as they are their ice creams!' said Bibi with a grin. Slightly over her shoulder, Vanessa was giving her sister an enormous eye roll, mouth agape at the cheek of their mate and a slight shake of the head, stunned at their friends complete lack of an apology.

The children did indeed all look happy. Freddie's strawberry-blond hair was clammy with sweat, sticking up at all angles, and his freckles were more pronounced than ever in the sun. His polo shirt was untucked, the collar askew. All his friends were in similar states of disarray, summer shorts stained with drips of ice cream, grass-stained knees and dirty fingernails from playing outside between matches.

Kristin raised her hands. 'Look, *I* never said it was a bad idea.'

'And *I* never wanted any part of these goddam pickleball deliberations. I'm here for the cake.' Vanessa leaned forward to look down the trestle table. The other two knew she was checking for her favourite – pavlova...

'I'm kidding, I'm glad it has turned out wonderfully. Can I do anything to help?'

Kristin shrugged. 'Not really, just enjoy yourself.' There had been plenty to do while setting up earlier in the day, but Bibi had never really troubled herself with an all hands on deck approach, relying instead on her charisma in an 'icing on the cake' sort of way. If there was ever setting up to do before a big match or event, Bibi could be relied on for one thing only: turning up just a little too late to contribute but bringing such fresh energy with her that she got away with it entirely. If there was anyone who could transform a boring table into the most raucous, it was her, and if her husband Garrett wasn't there – even more so.

They watched as their friend loaded her plate with food, enthusiastically commenting on each and every sandwich, scone and cake.

'Am I going to have to get these caterers to take over my party next week?!' she said with a broad grin as she brandished a paper plate piled high with assorted savouries and a scone groaning under an overdose of jam and cream. 'Garrett has ordered enough food to feed a small country but none of it comes with jam!' The sisters giggled. Whatever gags Bibi was cracking now, they both knew that her and Garrett's May extravaganza was going to be one of the highlights of the summer. It always was.

How does she get away with eating like this? thought Kristin. *And she never puts on an ounce of weight.*

Having amused everyone in the marquee, Beatriz disappeared to a table on the lawn next to some parents who were total strangers to her. Within minutes they were all roaring with laughter, Bibi's hands flying through the air, her gesticulations expansive and welcoming, and before long, the entire table was tuned in, listening to an anecdote, faces soft with curiosity. Truly, she had turned being unreliable into an art form. At least she had distracted everyone from Jeremy's 'little moment', as Petunia had called it. He had mercifully calmed himself down now and was perched at the corner of the bar, on his own, nursing a cold lager.

Kristin watched as Hailey smiled at Bibi. As predicted, Hailey didn't seem in the slightest bit put out by Bibi's tardiness, instead giving her a polite little wave and mouthing 'Hello there' as she passed her table. As unflustered as ever, she let it all wash over her, opting instead to seek out the Chappell sisters and crouching between them at their table, to ask how they thought it was all going.

'Oh, thank heavens you're here, Hailes. Please could you have a word with and suggest how great it would be to have a dog at the club,' said Kristin, who had sensed that the energy was on her side right now, and that this was the perfect time to bring up her plan to get a puppy. 'Freddie is absolutely desperate for one, bless him, and the Glassons have a neighbour with some adorable border terrier pups. They've got one put aside for us and I'm thinking of just saying yes and facing the consequences later.'

As she was speaking, Kristin was hoping that it would somehow escape Hailey's attention that there would be any repercussions to this plan. She turned to look at Jeremy, who was studiously ignoring both of them from the other side of the room, suddenly very focused on balancing some hummus onto a stick of celery and raising it to his mouth.

'I think it's a wonderful idea, as long as it's a good pedigree,' replied Hailey diplomatically. 'The kids will love it, and there's all sorts of research into the fact that being around pets is good for developing diverse gut bacteria and a healthy immune system.'

'Sure, that'll swing it with Jeremy,' muttered Vanessa with a snort. 'Gut bacteria.'

'Shhhh, Vee,' said Kristin with a shove on the arm. 'It's actually very important, especially when you're growing up.'

Hailey raised an eyebrow with a smile. She knew she was right; she could take the teasing.

'Anyway, these puppies are going to be Wilbur, the Glassons' dog's siblings. *So* gorgeous. And won't it be great for teaching Fred a bit of responsibility? You know – feeding, daily walk before bed and so on? And with no siblings it would be a bit of company for him. A buddy.'

Kristin's eyes were pleading. Hailey drew breath to respond but was cut off by Jeremy, who had now lost interest in his hummus and was hovering close by.

'He doesn't need any more damn company ...' His mouth was smiling but his eyes were blank behind his sunglasses. And he hadn't looked up at either of the women. 'He has us. And your parents are always around. And your sister. And Eleanor.'

'I'm talking about in the evenings, cuddles, you know, that sort of thing.'

'You two never stop cuddling. He'll turn into a mummy's boy if you're not careful.'

'Oh, come on, darling, you know that's not true.'

'I know what I see. And I know what prospective girlfriends will see too. Someone still clinging to those apron strings.'

'Jez, he's seven! I'm sure we don't need to start worrying about girlfriends just yet, let alone cutting the apron strings. He is actually supposed to still be dependent on us!'

'Or future boyfriends,' said Hailey, standing up from her crouching position as if to leave. Once again, she was right. Who was to say that it wasn't future boyfriends who might be commanding Freddie's attention? As she stood, Kristin saw Jeremy's head whip round. Even with his shades on it was clear that Hailey's comment had not gone down well. But whether or not Hailey had noticed too was impossible to tell; she ignored his face of thunder, and put her hand gently on his shoulder, leaning her head towards his neck and ear.

'Anyway, I have to go, but I do need a quick word later, Jeremy.'

Kristin frowned, curious about what business they might have together. Why was everyone best mates with Hailey all of a sudden? But she was distracted by Hailey's scent. One of her home-made natural potions no doubt.

'Sure thing, H,' said Jeremy. But he hadn't turned to meet her eye, full-focused once again on his plate.

'Thank you. I know Justin is so disappointed not to be able to make it today, to see you. It's been too long since we caught up. And, as you know, there *is* a fair bit to discuss.'

Kristin watched the beads of perspiration appearing around her husband's hairline and on his upper lip. She wished she was anywhere but here, next to him.

'I didn't know you and Justin had become such pals,' chipped in Petunia cheerily to her son, her cheeks already full of Eton mess. She dabbed at a dot of stray strawberry juice in the corner of her mouth. 'How lovely!'

'More business associates than pals,' said Hailey, her tone cooler than the one she usually spoke to Petunia with. 'Although, we *are* still waiting on that paperwork, Jeremy.' Her lips were smiling, but her eyes were looking accusingly at Jeremy.

'Oh, I see.' Petunia raised a concerned eyebrow and took a sip of Pimm's, warily lifting her glass as if to congratulate her son. Jeremy, however, was growing redder, a trickle of sweat now making its way down his left temple. He wasn't even sitting in the sun.

'I'll get the paperwork over to Justin this weekend,' he accused her. 'Had a lot on, you can see how it is.'

Kristin heard rushing in her ears, her blood pumping faster in her head. She had heard a couple of snippets of conversation like this recently. Hadn't the last one been with Garrett at the centenary dinner? She wondered if Hailey was saying this in front of her in order to bring her attention to something, but she couldn't work out what. Not today, not with so much else going on. She'd have to broach it with her soon, though, in the week maybe.

'I sure can, Jeremy.' Hailey was standing right behind him now, having taken a couple of steps back towards the table after she had started to walk away. 'But I'm sure he'd still appreciate that call. He *really* isn't a fan of having to chase people.'

Petunia gave Kristin one of her trademark shrugs, to which she responded with her customary eyeroll as if everything was entirely in order. Vanessa was trying very hard to look as if she had heard none of the conversation at all. But behind the flimsy chipboard of the hired trestle table, Kristin's stomach was in knots. Her clothes started to feel scratchy in the heat. The large frilly white collar on her blouse suddenly seemed ridiculous, a gimmick, rather than the chic bargain she had spotted online after some late-night Insta-shopping.

Things that she had told herself were her worst, three-o'clock-in-the-morning fears now seemed to have a glimmer of truth in them. Was Jeremy cutting business deals behind her back? And were those deals with her friends' husbands? She clenched her fist, her nails digging into the soft flesh on the inside of her palm.

'Crikey, look at the time!' Petunia took a final slug of her drink. 'We should really be getting everyone back to the courts in time for the final!'

She pushed her chair back, and began to stand up, but as she did, she lurched forward, throwing her hands out to steady herself on the lightweight table, which in turn juddered violently, drinks spilling across the white paper tablecloth. At first Kristin thought her mother-in-law had caught the strap of her handbag in the leg of her chair, but as Petunia stood, stooped a little, her knuckles white as she gripped the table, Kristin realised it was something more serious.

'Petunia?' She moved quickly, towards her mother-in-law, past Jeremy who hadn't moved an inch. He seemed more embarrassed than concerned.

'I'm fine, I'm fine. Don't panic. I'm sure it's just the heat. Too much excitement!' said Petunia, who was now back in her chair. But her voice was shrill, uneasy, and she seemed a little disoriented. She smiled bravely but was pale and dazed. Kristin hurried to pour a glass of water from one of the jugs on the table, leaving a ring of condensation on the white tablecloth as she lifted it. Jeremy stared pointedly at the Pimm's glass and stood up.

'I'm sure she's fine, Kristin, don't make a fuss. Just a bit too much to drink on a sunny day.'

He took his mother by the elbow and walked her towards the school buildings, as the rest of the table breathed a sigh of relief and returned to their conversations.

Kristin spotted Petunia's airforce-blue clutch bag under the table and reached for it. As she lifted it she realised it was unzipped, and two small white plastic pill bottles tumbled onto the grass. She cast a quick glance at them, realising she had no idea what they were for, and making a mental note to check in with Petunia about it, before stuffing them back into the inside pocket and chasing after her husband and mother-in-law. She was still walking towards the sports hall building when she saw Jez heading out again, round to the car park.

The children were gathering for the final, and Kristin had to weave her way through the crowd, trying to find Petunia but she had disappeared. Perhaps she had gone to the female washrooms to splash some cold water on her face. Especially if it was just a case of a little too much Pimm's. Kristin crossed the sports hall, and found herself on the other side of the building, a cut-through she vaguely remembered from perhaps a Christmas show. Something they'd attended when Freddie had been in Reception.

No sign of Petunia, but there was Jeremy, sitting in the open boot of their car, a bottle of energy drink in his hand. Facing him was Bibi, her back to Kristin, her hair blowing a little in the breeze. As she stepped a little closer, Kristin saw that Jeremy's hand was out in front him, resting on her hip.

She squinted, assuming she was mistaken. After all, they were in the shade while she was staring into the sun, struggling against the glare. She blinked. And in the split-second she'd had her eyes closed they had moved. Both were now facing her, waving in her direction.

'I've got your mother's bag,' she called, moving closer to them. Her voice sounded distant, as if it were coming from somewhere else. 'But I can't find her.' She smiled weakly at Bibi who looked straight back at her, as if everything was perfectly normal.

'She's in the ladies,' said Jeremy. 'I just came to get this out of the car for her. Some electrolytes to try to steady her a bit.' He waggled the bottle at her, while Bibi smiled, tipped her head to one side, then stuck her bottom lip out as if in sympathy.

'Poor Petunia,' she said, although Kristin wasn't quite sure who to. 'Jeremy was just telling me she's feeling poorly.'

Kristin put her hand out for the drink. 'Why don't I go and take this to her?'

Jeremy immediately handed her the clear plastic bottle. Kristin took it, turned and headed back in. She could hear the shrieks and applause from the pickleball final, but they weren't nearly as loud as the throbbing sound inside her head. She lifted the drink to her brow, hoping the ice cold condensation on the bottle might cool her down a little.

It didn't. So she closed her eyes and took a deep breath before heading in. But still, all she could see was that smudge of Bibi's blood red lipstick in the corner of Jez's mouth.

Now ...

Chapter 13

ELEANOR

Eleanor swallowed, unsure if she really had heard what she thought she just had. That Vanessa had *wished* Jeremy dead, and now ... he was? She stood up, smoothed the hem of her top down over the waistband of her slacks, not quite sure what to say.

'Of course you can have that milk,' she said quietly to Freddie, trying to keep her voice as neutral as possible, as she headed towards the kitchen.

She brought Freddie the drink he'd asked for and sat in the small armchair in his bedroom, staring out of the window at the tennis courts in the distance. Normally the place would be so full of people, life, joy, noise. The hours she had spent listening to the thwacks and shouts from those courts – what a pleasure it had been to witness some of the happiest hours of so many families' lives. And how different today felt. The sky was gloomy overhead, the tarmac still dark with damp from the rain that had continued overnight after the storm. The club felt desolate, as if it wasn't just Jeremy who had died.

The Chappells had been in their meeting with the police for nearly three hours now and when Eleanor heard Edward Chappell call her name she was almost relieved that there was an excuse to have a break from watching TV with Freddie. But as she entered the familiar kitchen, she felt her knees wobble a little, as everyone turned to look at her. Edward gave her a slight nod, Tamara smiled, taking a sip of tea from a cup in front of her, and Kristin gave her arm a squeeze as she encouraged her to follow the three of them back into the room.

Two policeman, different officers from the men she had met the previous evening, were perched on the edge of the pale yellow sofas, their big black boots denting the thick pile of the carpet beneath them, hats resting in front of them. Their police radios crackled intermittently, faraway conversations interrupting them with details of people up to no good.

'Eleanor, I'm so glad you popped up this morning,' said Kristin. Her face was pale, her lips dry. She looked distinctly more dishevelled than when she'd opened the door to the flat an hour or so earlier.

'Yes,' continued the younger of the two policemen, standing up slightly, seeming unsure of himself and then sitting back down as Eleanor herself did. 'We are talking about that cake – the one that Mr Hale seems to have eaten; none of us can work out who it was ordered by.'

'We have to answer some questions on how we normally handle any allergens at the club,' said Edward. His face seemed to be expressing to Eleanor that there was nothing to worry about. But his vague air of cheeriness was anything but reassuring. Eleanor had been up half the night weeping at the tragic loss this family had undergone, and now they were sitting around with cups of tea, almost making light of it.

'This isn't a formal interview or anything,' said the policeman. His radio crackled again from its clip on the front of his jacket, and he dipped his ear to it, listening in intently for a few seconds.

'Not at this stage,' chipped in his colleague, taking over.

'Right...' said Eleanor, glancing around. She felt four pairs of eyes watching her intently.

'No, it's more a case of trying to understand the sequence of events, and who knew what, and when.' The original policeman was paying attention once again.

It all sounded *an awful lot like an interview,* thought Eleanor, swallowing hard as her mouth and throat seemed to dry up in seconds. She noticed that everyone else in the room had a cup of tea but that she had not been offered one.

Prompted by the police, with all three of the Chappells watching, Eleanor told them about the chap who had delivered the cake, trying her hardest to remember the name of the bakery but only getting as far as 'some sort of Italian-sounding brand' that she hadn't heard of before. She explained how she had checked for a name or a card, tried to see who it was addressed to, but that when she had seen the four tennis team figures, she had assumed that it had been purchased by someone who was familiar with the club's rules.

'I am so sorry – those figurines all just looked so much like the four of you,' she said, gesturing towards Kristin. She felt tears prick in her eyes, desperately trying to contain them. She didn't even know if holding back would make her look more or less incriminated. 'I thought, how could someone have known you all so well, and yet not known about the club's allergy policy? It's stated on the website, all the club literature, the menus and in the changing rooms and so on. I was just so busy that day and it looked exactly like fondant icing or marzipan, but I should never have taken the risk. I'm so sorry.'

'Don't worry, Eleanor,' interrupted Kristin. Her voice was clear, untroubled by tears. Freddie's words in the bedroom crossed Eleanor's mind again. Kristin continued. 'We are not saying it was anyone's fault...'

'Well, we do need to find that delivery driver,' said the older policeman. 'As a matter of priority. Mrs Hale has our details, so please get in touch if anything springs to mind...'

'There's no reason to believe it was deliberate, though... is there?' Eleanor gasped. Kristin's mention of fault had been as chilling as her dry eyes. 'It was just someone's foolish mistake, wasn't it?'

Eleanor put a hand to her mouth, taken aback at the ease with which her nosey question had slipped out. It was just that she was feeling so scrutinised in here, seated on a pouffe three inches lower than the rest of them, all these questions about the cake, and Fred's words still ringing in her ears. Why was there no sense of, well, *grief*, in this room? It was all practicalities and no feelings.

The older policeman was looking at her directly, though. 'Well, the question of whether this was a mistake or not is very much what we're here to try to find out.' He took a quick glance at his colleague before leaning in to the group.

'Mr Hale's body is with the coroner. There are some test results we are waiting on, pending discussions with the doctors who treated Mr Hale...'

'What do you mean?' This was the first time that Eleanor had heard Tamara Chappell speak. She seemed to have aged overnight. Her skin was translucent, her hands never still. Her thumb was rubbing against her forefinger as she spoke, the nail bitten to the quick. Now she looked closer, it was clear Edward Chappell didn't look too good either. Then again, he had been pretty ill recently. It was impossible to tell what was on any of their minds, apart from the fact that no one had mentioned the fact that Jeremy was dead.

Gone. Forever.

The younger police officer looked down into his lap, clearly making way for his colleague to continue.

'Well, Mrs Chappell. We've received conflicting reports, you see. Your son-in-law was rushed to hospital on the grounds of an allergic reaction. And at first, it was treated as such. But having spoken to the team at East Surrey Hospital, we're now looking at the possibility that it wasn't his allergy that killed him. In fact, we suspect the crime happened much earlier in the evening. The doctors believe he was poisoned.'

Three weeks before...

Chapter 14

KRISTIN

Kristin flinched at the sound of the doorbell, the noise interrupting the lovely long stare she had been having out of the kitchen window as she folded clean laundry fresh from the dryer. One good thing about Jeremy hardly ever wearing 'proper' shirts and just the never-ending Royal Oaks branded sportswear was that her life was very rarely troubled by ironing. The meditative, repetitive task of folding the family's clothes flat against the kitchen island, daydreaming at the view of the courts in the distance, was one of those chores that she secretly quite enjoyed, in those rare hours when the flat was quiet. A brief moment to herself for once.

She padded down to the door, hoping it wasn't going to be a club member who wanted to 'escalate a complaint' about why Royal Oaks no longer provided dressing gowns in the changing rooms or bottles of water in the court-side fridges. But instead, she was relieved to see the impassive stare of a delivery driver fidgeting on the doorstep. He handed her a package, wrapped in a stiff white plastic bag, and asked her to stand and pose for the obligatory photo of it clutched in her hand. She always felt she should smile for the camera, even though she knew it was just of her slippered feet.

As the delivery man grunted and went on his way, she shut the door and headed back into the flat. She recognised the logo on the side of the bag and excitedly tugged at the plastic, ripping it in the process. She felt a flash of guilt, knowing she should have opened it carefully in case she wanted to send the contents back, but then again, doing things properly hadn't been going too well for her lately. She tore at the bag again and a bundle of silky material in pale pink tissue paper slipped out and onto the kitchen counter.

She let out a little squeal. It was exactly the shade she hoped it would be! Four nights ago, after hours of sleepless scrolling, she'd impulsively clicked the buy button on a stunning dress that Jeremy would have written off as 'far too expensive', hoping that it would be the perfect choice for Bibi and Garrett's infamous summer party. It was tonight: they'd held it on the second May bank holiday for years now.

Usually, this was an event that Kristin looked forward to, but this year the thought of it left her body filled with anxiety. Ever since she had seen that strange little encounter between Bibi and her husband at Freddie's pickleball match.

She had wanted to talk to Bibi about it, but it had been a frantic week for both, and this was definitely not a conversation that was going to work by text. In daylight, at the kitchen island with a cup of coffee, she knew she trusted her friend. *They had known each other for a long time, and there had never been any hint of flirtation between her and Jeremy, nor,* thought Kristin, *any sense that she wasn't happy with Garrett.* She would have said something, wouldn't she? Then again, when her thoughts started whirring in the small hours, it seemed entirely possible that Bibi might not talk to her. Maybe she had misunderstood the closeness of their friendship? Or been inattentive to what Jeremy needed, or what they were up to? She thought she trusted them. But she also knew what she had seen. And the two didn't add up.

So how could she have fitted all that into a text message? Which meant that now she was faced with seeing them both together, at a huge and notoriously glamorous party. The bile swished in her stomach. She probably should have had something more than coffee by now. Protein, that's what Hailey would advise. *Was there protein in a crumpet?* she wondered, as she slammed one in the toaster and went back to her parcel.

There was just so much to do at the moment, how could she manage to turn up tonight looking like anything less than a frizzy, frazzled nightmare? Half term was looming, play dates needed to be sorted, birthday gifts for various parties needed to be bought and wrapped, and then there were arrangements for further introductory pickleball events at the club to be getting along with. For someone who talked so much about being a 'modern, hands-on dad', Jeremy didn't seem to know about most of this, let alone be helping with it. What was it she'd heard it called online? *Weaponised incompetence.* And with each day that passed, the summer seemed to be getting hotter, everything moving just a little too slowly.

Daydreaming about the dog was the only thing that had kept her positive. She had quietly discussed it with her parents, making sure they might be on hand for the odd bit of puppy sitting and dog walking. But she hadn't let on about her determination to go ahead with the plan to Jeremy. He'd made it quite clear that he hated the idea, and his mood had been erratic ever since the success of Hailey's pickleball tournament. He'd love the thing once it was home, wouldn't he? ... Wouldn't he?

This is how she had ended up two nights ago, one leg kicked over the duvet, trying not to wake the snoring Jeremy, falling prey to the lure of an algorithm that seemed to know what sort of a night she was having. Before she knew it, a 'mid-life style' influencer was promising that *this* was the dress that would make the summer 'pop'... Hmm.

She ripped the tissue paper apart, lifting the dress to hold it up against herself. And what a dress it was! Soft, flowing pink silk, which hit her ankles. A high neckline with cutaway shoulders that would show off her arms, toned to perfection from years of tennis. And the back, slashed from the nape of her neck to the base of her spine. There was no way she could wear a bra with it, maybe no underwear at all. Dare she?

She swayed a little, watching the silk move against the pilled fabric of her everyday housework leggings. She imagined herself walking down the patio steps at the O'Briens', heading onto their immaculate lawn, a cocktail in her hand. Maybe she'd wait until the party to tell Jeremy about the puppy, do it when other people were around, just in case.

'What on *earth* is that?'

Jeremy was leaning against the kitchen doorway. A thin sheen of sweat was slicked across his face. He was wearing tennis shorts and a polo shirt, sweat bands on his wrists. But Kristin barely noticed these details. All she could see was the smirk.

'It's a dress I bought for Garrett and Beatriz's party.'

'For you to wear?'

'Of course, for me – who else?'

'Well, I'll be honest, darling, it looks better suited to some backstreet dive in Miami than the Home Counties. Just because we're going to Bibi's doesn't mean you have to play dress-up as her.'

Kristin's cheeks turned the same colour as the silk as she stared into her lap.

Chapter 15

BIBI

Three miles away, Bibi O'Brien was just finishing her morning yoga session in the studio overlooking the manicured lawns, when she saw the same delivery courier crunch up the driveway towards the front door. *Just in time,* she thought.

As she lay in her savasana position, breathing slowly in and out, she heard their housekeeper, Mrs Forbes, take delivery of the package. A final exhale and she pulled herself upright, grabbed her unnecessarily large bottle and took a long swig of the icy cucumber water, before heading through to the hallway.

The fifty-year-old woman was puffing slightly as she carried the heavy cardboard box towards the kitchen, her legs shuffling beneath it.

Bibi strode towards her, the tiles cool on her bare feet. 'Mrs Forbes, I'll take that from you.'

'Oh, Miss Bibi, I didn't see you there.'

Bibi laughed and prised the box from her grasp, placing it on the bright ottoman at the side of the hall. 'Don't tell my husband I've ordered something else; he'll murder me!'

Mrs O'Brien raised one finger to her lips and headed back into the depths of the house.

Bare feet on clean, cool tiles still felt as satisfying to Beatriz as they had done on the day they'd moved into this house eight years ago. As a child in Puerto Rico, Beatriz had sworn to herself that she would one day have a home – a beautiful home – that would stay cool during the summer and warm during the winter. Somewhere she felt safe and comfortable, where she owed no one a thing. Having grown up in a tiny apartment, which only seemed to feel anything even close to cool between the hours of 2 and 5 a.m., she had long used this dream of a 'real' home as motivation as she fought to get out of San Juan, making it to Miami as a teenager. Once there, she had picked up whatever modelling or waitressing work she could, flirting whenever necessary along the way to securing the gigs she needed. After all, she had known long before she left Puerto Rico that she was both beautiful and alluring, and by the time she made it to Florida, she was using that charm like a weapon.

Saving every penny she could, she worked, smiled, gyrated all the hours that God sent until she had the cash to head for the West Coast and reinvent herself as a high-end sports model. When she arrived in Los Angeles with a new wardrobe, new teeth and a new, less obvious accent, she picked up work faster than ever before, all the while remembering that her looks, her charm – and her savings – were her superpowers.

By the time Bibi met Garrett she was wealthy enough in her own right that she never needed to ask him for a penny. She was done with gratitude and made sure that he never took her on a date for which she couldn't pick up the tab if she felt like it. Because by now she had learned that the only thing more powerful than a killer body with the charisma to match was knowing you had enough cash to buy any favours you needed – rather than having to flirt for them.

Garrett was Irish American but had grown up in South Dublin under similarly challenging circumstances. He immediately found her independence (as well, of course, as her beauty) intoxicating. He had made the very best of Ireland's once-booming tiger economy, but managed to get out before any of his property deals came back to haunt him.

Twenty years later, no one seemed quite sure what he did to make his money. There was talk of investing, and he certainly seemed as nimble on the stock market as Beatriz now was on the tennis court. He also appeared to be connected to the sports industry, possibly related to the gambling industry but also perhaps investing in players. Or was it some sort of sponsorship set-up? Whatever the truth was, it all seemed to be manageable from the lavishly upholstered lounges of Californian golf and tennis clubs, with little more than an iPhone and the occasional laptop. The man didn't seem to have an office, much less an actual company. And it was this relaxed approach to life – combined with his dark curls and mesmerising clear blue eyes – that meant he was the first man in a decade who had really, truly turned Beatriz's head.

She quickly learned not to ask too much about his work. He never gave her a straight answer, claiming it was boring anyway, and she had no argument with that. But she had a secondary consideration: if she didn't ask him too much about the provenance of his fortune, she wasn't obliged to answer any questions he ever had about some of the work she had done on the way up. Particularly ten years ago in those first few months in Miami.

Years later she had managed to buy up most of the images from early shoots which might come back to haunt her, but there were still hostessing jobs that made her wince if she dug too deeply into her memories. So if she didn't want to *be* asked, perhaps it was best not to ask herself.

The couple quickly recognised each other as birds of a feather, self-made creations existing in a world of exclusive clubs, inherited wealth and Californian nepo babies. They built a mutual trust that was as much to do with what they didn't want out of life, as it was to do with actual goals or ambitions. They each understood about the other that it was money that made them safe. Not just cash for the nice clothes, the great hotels and the fantastic seats at their shared passion – Grand Slam tennis. But enough cash not to be answerable to anyone, least of all each other. All of which meant that it had taken years for Beatriz to trust Garrett, to surrender even an inch of her independence to him.

Of course, this independence only served to make Beatriz even more intoxicating to Garrett. Once he realised that she had real money – perhaps even more than him now that she had learned to play the stock market herself – he begged her to marry him. She had said no for over a year, still not sure that she wanted to tether herself to anything or anyone. Eventually, it was polo that swung it for them. Garrett had started playing, and Beatriz had longed to live in England since she was a little girl. So, the wealth of the leafy suburbs southwest of London were the obvious answer. Beatriz had her tennis, her cool green woodland walks with beloved dachshund Barney, and Garrett had all the polo-playing contacts he could dream of.

They had made the leap eight years ago and been happy ever since. Or at least as happy as two people who had been married nearly a decade without ever being really honest with each other could be. The one thing there was no question about was how happy their enormous mock-Tudor mansion made them. It had taken years, but they had stripped the house to its bare bones, even moving the central staircase so that it caught the best light in the morning. There was an underground gym and screening room, a steam room and sauna and soundproof dancing room with state-of-the-art decks and a sprung floor.

Every room had voice-automated lighting, as well as similarly obedient blinds, curtains and music systems. Security relied on a series of fingerprints, and of course those beautiful, tiled areas were as warm during the winter as they were cool in high summer.

Then there were the grounds: a manicured lawn, a barbecue area where Garrett spent many happy hours grilling steaks, prawns and asparagus, a swimming pool and hot tub complete with pool house, and of course a discreet private tennis court tucked away behind the double garages. If they hadn't been as sociable as they clearly were, they would rarely have had to leave. Their home was built for pleasure – all day and any which way.

So when Beatriz skipped down the stairs that morning, the marble tiles cool under her feet, she felt the contentment of someone who had fought for her home, and enjoyed sharing it. She knew that their summer party was a 'must have invite' and the one that their social set looked forward to the most. Held on the last weekend of May every year, it kicked off the summer, setting a standard in food, drinks, service and entertainment that others spent the rest of the season trying to live up to.

Smiling with pleasure when she recognised the label on the box, Beatriz lifted it from the ottoman and carried it into her office where she sat on the grey velvet sofa that faced her desk. She picked a silver letter opener from the desk drawer and jabbed at the cardboard to open a corner, then pulled at the contents, brightly coloured silks and satins spilling out of the box and onto the sofa. Light poured in through the French windows as she sat, yanking at her dresses like a magician pulling hankies from a closed fist. The fabric seemed to glow as the sun dappled against them on Beatriz's lap. There was bias-cut emerald-green silk, a gold beaded satin mini-dress, which looked like something worn for carnival, and a long silk backless frock whose bright-pink fabric ran across her hand like water.

Holding the last dress by the shoulders, she raised it to see the movement of the fabric against her body. It was perfect. She wouldn't bother trying it on: it would fit. She'd bought enough from this brand over the last couple of years to know that. She shoved the rest back into the box and made a mental note to get Mrs Forbes to return them as soon as possible.

She slung the pink dress over her arm and headed back upstairs. Garrett was getting out of the shower as she entered the bedroom, holding the dress against her body to have a look in the full-length mirror. He was dripping wet, rubbing at his hair with a white towel, leaving wet footprints on the thick pile of their cream carpet as he headed over to his wardrobes.

Beatriz swayed a little, hoping the movement of the dress against her hips might catch his attention. But he walked straight past, apparently oblivious. Humming to himself, he was butt naked, flicking through his admittedly impressive collection of designer shirts.

It was hard to know what might make Garrett notice her if not this dress, Beatriz thought as she slumped onto the bed, and stared out into the garden. The first of the fleet of caterers were arriving, carrying boxes of wine towards the marquee. More men. And she knew she could have any one of them in the palm of her hand in an instant if she went outside and turned on the charm. But it was Garrett who she really wanted to notice her again.

Something had shifted lately. It was only a whisper of discontent. But Beatriz knew men, and she knew it was there. A sense that as far as their marriage was concerned, someone in a faraway room had closed a blind, only she wasn't sure where the room was or how to reopen it. More than anything, she wanted to let the light in again, and most frustratingly of all, none of her usual tactics seemed to be working.

For years, decades even, it had been like an instinct, the flexing of a muscle for her – to make a man pay attention by making him jealous. Once or twice, it had even put her in dangerous situations. But she had never really needed to do this with Garrett, he had always been besotted by her. Her past tactic of dangling another man, like holding a match close to a flame until it burst into fire, had rarely been needed. Even when she wasn't flirting, was just passing the time of day with whoever she was around, sometimes it would create a heat in his blood that only one thing could quell. But recently, the fire was barely embers and Bibi was more than a little concerned.

Chapter 16

VANESSA

Vanessa pulled open her new suede clutch and checked her teeth for lipstick as her cab pulled into Bibi and Garrett's gravel driveway.

'Looks like quite the party,' announced the driver, suitably impressed by the sprawling lawns, elegantly dressed guests and a brass band bedecked in red, white and blue playing beneath one of the magnolia trees.

'Let's hope no one gets up to anything too scandalous then,' she replied, grinning. She passed him a couple of notes and climbed out of the car, her wedges sliding slightly on the pebbles, and waved to Garrett who was waiting on the top of the patio steps to greet guests. She spotted Bibi with a cluster of women down by the fountain, their tinkling laughter ringing out across the balmy evening air.

Standing high above the lawns, Garrett must have seemed the picture of a relaxed, gregarious host, but as Vanessa often found as a solo guest at these sorts of events, she had more time to observe than the rest. She climbed the steps up towards Garrett and put a hand on his shoulder, enjoying the lush velvet of his dark green jacket, and he pulled her in close to plant a kiss on each cheek. He'd had his filler redone, she noticed. They had done a good job. No lumps. It only endeared Garrett to her more, the fact that he seemed so reluctant for anyone to realise he was nearly a decade older than Bibi.

'Great to be back, my friend,' she said with a grin. 'It must be May!'

'It must indeed be May,' he said, laughing. 'And it's great to have *you* here. Looking as good as ever, I see …' Garrett looked her up and down appraisingly. In any other man, Vanessa would have found this mortifying, insulting even, but Garrett was an honourable man, and with one whom she had a comfortable, fraternal relationship with. They would text each other podcasts that one thought the other might enjoy. They sometimes discussed the best ways to cook steaks, getting each other increasingly specific and scientific bits of equipment for the barbecue. One thing they didn't do was flirt with each other.

This was why, when Garrett said she looked great, Vanessa took the compliment at face value. Well, that and the fact that she really didn't think she looked that great. Or at least she had barely made an effort: she was wearing an old frock and a pair of wedge sandals that she knew she'd find easier to dance in later. She'd made the mistake of wearing stiletto heels on this lawn before, and it wasn't one she'd repeat, even if she had decided not to drink as much as this year. This was an outfit for having fun in, one which allowed her to show off her natural tan and undeniably athletic figure. It would have to do, she'd told herself with barely a glance in the mirror – it usually did.

Over the years, Vanessa had always enjoyed this party. Yes, there was great booze and great music, but she genuinely liked the O'Briens too. They were considerably more straightforward than most of the members who frequented the club, particularly the English ones. And she liked how little they always asked about what had become of last year's date. Hailey and her family always seemed so *concerned* when a boyfriend disappeared, and

Kristin of course was always monitoring the situation like a hawk, as if she were seeking validation for her own marital choices in the hope that Vanessa might one day take the plunge.

But Garrett and Beatriz knew that Vanessa's romantic life was none of their business, and it was aways an enormous relief to enter their house knowing that no heads would be tipped sideways in sympathy, no platitudes would be offered, and no questions would be asked. In fact, this year, she had decided not to bring a date at all. Why spend the night babysitting some bloke from an online dating app when she could talk to her real friends and enjoy the night?

Vanessa rocked back on her heels, surveying the party, with its troop of servers, stunningly decorated garden and champagne cocktails in full flow.

'I see you've made as little effort as ever,' she said, with one eyebrow raised.

'Ha. You know Bibi … she hates a party. And me. We're the boxset type.' He chuckled, the deep rumble of his voice as masculine as his immaculate, deep-black stubble. The two of them stood in silence for a minute. 'Where's your sister? She here yet?'

'I don't think she is. Running late apparently – Jeremy probably had a meltdown.'

'Oh, I see.'

He was non-committal, staring ahead. Vanessa had long suspected that Garrett didn't think much of her brother-in-law, but she was damned if she was going to ask outright.

Guests continued to pour into the garden, a steady flow of the healthy and the wealthy. A particularly well-spoken couple who Vanessa recognised from various tennis fixtures appeared at Garrett's side and commandeered his attention. She was as fine with being entirely ignored by them as she was with wandering off herself. As she turned to go, gently tapping Garrett's forearm goodbye, a Long Island iced tea was offered to her by a smiling waiter. She took it, along with the chance to take a walk. She was far from ready to dance yet and hadn't spotted anyone else she really fancied chatting with.

Outside the marquee, the band was picking up tempo. On to some country music now, they were swaying as one, occasionally yee-haw-ing at each other, which in turn was emboldening some of the guests to slap their thighs in a moderately mortifying faux-cowboy manner, as they readied themselves for the dance floor. The sun was still beating down though, and Vanessa had long held a personal rule never to dance until after dark. Instead, she set off on a loop of the garden, before heading towards the swimming pool where she slid a foot out of one of her sandals and dipped it into the cool, still water, sending ripples across its surface. She checked her phone. What on earth was going on with her sister? She had seemed stressed, distracted all week. And so had Jeremy – even by his already abrasive standards. She recalled seeing them heading into the flat earlier in the week, his hand yanking two heavy shopping bags out of Kristin's when he caught sight of Vanessa.

Too late, mate, she'd thought. *I already saw you not helping.*

She'd spotted him earlier in the week too, heading off court with one of his clients, referring to tennis as a '*proper* racket sport' as Vanessa headed onto the adjacent court. Why did he have such a bee in his bonnet about bloody pickleball? Was it just that he'd been out-voted by his wife, her friend and his mother?

When she'd tried to fish around to the subject with Kristin, she had said something about them being worried about Petunia's health. That tumble at the tournament had shaken them both up apparently. Vanessa wasn't convinced. Jeremy's behaviour, which had been cold and abrasive for a while, was starting to curdle into something more akin to bullying. There was an edge to him lately, and she suspected Kristin was desperately hoping she hadn't noticed.

She leaned to tie up her sandal and accidentally knocked her drink over, the cocktail trickling out of the glass and towards the water's edge. As quickly as she could, she picked up the glass, realising it was time to head back to the party before someone accused her of hiding. In truth, she *was* hiding a bit. None of her gang seemed in the mood for a party, as if something uneasy, unspoken, was permeating in the air between them. So she decided to take the long way round, via the tennis court. Garrett wouldn't mind her enjoying his grounds; she might even swing by the barbecue area and check out his latest set-up.

As she left the pool, she spotted Bibi, slipping between the hedge that separated the court from the main grounds and into what Vanessa knew was a discreet area where she liked to sunbathe naked – on the two or three sunny days of the year that she could. Her dress caught the breeze a little as she stepped towards the main party, running a hand through her hair, ensuring it was in place. The pink silk billowed, showing her bare back, and then she was gone.

Vanessa crossed the grass and scanned the party. The guests seemed to be having fun now, judging by the noise from the terraces and the buzz from the dance floor. Discarded cocktail glasses and beer bottles were starting to dot the lawn, indelicately toppling into flower beds faster than the serving staff could pick them up.

'Vee!' Her sister was finally here, heading down the steps now. 'You beat us!'

Well, it didn't look as if she was late because she'd spent an eternity getting ready. Kristin was in a tea dress that seemed more suited to a midafternoon garden party. On her feet was a pair of ballerinas that Vanessa knew she had worn on the school run more than once. Even her hair looked uncharacteristically unruly, as if she hadn't had time to run a brush through it.

'Everything OK?' Vanessa asked tentatively as she leaned in for a kiss. Her instinct was to tilt her head as she asked, but she didn't want to be one of *those* people. She felt her own concern rising in her like a blush but was desperate to hide it.

'Yes, of course, why?' Kristin flicked her hair from her face and smiled at her sister. Her lips were pulled a little too far back from her teeth as she smiled. For someone else the act might work but there was a manic energy to her tonight. There was a fleck of cerise lipstick on one of them. Her voice was noticeably higher than normal.

'Oh, you know, it's me who has the terrible reputation for time-keeping, I didn't know what to do with myself!'

To her discomfort, Vanessa heard her own voice and realised that it was just as shrill. Every bit as unconvincing.

'Anyway – how are things?' She scrambled for something fun to say. Why were they talking like two polite colleagues? 'Still going ahead with the puppy plan? Does Freddie know yet?'

'Sshshsh!' Kristin's head darted round. Again, she looked close to manic, the whites of her eyes flashing in the shade.

'What's the problem – are you trying to *keep* this from Jeremy? Because I'm pretty sure he'll notice if a puppy shows up in the flat...'

'It's not that—'

'Well, it *seems* like that...' Why was Kristin behaving like this? Strangely imperious, defensive... And why was Vanessa's mouth running away with her? She hadn't come here spoiling for a fight – she just wanted to check her sister was OK and now they had lapsed from faux-formality to snapping at each other in a matter of seconds.

'I just – I just haven't had the conversation yet. And the last thing I want is to be having it here,' said Kristin, with one hand out as if to keep the chat at bay.

'Fine,' replied Vanessa. 'Where is he anyway?'

'I've no idea, he disappeared the minute we got here.' Kristin rolled her eyes, trying to make light of it.

'Never mind, more chance for us to have some fun not talking about work for once. Have you got a drink? Where are the waiters? The weird American food will be out soon—'

'Oh, God, not the corn dogs...' Kristin smiled and the sisters each took a glass of champagne from a passing tray. They clinked the glasses and smiled. It was going to be OK. Wasn't it?

'Yes, the corn dogs – I love them!' Vanessa wrinkled her nose disapprovingly.

OK, they were back on even ground again now. *Just keep things calm, you catch more flies with honey.*

'Well, so do I, but I need to be careful.'

'What the ...? For starters, you don't need to be careful – you're like a rake! And then – do you really think this party is the time to start? It'll be a festival of fried food in twenty minutes!'

As Vanessa was saying this, she realised that Kristin had stopped paying attention, her gaze instead following Beatriz who was emerging from the hedge by the tennis court.

'Oh, God, she looks amazing,' muttered Kristin, almost to herself.

She really did, but it was more than that. Bibi carried herself as if she knew that she did. The pink moved with her body, accentuating curves while seemingly in constant motion in the evening breeze. Her tanned shoulders looked immaculate

– powerful yet elegant – and when she turned to wave across the garden, Kristin seemed to sigh as the dress revealed a daring slash in the silk, zero bra and a perfectly tanned back.

'Ladies!' said Beatriz as she leaned in to hug both sisters at the same time, an arm around each. Are you having fun, do you have everything you want? What's the news? And is it true about this puppy that you are getting from Tina?'

Vanessa nudged Beatriz. 'Shhh, she hasn't told Jez yet…'

'Seriously?' She flung her hands in the air in mock despair. 'Where is he anyway?'

Vanessa noticed her sister flush at a second asking of this awkward question. 'Oh, I don't know – he seems to have vanished the minute we got here. Probably talking shop with Garrett or something.'

Garrett, however, was still standing at the top of the terrace steps, quite clearly not talking to Jeremy.

Then, out of the corner of her eye Vanessa saw him coming from exactly the direction that Beatriz had just emerged from. She said nothing as she watched him head up the side of the patio, then skip down the steps as if he had just come from the house itself. He approached them with a leonine smile. His tongue flickered across his lips.

'Ladies…'

'Aaaah, here he is!' cried Beatriz while Vanessa wondered if this really was the first time she'd seen him this evening. 'Welcome, welcome. You want a beer?' She leaned to reach a cool bottle from a passing tray, and as she slightly turned, Vanessa spotted his hand on her back, nestling between the fabric, his thumb gently stroking her flesh.

The shadows were long on the lawn now – the sun had almost vanished behind the immaculate hedges that lined the

O'Brien estate. But the evening was still warm, clammy even. Vanessa felt damp around the back of her hairline.

As the night got darker, the beat of the band became more insistent, as if they were a heartbeat getting faster and faster as the air seemed to close in around them. Vanessa still wasn't sure she was up to dancing, even when Bibi grabbed Kristin's hand and demanded she head into the marquee with her. To Vanessa's surprise, her sister headed off willingly, giggling a little as she grabbed another drink en route. There was still something off about her – her attempt at looking relaxed seemed forced and unconvincing.

Instead, Vanessa stepped back inside where she found Garrett sitting in the half-light of a side sitting room. The French windows were open, letting in the hubub of the party, but Garrett was sat so far back, slouched on a brown, buttery-soft leather sofa, that he was almost out of sight, an alligator in the shadows. On noticing Vanessa, he patted the cushion next to him.

'Hey.'

'Hey.'

'Another great party,' said Vanessa. 'I don't know how you guys do it.'

'I do,' he replied with a slow, confident smile. His shirt was tight against his chest, sweat starting to show on it. 'You just throw the same party year after year, chuck a bunch of booze at youngsters, a lot of music and people get more and more relaxed each time. They probably don't remember much of it.'

Vanessa thought about Jeremy's hand on Bibi's back.

'They sure do.'

She dared herself to go a little further. Perhaps she, too, was one of the ones getting more relaxed, year on year. Or perhaps it was just the alcohol. But almost without realising, she heard herself reference the past.

'I suppose it helps when you've seen worse behaviour back in the day than the Home Counties tennis set could ever throw at you. This lot are tame in comparison.'

Garrett chucked the rest of his scotch in his mouth, complete with the huge cube of ice that had been in it. 'Seen it? Darlin', back in the day it was me doing it.'

He crushed the ice with his back teeth, mouth open in a sly, knowing smile. Then he got up and walked away, patting Vanessa on the knee as he did.

She didn't know why she was so surprised. Vanessa had heard many stories about him over the years. There had been talk of gambling and match fixing. Of finding young players in trouble with debt and persuading them to throw matches to settle scores. Of getting a grip on more established players and finding other, less charming ways to persuade them to create final scores that suited Garrett. But she'd never paid much heed to it; it all seemed a bit far-fetched, frankly. She had only ever seen Garrett as a good husband, a charming host, someone who caused no trouble and kept himself to himself. He didn't even throw his weight around at the club, which most husbands liked to do the minute that their wives started winning titles.

What a strange evening it was proving to be. As if everyone was pretending to be themselves and failing miserably. Even all this talk about how it was the most relaxed night of the year was falling somewhat short.

Vanessa tried to haul herself off the leather sofa, struggling a little as she tried to stand. She peered out of the French windows, but instead of heading to the dance floor, where she thought she could see a silhouette of Garrett dancing with Kristin, their faces close together, she headed back into the house and found the bathroom.

She splashed water on her neck and stared at her reflection in the mirror. What did Garrett see when he looked at her? Had he really been confiding in her just then, or was he doing a bit of myth-making, knowing she'd spread the word?

Chapter 17

HAILEY

The worst thing about Justin's illness was not the burden of trying to keep ahead of medical advancements or the exhaustion from a night of checking that he was comfortable even if it meant her being woken several times. It wasn't even the endless worry about his condition and when it might take a turn for the worse.

It was the loneliness.

It was missing him when he was just too tired to go out, or even, as was the case tonight, missing him while he was at the party but just too weak to take part the way he used to. She remembered dancing to this very band with him only five or six years ago. Him whirling her around to 'American Pie' until she was dizzy. She still had the heels she had been wearing that evening, the grass stains still on the expensive Italian leather of the soles. Tonight, he was in his wheelchair, resting in a quiet room with a view of the garden, with a constant stream of friends passing through to say hi. Yes, he was here, but he wasn't by her side, not like he used to be.

Oh, how much fun they had had at parties back in the day. They had been to the best clubs in some of the most glamorous and exciting cities in the world. He had taken her to karaoke bars in Kyoto where they were the only non-Japanese customers in sight. She had taken him to country bars in Nashville where he had been the only Brit. They had used contacts in the Senate to get bookings for the best ribs in Washington and taken Bibi's advice on the very best sushi in Miami. Garrett himself had even set them up with a night to remember in Dublin.

When they were even younger, during those few months of backpacking they had managed to sneak in between Oxford and the start of their glittering careers, they had travelled around Mexico, enjoying a couple of weeks in the then-undiscovered paradise of Tulum. These days Hailey rolled her eyes when yet another intern announced their intention to head there for life as a 'digital nomad'. She remembered when the place barely had working toilets, let alone enough Wi-Fi to run a career through. One night, they had used a tip from a university contact and set themselves up with some extraordinarily pure cocaine. Neither of them had ever taken it before – exams (and common sense) had taken precedence over everything for the past few years. But that night, as they had lain on their backs on the warm Tulum sand, the stars glittering brighter than they ever had before, they had both agreed that they could never do it again. Because nothing could compare to this. They had to keep this experience sacrosanct, a forbidden night that no one else would ever know about. Perfect, preserved in the amber of their memories forever. Their secret.

Hailey had stayed true to her word, as had Justin. They had never tried the drug again, and neither of them had mentioned their night under the stars to another soul. Tonight, feeling more than a little lost, Hailey wandered slightly aimlessly from group to group, never quite managing to muster enough party spirit. She found herself missing the old Justin more than ever. She was lucky to have known that man at all, she reminded herself, and she was lucky to still have the man that he was today. It had been an incredible journey. A true love story. But tonight, her heart was aching.

From the glass-walled kitchen extension, Hailey watched the partygoers starting to warm up as the infectious beat of the band made even those not inside the marquee start to tap their feet and nod their heads. She saw a couple snatch a kiss as they stopped to sit on the patio steps towards the lawn and found herself wondering if anyone there tonight had a marriage as strong, as vibrant, as hers and Justin's. Perhaps Bibi and Garrett did – they certainly still had a lot of heat between them. But did they share the unspoken communication that she and Justin did? They were so instinctively in tune with each other's thoughts and worries. The way they anticipated each other's needs and wants. The way they always seemed to find each other the perfect gift despite them earning enough to buy whatever they wanted whenever they wanted. It was uncanny but oh so special.

She heard Jeremy braying somewhere in the distance. Boring the pants off some disinterested newbies no doubt. God, she dreaded to think what his and Kristin's marriage was like. These days it seemed like a dog-eared old novel, well past its sell-by date, the spine barely managing to keep the pages in. *They seemed so wary of each other all the time*, she thought. Kristin was continually second-guessing him or defending him. It must be exhausting. Then again, everyone seemed somewhat wary around Jeremy these days, even his own mother.

Hailey left her snooping spot in the kitchen conservatory and realised she could stop daydreaming about Justin and their unbreakable bond and just go chat to him for a bit. No one would mind if they hid away for a little while, would they? Maybe he was even ready to leave. She couldn't see either of them summoning any more party spirit than this, and they'd put in a good shift already.

As Hailey turned from the window to cross the kitchen, Vanessa came in, looking a little green around the gills. Hailey was about to greet her, but the numerous catering staff buzzing around the enormous kitchen island kept getting between them. Vanessa opened the huge American-style fridge, grabbed a small bottle of water, and headed back out again without even noticing Hailey behind all the aproned servers. Hailey went after her, but stopped at the doorway when she noticed bloody Jeremy heading their way. She dipped into an alcove, hoping he'd turn and go to the bathroom. No such luck: he'd spotted Vanessa.

He had stopped when he saw her, and was now casually leaning against the hallway door. One leg was bent, his foot flat against the wall, as he grinned at his phone like a teenager.

'All right, Jez?' said Vanessa, a little blearily.

He looked up, feigning surprise.

'Oh, it's you. Yeah, of course I'm all right,' he said, with a small shrug. 'You having fun?'

'Of course. I was just looking for some water,' she explained, waving her water bottle at him as if he wouldn't believe her otherwise. 'What are you doing snuck away in here?'

'Oh, just, you know. Taking a moment.'

Hailey, straining to hear them, considered that Jeremy had never been known to 'take a moment' in his life; *he was more often found commandeering them*, she thought.

The champagne seemed to have made Vanessa bold. She was leaning forward a little, almost taunting, 'Not avoiding Garrett, are we?' Now it looked like she was trying to smirk, to brush away the boldness of her question.

Too late. His eyes flashed angrily as he glared at her, his chin tipped to his chest. He slid his phone into his back pocket and lowered the leg that had been bent against the wall.

'Oh, Vanessa. We don't *all* have to spend our lives avoiding men, you know.'

Vanessa was chewing the inside of her mouth. She grimaced as she bit a little too hard. *That'll be a mouth ulcer in the morning,* Hailey thought.

'Well, you certainly weren't avoiding his wife earlier – your hands were all over her.'

Hailey had no idea what this was about, but Vanessa was defiantly staring at him now. She was transfixed by the tension between them. Actually, she recalled she had noticed Jeremy and Bibi seeming to flirt a few weeks ago. She'd seen them walking into the clubhouse together while she'd been at reception. He'd been coaching her a lot this summer, and they seemed quite close. An image of him kneading her shoulder on one of the courtside benches sprang to mind, but Hailey couldn't remember now when she'd seen it.

Jeremy moved away from the wall entirely and turned towards Vanessa. His face was only an inch or two from hers. Hailey could imagine that Vee could smell the black-pepper bodywash she knew was used in the men's locker rooms at the club. Tinged with sweat. Perhaps a little cigar smoke.

'Well, well, well, Vanessa Chappell. Are you involving yourself in my marriage?' Jeremy was speaking slowly now, softly, but with his face so menacingly close that every word cut like a knife. 'Because I don't think that's a very good idea – do you? Not with the secrets you've been keeping for over a decade. Play nicely now, it's a party, not a Grandslam final...'

He turned and headed into the darkness of the garden, and finally Vanessa dared to breathe out. Once he'd passed the hurricane lanterns and reached the far end of the lawn he was lost in the shadows.

Vanessa shuddered, and Hailey hesitated in the doorway a moment, unsure whether to let her friend know what she had just witnessed. She took a breath, then walked towards her.

'Hello, darling,' she said, trying to keep her languid drawl as relaxed – and relaxing – as possible after the whispered threats of Jeremy. 'How are things?'

'Urgh, do you know, I'm not quite sure,' replied Vanessa, nodding her head towards the garden to indicate that she was heading out there. Hailey walked alongside her, and they sat on the terrace steps, looking down at the silhouetted bodies moving to the music in the marquee. The grounds were alive with revellers; it was hard to imagine the property in any other state than this perpetual, thumping beat of a party.

'How so?' asked Hailey softly.

'Oh, you know, it's weird working with family. Obviously, it's wonderful too – and I'm so proud of them all – but sometimes, well, it all gets a bit claustrophobic, doesn't it?'

Hailey nodded thoughtfully.

'Oh, God, Hailes, I'm so sorry. That was thoughtless of me. I know your family are on the other side of the Atlantic, and then there's the whole Justin situation—'

Hailey put a hand on Vanessa's arm to stop her. Her fingers were cool, and as slender as the rest of her.

'Don't—'

'It's just all been a bit much, you know. Working with Kristin and—'

'Jeremy?'

'Yes, Jeremy.'

'I can imagine it makes things a little ... stifling.' Hailey was treading carefully now, still unsure what she had just witnessed and whether she could be of any help to her friend.

'I mean, we're sisters, but we don't need to be in each other's pockets all the time,' continued Vanessa. 'But I think we'd cope if we had to be. It's him. It's the way he casts a mood over things. Like I can't get my sister out from under a heavy blanket or something.'

'He seeks to exert influence where he can. Because in truth, he is not a man of importance, although he would very much like to be.'

Hailey sensed Vanessa felt a frisson of delight at her sanguine manner. She was more than a little pleased with her own comment too and let a smile of satisfaction creep into the corners of her mouth.

'That's exactly it,' said Vanessa. 'I'm more than a little concerned. It feels like there's ... something brewing.'

'It certainly does,' replied Hailey. 'For starters, he owes Justin a considerable sum of money and has done for a while.'

Vanessa's eyes widened. She blinked, hoping Hailey wouldn't notice.

'Does Kristin know?' Her voice was barely a whisper.

'I haven't said anything. But Justin is losing faith that he's ever going to see his investment again, and as you know ... well, he's a man with a deadline.'

She was pleased to notice that her euphemism was not lost on Vanessa, who swallowed the rest of her bottle of water. The volume from the dance marquee seemed to be increasing yet again. It was starting to feel like more of a headache than a heartbeat. She had been ready to pursue this line of conversation a little, and was on the verge of asking what Vanessa thought, when Kristin appeared from the tent, her shoes in one hand, her phone in the other.

'Vee! Vee!' She was yelling as she ran towards them, eyes wide. 'Where's Jez?'

Vanessa stood up and tried to scan the garden in the dark. 'I don't know. He was here a moment ago. What's happened? Are you okay?'

Her sister's hair was wild. Damp around the hairline and nape of her neck, a makeshift topknot on top of her head, held together with a couple of bamboo straws from discarded cocktail glasses. Her chest was heaving. Hailey stood too, but stayed back from the sisters, not wanting to interrupt.

'It's Petunia.'

Hailey gasped. Her friend.

'She's been hospitalised. I've only just seen my phone. I had it on silent. And no one can find Jeremy.'

Now ...

Chapter 18

ELEANOR

The coffee Eleanor had just put onto her desk spilled over the edge of the cup and then the saucer as she slumped into her chair. She sighed. The last few days had been exhausting.

The police were still popping in and out as they pleased. Poor Kristin was doing her best, but of course she was tearing her hair out. Eleanor had been left with the lion's share of the day-to-day running of the place and frankly she was run ragged. She longed for things to get back to normal, for her to know less about this whole situation than she did, and most of all, for the members to stop asking her so many questions.

They had reopened the club yesterday, but the Royal Oaks was far from functioning normally. There were the people that she *had* managed to contact discreetly. And then there was the fact that half the members had no idea what had happened – people constantly turning up at reception wanting to know why their sessions with Jeremy had been cancelled, or others wanting to get access to the pro shop, which was his domain. Eleanor had had to put her foot down about that in a more than awkward conversation with the Chappells. She only had so many strings to her bow and running a sports shop was not one of them.

Vanessa had been an absolute star though, taking on some of Jez's classes herself, speaking to confused club members at other times, and acting as a kind and efficient go-between for her family and the staff. Eleanor had nothing but admiration for her. She was a trouper, an absolute trouper.

Eleanor opened her emails and sighed as she realised how many more people she had to reply to, explaining the interim arrangements, batting away the indiscreet questions of gossips, and all the while wondering what she should be telling the police about, and why. Outside, she heard the throaty roar of an expensive sports car. She pushed her chair back and tipped her head so she could see the staff car park, immediately recognising the fire-truck red of Bibi's car. Well, it was Garrett's really – Bibi usually drove a neat little electric thing. There was a blur of hair and gold accessories as she got out of the car, slung her handbag over her shoulder, whipped her hair out of her face and strode towards Kristin and Jeremy's flat. Kristin's flat, she corrected herself.

Eleanor ran a hand through her hair and took a gulp of coffee, then saw Bibi flash past the window again. Wearily, she stood up and headed into the club's reception to greet her, just as the bell on the welcome desk rang out.

Bibi was standing there, one immaculately manicured hand around her huge phone, the other rifling through her handbag.

'Hello, Bibi, can I help—'

'Oh, Eleanor, thank heavens you're here. I can't get hold of Kristin at all, but Hailey's called me in a state.'

'Why, what's happened?' Eleanor tried to keep her hands very still, at her sides, to give the impression that she remained entirely calm. Seeing the panic on Bibi's face was making it hard, though. She was too used to the woman floating in and around the club like an expensive cat, the sort who could leap onto high shelves effortlessly, or slip though gaps like liquid. Today, she seemed more like one who had slipped in the bath. Wide eyes. Dishevelled hair.

'It's Justin …'

Eleanor's hand flew to her mouth. *Surely not?* Surely not another death?'

'No, no, it's not that.' Those flame-red nails waved in her face as Bibi dismissed the idea. 'It's the police, they're at the de Veres'. It's why Hailey called. She wants me to speak to Kristin as soon as possible.'

Eleanor frowned. 'What, do you …?'

'They're interviewing Justin. They think *he* ordered the cake!'

'What, the League celebration cake?

'Yes – but, darling, you know of course *he* didn't order it. He hasn't done anything for himself this decade.' Another flash of red as Bibi waved a dismissive hand.

'I'm terribly sorry, Bibi, I'm not sure I understand. I thought the police no longer thought the cake itself was the cause of… the cause of, well, the death.'

'It was ordered on his card. Hailey says the bakery have now confirmed it. It's a new place, up on the road towards Freddie's school. But it can't have been him, it just can't. She says it *must* have been a mistake, stolen card details, ID theft or something. They're with the police now, trying to figure it all out – but Hailey is in a state, and no one can track down Kristin. It's obviously a huge misunderstanding but, well, it's not the sort of misunderstanding friends need right now.'

Eleanor remembered her hands. If she could keep them still, she could probably keep her face impassive. So had the rumours about Hailey and Beatriz been true then? She remembered the afternoon of Jeremy's death, when she had heard two of the clubhouse staff talking about it. Some sort of falling out.

But they had always been such solid friends. What was she to know about the lives of these indulged women? Eleanor was shocked to find herself thinking. Perhaps she had been too close to all of this. Had one of them upset Jeremy?

'Anyway, Hailey is worried that this is going to impact Justin; he's frail enough as it is. So if you could let me know where to find Kristin? She's not in her flat, I've just checked.'

In that moment, with Beatriz so close to her face, all noise and nails and panic, Eleanor found herself wishing she could just crawl under her desk and hide. And that's when she remembered. A week or so ago. Her pen had rolled clean off the reception desk when she'd been in for the early shift. The club opened at 6 a.m. sharp during the week for the commuters who liked to get a workout in with enough time to get into Central London. It was usually the same group of regulars, which meant reception was deathly quiet for a couple of hours before the post-school-run mums started to arrive.

Eleanor was bent under the desk when two of the regulars came out of the men's changing rooms. She was crouched, patting the floor by her feet, trying to eke the pen out from under the edge of the desk. She must have been entirely invisible or surely the two men wouldn't have carried on talking. But they had, so she had felt compelled to stay hidden – to preserve the blushes of all three of them.

'You're kidding, he's asked you too?'

'Yeah, and it's not just me he's been trying to tap up. He's asked Garrett O'Brien as well—'

'No way, the big Irish guy?'

'The very same...'

Eleanor felt the butterflies fluttering in her stomach. She should not be listening to this. She still hadn't retrieved her pen, but she could see light reflecting off a smart metal water bottle on the carper under the front desk, tucked into the corner.

'I think he's in trouble, man. It's not a good look, hitting clients up for cash. And that Garrett guy – people talk about him. He's got some kind of seriously shady past, you don't want to get on the wrong side of him.'

'I hear you. Have you seen him working out? He looks like he could take your throat out with one hand.'

'Exactly. And I don't think he'd hesitate to.'

Eleanor had waited until she'd heard the gentle slam of the clubhouse front doors before standing up from behind the front desk. Her ears had been buzzing at hearing what the men had said, but to be fair they'd been just as uncomplimentary about Garrett as they had been about Jeremy, so she had dismissed it as some sort of hyper-masculine gossip.

This morning, as she found herself feeling steamrollered by Beatriz and her enormous sense of urgency, she was remembering the moment in a different light. Why was Beatriz so keen to tell her that the police were interested in Justin? How did she know so much about this cake? Who had she been speaking to?

She stopped herself, her mind racing, and stood, paralysed, unsure whether to let Beatriz into the flat or not. Because in that instant, the unimaginable had happened: she had realised that she didn't trust Bibi O'Brien. Not one little bit.

Two weeks before...

Chapter 19

HAILEY

Hailey curled her legs under her on the soft leather of the sofa, creating a cozy little nest in her lap for the ball of fluff that was Baxter. Outside, the club was quiet, making everything seem much further away than it actually was. As the sun moved round and the light hit the window behind her seat, she was glad of a moment to herself after the last few frenzied hours.

She stroked the tiny border terrier's button nose and wrinkled her own at him.

'What a day to join the family, little one,' she said, her voice uncharacteristically gentle, singsong even.

Here she was, in the Hales' family kitchen, waiting for Freddie to return from school with his grandma. Mrs Chappell, that was, not poor Petunia – who was still in hospital, having been rushed there the previous night while Kristin and Jeremy had been at the O'Briens' shindig.

Hailey, Beatriz and Vanessa had been asking Kristin for updates in their group WhatsApp, but they had been few and far between. Of course, she had also had her hands full consoling Jeremy. Then, at the crack of dawn – early, even by Hailey's industrious standards – Kristin had called Hailey directly for help.

'Hailes, I need a favour – and it's an enormous one – but you're the only who knows the Glassons...'

Hailey had paused when she realised what she was being asked. Because it really *was* something she'd rather avoid. Not because of the puppy, but because of the social responsibility that this favour would entail... Kristin was right, Hailey did know the family who had the puppies – they were school friends who Hailey had met through the pickleball activities. She had even considered taking one of the puppies for herself and Justin, but had ultimately backed off at the thought of one getting into her sacred 'herb garden'. Still, they had melted her heart when she and Kristin had gone round to visit them, and Hailey couldn't deny that she was secretly delighted by this chance for a little cuddle with Baxter before he met his new family.

The Glassons were heading off – this morning – for a half-term holiday, and Baxter was the last puppy remaining. It was now or never, Kristin had explained, and Freddie would never forgive her if they missed out, especially when his granny was so ill. The pup had now had all his vaccinations, and had just been staying at the Glasson home until Kristin had had a proper chance to explain the purchase to Jeremy.

And this was the root of Hailey's hesitation: it wasn't the disruption to her already busy working day or the daybreak hour of the call. It was the prospect of getting involved in the potential fallout surrounding Baxter's arrival, once Jeremy realised he had been overruled and the purchase was a done deal.

Hailey had never really bought into the treacly charm that Jeremy displayed around the club – his tales of 'his pro career' and adventures on 'the Tour' made her cringe. She could even put aside his unnerving assumption that every woman whose path he crossed was thrilled to be flirted with by him; it smacked of insecurity, to her. But she didn't trust his temper. He had the shortest of fuses and she wanted to keep herself and Justin as far away from that as she could.

She had seen the way Vanessa avoided eye contact with the others when Kristin referred to a difficult weekend. And she had heard his voice, carried across several courts when Freddie messed up an exercise during a coaching session. Personally, Hailey didn't think Jeremy should be allowed to coach Freddie. It seemed like way too much pressure for the child. Jeremy seemed both overinvested in it and impatient. She suspected that the same need for validation that meant his son's tournament mini tennis league results were already something he bragged about, the same energy that kept him canoodling with every female club member aged forty-five or older, was the sign of a personality that could become vicious when he felt threatened, or belittled. And now that Justin had got himself tied up with him in some kind of financial arrangement, it was all feeling more than a little uncomfortable.

Perhaps I am being neurotic, she thought as she looked down at little Baxter, snoozing in her lap. A perfect curled croissant of fluff. She stroked his black-and-tan fur, rubbing one of his velvety ears between her thumb and forefinger, instantly feeling more relaxed as she did. *How big a favour could it possibly be to sit with the new puppy of a little boy who might be on the verge of losing his grandmother?* she had asked herself. So of course she'd said yes.

She heard her phone buzz on the far side of the sofa and reached for it.

All OK? Please ring the clubhouse to send you up some food if you need it? Kx

All OK. How are things with you? H x

It's not looking good, H. Jez incredibly stressed too. Xx

The mention of Jeremy made Hailey queasy again. God, she hoped he'd stay at the hospital. Just a few hours longer, until Kristin could at least get back, or maybe even tell him about the puppy while they were there. How had she let things get this far? And why was she so afraid to confront her husband with anything? She'd been a fool to trust Jeremy in Justin's company at all. But it had seemed like a nice gesture when she'd been spending all that time with dear Petunia.

She thought back to the evenings he had popped round, all smiles. Halfway through dinner and there would be the crunch of wheels on the drive followed by the doorbell, and his cheesy grin.

'Hey,' he'd say, who didn't have a young son to be getting to bed. *Did he tell Kristin where he was going?* Hailey had wondered occasionally. She had learned the hard way that Brits don't take kindly to being questioned about how their marriages operated, but after working full-time at the club was Kristin really OK with Jeremy wandering off, avoiding homework, family mealtime, bedtime even? There was never any mention of her when he arrived, just a smirk that seemed to say, 'I dare you ...'

'Just popping in to see the J-man,' he had told her once as he'd brushed past Hailey at the front door.

And so it had continued. Somehow, he had managed to convince Justin to become his friend. By bringing him titbits of sporting gossip. Or news about something or other he'd read that might help (pretty much always based on research Hailey had read weeks ago, or, failing that, some crackpot pushing snakeskin supplements). Once or twice, he'd even suggested that 'the big man might like a trip to the pub, a bit of real food'.

How could Hailey refuse? Justin would work hard all day, but his social life was shrinking as his condition worsened. If Jeremy was going to go to the effort of bringing a car that would accommodate Justin's top-of-the-range wheelchair and arrange with the local pub that they'd be in for steak (grass fed of course) and chips (cooked in tallow), then what was she supposed to do – hold him hostage?

At first, Justin seemed to enjoy the camaraderie, even if it was one with a man so transparently desperate for acceptance that it was mortifying. But Jeremy seemed to have no boundaries. He'd stay later, appear more often, forcing Hailey into the position of being the jailer – worrying about when he'd be back, if he were over-tired, what they were discussing. And she'd hated it.

The more she'd looked at Jeremy's wider behaviour, the more she saw that his lack of boundaries spread far beyond just Justin. He once told his mum that her frock was 'pretty sexy actually' and that it would 'get the pensioners going' as she left for a garden party last summer. There was the time they'd been lined up on the court for a formal photograph, one of the classic images used to line the reception walls, and while their hands were behind their backs, he'd slapped Vanessa on the bum shouting, 'Say cheese ladies.' Hailey had chalked it up to the hijinks of an almost-sibling, but when she thought about it a little longer, she couldn't shake the moment off.

No one had laughed, but no one had reprimanded him either. What could Vanessa have done in that moment? Cause a fuss in front of everyone? Shame her sister's husband in their mutual place of work? Then there was the way he spoke to Kristin in front of people. The words themselves were always flattering, but the tone ... the tone suggested something quite different. Insincerity and more than a hint of sarcasm.

Eventually, the truth behind the two husbands' friendship started to emerge. To Hailey's eternal shame, it caught her by surprise. She had tried so hard to convince herself that she was a hard-hearted harridan for wanting to deny her husband a bit of freedom and a change of scene that she'd let her guard down – and exactly what she'd dreaded had transpired. One evening, Jeremy let slip that he and 'the big man' were now business partners. They had gone in together on a property deal, he'd told her with a self-satisfied grin as he'd wheeled an exhausted-looking Justin up the entrance ramp after another of their lads' nights out.

Hailey's jaw clenched as she forced herself to pause before she spoke.

'I see,' was all she managed before Jeremy interrupted her.

'Now don't panic, I've been through all the numbers with hubs here and it's a no brainer.'

Hubs. The patronising creep. Hailey had pursed her lips together, as if trying to keep what she wanted to say from flying from her mouth in a torrent of disgust.

She said nothing, but pointedly reached towards Justin's wheelchair, making a pointed attempt to grab the handles from Jeremy and steering her husband into the drawing room. God, had it come to this. Her once proud, virile husband now something she was squabbling over with this callous man-baby. But Jeremy didn't surrender, his strong wrists flexing as he gripped tighter on the handles, taking Justin straight past the drawing-room door and into his study.

'We're going to have a quick snifter to celebrate,' he said over his shoulder, before spinning Justin round to face them both. 'Aren't we, J?'

'But Justin doesn't drink. He c—' Hailey was having to try very hard to keep her voice steady.

'Oh, but I bet he'd like to. He's told me all about the cracking collection of Japanese whisky that he hasn't had a sniff of the last couple of years.'

It was true. One of the many griefs that Justin had had to suffer in recent years. But he had been keeping them in his study, pristine, collectors' items. Hailey had long told herself that she'd have a glass of his favourite the night he finally died. She knew if she admitted it to anyone, they'd call her morbid or accuse her of wishing Justin gone. But the truth was very different: she knew that day was coming, and she knew that when it did the loneliness would come for her like a hurricane. It consoled her to know that there was a ritual she had planned for herself, that there would be steps she could follow when the terrible moment arrived. She lived every day with the crushing dread closing in on her with every milestone Justin passed. Knowing that she had a plan for those first few moments, and that it was something her beloved would so thoroughly approve of, gave her great comfort. So now, her guts lurched at the prospect of Jeremy of all people getting to that precious bottle first.

'Relax, Hailey,' Jeremy said, his voice calm, confident. He now put an arm out, resting his hand on her shoulder as if she were in need of some reassurance. She tried to shrug it off, but he resisted, the weight of his hand firmer than ever against the thin fabric of her T-shirt. 'It's not as if I'm going to be stuffing him full of illegal substances now, is it?'

His eyes looked directly at hers, confrontational, holding her gaze. How did he know about her herb garden?

'Those are medicinal, not recreational,' she replied. Her voice was calmer than ever. But her eyes flitted from Jeremy's to Justin's, almost pleading. Why had he told Jeremy about it? Of all people? There was no reassurance in Justin's eyes. There was not much of anything – instead he looked resigned, exhausted.

'But Hailey my dear, I'm sure His Majesty's Constabulary don't care one way or the other. Medicinal, recreational – either way they're illegal.'

She knew he was right. He could call the police on her at any time, and it would threaten not only the way that she managed Justin's pain, but her career, her income, and her reputation. She shoved thoughts of a custodial sentence to the back of her mind as she was confronted with the enormity of the risk she had been taking. How would Justin cope if she were to be incarcerated? She was the one who managed his meds, his schedules, everything.

So she had smiled sweetly and waved them through to the office. A quarter of an hour later, when she'd heard the clinking of a glass she knew.

He'd opened the single malt.

In that moment, she had felt trapped, as if someone were tightening a belt around her chest. And over the following months that belt had only tightened even though the friendship itself had seemed to wane. The trips to the pub had petered out a little once whatever deal it was had been struck. Justin, who had for so long seemed to treasure their evenings together on the terrace, watching the sun set over their gorgeous grounds, had become withdrawn, embarrassed even. And Hailey, who had had to work so hard to maintain a sense of being a wife, a *woman*, even though she had become more of a carer, had started to feel every bit as lonely as she had always dreaded she'd feel once Justin was gone.

Eventually, a couple of months ago, Justin had admitted that he feared he would never see his money again.

'It's my own foolish fault,' he'd said, his voice tremulous, barely audible over the sound of the sprinkler taking care of the lawn.

'Darling, don't be silly—'

'Don't call me silly. I feel enough of an idiot.'

'Darling, *please*. That's not what I mean. This is entirely *his* doing.'

'*I* fell for it. Thinking he really did see me as some sort of mentor. Letting myself believe my knowledge and experience was "inspirational", or whatever he said. Do you know he wanted to get me on TikTok, some sort of investor guru. For pity's sake. It was all a line.'

'It's excruciating. But we will get that money back. If for no other reason than that Kristin would be absolutely mortified if she knew this had happened.'

She'd meant it, she realised, as she took a sip of the ice-cold kombucha they were sharing. So much so that as she'd put her lead-crystal tumbler down with a clank on the wrought-iron terrace table, she had thought about the damage it could do if broken. And she had often thought of it since. The ways she might harm Jeremy. Just to give him an inkling of the pain Justin went through every day. What he endured, and what Jeremy had exacerbated worsened with stress of this 'deal.'

That morning, as Hailey sat on Jeremy's sofa, his puppy in her lap, those thoughts came back with a shudder. Up until now, it felt as if it had only been her closeness to Petunia (who really didn't deserve a son like this) that had stopped her from dwelling on these thoughts too much. Oh, how she hoped her friend would pull through. She picked up her phone to check in with Kristin.

Chapter 20

KRISTIN

The ward was unbearably hot and smelled faintly of boiled cabbage and the brand of disinfectant used when someone was sick on the school bus. Still, it had taken over twenty-four hours to get Petunia on to a ward, so Kristin experienced a feeling of triumph as she helped her to adjust the incline on her bed, wheeling the little table into a comfortable position across her lap, and pouring her a glass of water.

'At last,' she said, although she still wasn't quite sure if Petunia was listening. Her eyes were closed, her hands like marble, folded in her lap. Kristin thought of her holding court at school only a couple of weeks ago, thriving as she welcomed people in to enjoy the pickleball tournament.

Had that moment, that wobble she'd had getting up from lunch, been a sign of things to come? Kristin now wondered. At the time she'd put it down to a hot day and one glass of Pimm's too many. Perhaps they should all have taken greater note.

'Good time?' asked a smiling doctor, as she put her head round the edge of the blue curtain surrounding Petunia's bed.

'Well, yes, but I think Petunia's asleep and I'm not quite sure where her son has gone. I'm only her daughter-in-law.'

Jeremy had declared that he needed 'some air and a proper

coffee' nearly an hour ago when Petunia had still been left marooned in a corridor two floors away. Phone reception in the hospital was patchy, so she wasn't sure if he had received her messages explaining where they were now, or if he was simply taking his time in a cafe somewhere in the bowels of the building.

'If it's OK with you, I'll explain things now, otherwise you could end up waiting until tomorrow's rounds.' The doctor looked as if she hadn't slept for a week.

'Of course,' replied Kristin. 'Please, fire away. Is Petunia going to be OK?'

'Well, as I think you now know, she had a stroke a couple of days ago. We've done all the tests we can at this point and it does all look very positive. And this in turn means that she doesn't seem to be experiencing any physical symptoms – mobility, that sort of thing. But it was a serious event to experience. She is lucky we got to her when we did.'

'Right, so this is ... good news?'

'So far, so good,' replied the doctor with a smile. 'But we're going to have to keep her here for a few nights, to make sure that there isn't anything that's gone on which we haven't been able to spot yet. And she's going to have to take some medication too. Someone will be round later to talk to your husband – or you – through that.'

'I wish I knew where my husband was ...'

Just as she said it, Petunia opened her eyes and smiled.

'Oh, don't worry about him, sweetie,' said Petunia. 'It sounds like you've got this covered.' Her voice was weak, but Kristin found herself strangely surprised that it sounded exactly like her. *How else was she expecting her to sound?* she wondered – but the relief was enormous.

'Petunia! How lovely to have you back with us! You had everyone worried...'

'Thank you for all you and the team have done, doctor...' Petunia leaned forward, wincing to read the name on the doctor's badge, but the woman waved a hand at her.

'It's what we're here for – now you just need to make sure that you rest up and take your meds on time.'

'Of course I will, Krissie here will keep an eye on me. She's a treasure.'

Swimming alongside the relief that Petunia seemed so close to her old self, Kristin felt a gentle tug of anxiety that she seemed to be acquiring a whole new set of responsibilities. Where the hell was Jeremy?

'Well, Mrs Hale, it's great to see you awake while I'm here. And wonderful to know that I'm leaving you in such good hands with your daughter-in-law.'

Instinctively, Kristin's hand reached over and took one of Petunia's. It was cold. Her skin felt like it could fall away at any minute. She smiled at her mother-in-law.

'I think we've got a handle on things, don't you?'

'Oh, absolutely,' replied the older woman weakly. 'I'll be fighting fit in time for Wimbledon.' She laughed a little and closed her eyes.

'Then I'll leave you to it...' With that, the doctor left.

As soon as she had gone, Kristin stood up and started rearranging things again. Topping up the water that Petunia had yet to take a sip of. Straightening the thin hospital covers over her legs, readjusting the TV, which was on a flexible arm above the bed.

'Krissie, please, sit down.'

'I just feel so useless. Is there anything you want me to get from the shop? As soon as Jeremy's here I can go to yours and get some nice comfy pyjamas and bits like that for you. Magazines? Books? Toiletries?'

Why couldn't she stop moving? All these hours of sitting on plastic chairs breathing third-hand air were suddenly making her feel claustrophobic in the extreme. She tugged at her top, trying to get some ventilation against her skin.

'Krissie, *please…*'

'God, sorry, I'm making things worse now, aren't I? I'm just so glad you're OK!'

'It's fine, but listen, there's something I want to talk to you about.'

'Anything.'

'And I really want to talk to you before Jeremy gets back, you know, just in case.'

Kristin frowned. Somewhere in her gut she realised she was heading into a conversation whose direction she was unsure of, a skier heading downhill out of control. Petunia gestured towards the chair. Even doing that seemed to tire her a little, as her hand rested again, limp on her lap.

'Now I don't want you to panic—'

There's no faster way to make me panic than to start with that, thought Kristin.

'…and I don't want you to think that this is some sort of impulse thing. It's a change I made earlier in the year when I first had one of these funny little turns.'

'You—' But Petunia held up her hand a second time to stop her.

'It's about my will, my last will and testament.'

'Oh, Petunia, you heard what the doctor just said, you don't need to be thinking about all that!'

'But I do. I want to.'

'OK, but wouldn't you rather wait for Jeremy?'

'Krissie, please, just listen. The will. I want you to be prepared.'

There was a pause as Petunia slowly reached for the beaker of water and took a sip.

'Because I'm not leaving anything to Jeremy.'

Kristin felt the blood drain from her hands. She knew full well that Jeremy had long been counting on inheriting what was left from the proceeds of the empire his father had built. She wished she didn't know, because, God, was he reckless with money. Her mind started racing. How would they cope? Would they now be tied to the club forever? What about all the renovations Jez always said he wanted to do once they were in charge? And what about taking some time off, their already-postponed chance to travel as a family?

'…because I'm leaving it to you.'

It felt as if the air had been sucked from her body in an instant.

'What on earth do you mean? What about your son?'

'I know you might think it sounds callous. But if you think you know the man, remember that I know him even better. And he's just not someone who is cut out to handle a big sum of money like that.'

Kristin felt sick. The dizzying combination of open-hearted trust in herself and total betrayal of her husband. And she was stuck right there, being pulled by two separate loyalties, two possible lives. There was only one thing that she knew was true: that Petunia's assessment of Jeremy was correct. That didn't mean it wouldn't prompt a reaction, though.

'But, Petunia, what will Jeremy say?'

'Well, that's why I'm telling you now, so you can be prepared. I haven't done anything daft, of course. I've earmarked a little bit for him. And obviously some of the sentimental bits. His dad's watch and so on – not that he's shown any interest in it since I told him that he couldn't sell it while I was still here. But I can't leave him what I know he's expecting. No good can come of it.'

Kristin had no idea that conversations like these had ever taken place.

'I'm so sorry. But I don't understand. We have never been short of money, we're both on decent salaries. Why would he…?'

'Well, he has asked. More than once. I don't know, perhaps it was that he had some sort of taste of the good life while he was on the Tour back in the day. Proximity to that kind of cash, success and, I'm sorry to say it – *women* – it does things to a young man's head. Especially one as easily turned as Jeremy's.'

Petunia was speaking slowly, quietly. But she wasn't leaving any pauses long enough to let Kristin step in. In truth, the softness in her voice was only serving to keep Kristin totally focused on what she was saying – rather than on what her own reply might be.

'There's always a scheme, there's always *been* a scheme. His dad got him out of the hole with that gambling business, decades ago, but he swore he'd never help like that again.'

What gambling business? What schemes?

Questions swirling round her head. The room was swirling around Kristin now. This was all news to her.

'So, you can imagine, ever since his dad died, he's been trying to persuade me to go along with various misadventures. And I've always resisted. But in all honesty there have been days where I've felt like he's just been trying to run down the clock until I go. As if it will afford him some sort of freedom.

'Well, it's *you* I want to be free. You and little Freddie. You don't deserve to be held back by any misadventures of his. I don't want him frittering away the money his father worked so hard for – and which I have maintained so carefully. It was there to create stability, not to be tossed into madcap schemes and reckless investments. It's for *you*, and for *my grandson*. I know you will do the right thing with it, and I do trust that you can and will keep Jeremy on the straight and narrow.'

The heat was stifling now. Kristin wiped her brow with the back of her hand, then ran a finger across her top lip, trying to shift the beads of sweat gathering there. Why was there no air in here? And why could Petunia not see that however noble her intentions were, she was effectively lobbing a hand grenade into her marriage.

How could she keep such a secret from Jeremy? And yet, how could she not?

'Oh, Petunia, I hate that you have been worrying about this. I wish you could have talked to us sooner.'

'Not "us". *You*.'

'But what do you want me to tell Jeremy?'

'You can tell him about it or not. I have decided that I won't actively lie to him if he starts to press me on things again. On the other hand, nor do I have any intention of telling him if I don't have to. I hope that – at last – he has grasped that discussing finances with me is now a closed book. And frankly, I'd like to enjoy our time together instead of spending it bickering about hypotheticals.'

Kristin looked at Petunia. Her almost translucent skin, so vulnerable without her usual, carefully applied foundation and blusher. Her normally immaculate blow dry askew against the NHS pillow. She didn't feel as if she could fight Petunia on this one. Her mother-in-law had clearly made her mind up.

'I hate the thought of keeping a secret from him ...' said Kristin, but her voice petered out halfway through the sentence. Because she knew as well as Petunia did that there was no way she could tell Jeremy.

Ever.

Chapter 21

VANESSA

Sweat was already trickling down the back of her neck. She shrugged, trying to ignore it. She didn't mind too much though: the early morning heat had meant she was able to start her workout without having to do a thorough warm-up. A few dynamic stretches and she was good to go. Tapping her racket against her tennis shoes, she took a deep breath and waited for the first ball. As she moved from side to side across the baseline, whacking forehands and backhands sent from the club's state of the art ball machine, she knew that this was the only thing that could have lifted her mood today. No matter what was going on in her life, fresh air and exercise, especially tennis, had always been there to rescue Vanessa. She could lose herself in the mindless satisfaction of thumping balls over the net.

She'd stayed at her parents' home last night, taking over from them as babysitter when Kristin and Jeremy had gone straight to hospital to check on Petunia. Last night as they'd stood in the driveway at the O'Briens', the party still in full swing in the garden behind them, Kristin had frantically barked instructions at her while she tried to write it all down as notes in her phone. Vanessa's hands had felt as if she were wearing thick gloves, her fingers moving slowly as she tried to type, straining to hear over the incessant din of the band.

'Mum's taking Dad for blood tests first thing. I said I'd be round to collect Fredster before that.' Kristin was reeling off the daily schedule in chronological order, tapping her fingers as she tried to include everything Vanessa would need to know. Jeremy was scrolling on his phone, ignoring both of them. 'Freddie's got football at nine, and he's got all his kit with him at Mum and Dad's. He finishes at ten and then I usually take him for a hot chocolate in town to keep out of Jeremy's hair for a bit. Oh, no, sorry, never mind, he'll be with me – Jeremy, I mean.'

Vanessa looked at her, waiting for the next instruction. The fact that Kristin organised her weekends in such a way that Jeremy had more than a little 'me-time' was left hanging between them, its absurdity seeming to grow in the silence. They were saved by the sound of a cab's tyres crunching up the gravel before hugging each other goodbye and going their separate ways.

After a few hours of restless sleep Vanessa had got up with Freddie, made him some pancakes, recounted to her folks – who were confused but not alarmed to find that their elder daughter had let herself in to stay over – what had happened the night before, then taken her nephew to football in a cab. She was, after all, not sure she was fit to drive after the party.

She hadn't really had that much to drink – three cocktails and a glass of champagne. It was more that she'd had barely any water all night, followed by far from enough sleep. But as the sun had come up hours ago, streaming through the windows of her parents' spare room, she had woken feeling more like she'd been to a poisoning than a party.

'Where are Mummy and Daddy?' Freddie had asked her, padding into the bedroom and peering at her, as if expecting his parents to be in there too.

'Oh, sweetie, they've gone to the hospital, Grandma P is ill. But don't worry, I'm here to look after you: I'm going to take you to football.'

'Amelie's grandma died, and they all got to go to Scotland to see her body,' replied Freddie with typically unnerving candour.

'Wow, really?' replied Vanessa.

'Yeah, she told me at break that she misses her a lot and sometimes her mum cries, and I told her my mum cries too.'

Vanessa had not known that Freddie had seen his mum crying. Or that it had become commonplace for him. She hadn't been able to shake off his comment all morning, whether she was flipping his pancakes or chopping up carrot batons for him to take in his bag to footie, it preyed and preyed on her mind.

She had instinctively asked the cab driver to wait while she dropped him, before taking her straight back to Royal Oaks.

Now, as she returned shot after shot from the machine, towards the targets she had laid out on the other side of the court, she felt the force of each one through her whole body. She focused on her footwork, ensuring she was in position before the ball bounced so that she could control its trajectory. Rhythm and timing was everything. She reset the machine to its highest tempo, forcing her to pick up the pace and challenging herself to the max. She needed the game to test her and to give her the feel-good factor that a truly punishing workout provided. And she needed to be distracted from her worries. At least for a while.

Slowly, as she sipped from her Royal Oaks water bottle, she felt the tension from the last twenty-four hours start to leave her body, one type of exhaustion replacing another. She kept going though, sweat stinging her eyes, muscles aching, her breathing louder as she strained make every ball. Again, and again. Until this panicky feeling passed.

The sun was right in her eyeline now, almost dazzling her. Images from last night started to whizz through her mind. Jeremy smirking at her as he delved into her past. God, she hated that he had known her back then. At a time when she'd been so dependent on the approval of others. She had learned the hard way that you will never achieve much if you're too hung up on people liking you. And he *had* made her life a misery.

Then came the flashback: Freddie nonchalantly stating that he knew his mother cried a lot. Vanessa couldn't bear it if the same thing was happening all over again. The coercion. The control. The bullying. But how could she let her sister know she'd seen it all before?

Chapter 22

HAILEY

The puppy yelped like a newborn at the sound of the front door opening, startling Hailey out of her nap and leaving her clutching her lap to comfort the little thing. She had barely opened her eyes when the jangle of a set of keys being hurled on to the kitchen counter set Baxter off again.

'Shshshsh,' she said, stroking the puppy's head. Then she saw him.

'Jeremy!'

'*What are you doing here?* Where's Kristin?'

Hailey couldn't work out if it was her or the dog who was quivering. Her heart had been sent racing at the abrupt wake-up and then – Jeremy? Wasn't he meant to be at the hospital? She glanced around, noticing the light in the room and realising that it was later than she'd thought – it was already getting dark. She must have dozed off for at least an hour. What was she supposed to tell him about—

'And what's *that*?'

'Well, this,' she said with a smile that she feared was more of a grimace, 'is Baxter. He's a border terrier puppy, twelve weeks old.'

'Very nice, but you haven't told me what you're doing here.'

'I was waiting for Kristin and Freddie. I thought you were at the hospital – how is your mum? … Anyway, I picked Baxter up for them.'

Hailey wasn't used to babbling like this, it felt totally alien to her. She was always so measured in both her public and private life. She forced herself to take a very deep breath.

'I beg your pardon?' Jeremy's face was blank, impassive, but his tone was furious. He was standing over her now; she felt trapped on the sofa. She'd be an inch from his face if she stood up and that would be a very uncomfortable place to be.

'The puppy. He's yours. Well, Freddie's, I suppose. Isn't he the cutest little guy?' She tried to smile up at him, steeling herself for his reply.

'Sorry, Hailey, but I think you have got this all wrong. We're not getting a puppy. Never have been, never will be.'

Baxter was sitting up in her lap now, wriggling as if he wanted to hop down and lift his leg against this strange new man.

'I see. Seems like Kristin didn't have a chance to discuss this with you. I appreciate that this is a very difficult time for you and the family—' began Hailey.

'Everything's fine, Mum's fine, she's on a ward now,' replied Jeremy irritably. He took his faded baseball cap off, slung it on the kitchen counter and ran a hand through his hair. He did look shattered. Maybe this anger and intolerance was the result of stress, and fatigue.

'Well, that is great news! But Kristin asked me to collect the puppy today for her. It was the last chance to get him, or he'd have been sold to someone else, and she didn't want Freddie to be disappointed. Look, he's dying to say hello.' She smiled again, hating herself for doing so.

Jeremy crossed his arms and leaned back against the kitchen counter, so she gently placed Baxter on the cool of the kitchen tiles allowing him to scurry across towards Jez, his claws making a tiny clickety-clack sound on the floor as he went. Jeremy, disinterested, began to fill his Royal Oaks water bottle from the tap on the refrigerator, his back turned.

'Look, I just don't have time for this right now. It isn't my puppy, and it isn't my problem.' Just as he was dropping ice cubes from the freezer compartment into his water bottle Baxter reached him, tugging playfully at the hem of his faded jeans with his mouth. Jeremy jumped at the contact, swivelling on the other foot, trying to shake the little dog off, almost kicking him away. The puppy howled in pain and confusion.

'Jeremy, no!' Hailey leapt towards Baxter as he skidded on the unfamiliar surface, hitting the leg of a kitchen chair as he did. 'What the hell do you think you're doing?!' She grabbed the pup, returning him to her arms and stroking his head as he whimpered.

For a second, she thought Jeremy might look remorseful, guilty even. But then she realised: Jeremy wasn't annoyed just about the arrival of the puppy, he was scared of it. She tried to cast her mind back to times she had seen him with any other dogs at the club, or the school, or anywhere really. She had no recollection of Jeremy bending to pet the head of an excited lab or ruffling the fur of the myriad labradoodles and cocka-poos that the members seemed to possess. Everyone else, she could instantly call to mind. She knew Vanessa sometimes took a mate's lurcher for long runs in the South Downs National Park. She had heard Garrett talking about how much he missed the huge German shepherds that had guarded their Los Angeles mansion. As she flicked through her mental Rolodex, she had something for almost everyone in her friendship group, but nothing for Jeremy. She'd never seen him with a dog or even anywhere near one. Was he afraid of the dogs themselves, or the responsibility that came from owning one?

And did it really matter, given that he was still on the far side of the kitchen, refusing to come near or apologise to either her or Baxter? Intent on wiping the water he had just spilled, he was avoiding them both. On the countertop, his phone buzzed briefly, its screen lighting up.

Jeremy sighed. Resignation, exhaustion, impatience? Hailey didn't know. He necked the water, slammed the glass on the workshop and made for the kitchen door.

'I can't deal with this right now,' he muttered. 'You need to leave. And take that thing with you.'

Hailey said nothing, focusing instead on the puppy, who was still whimpering. She muttered at him not to worry, that she was here, that they'd get it sorted. But in truth she had no idea what to do. She didn't know where Kristin was or if Jeremy had even been telling the truth about his mother. But it chilled her to realise that for the first time she had felt a prickle of fear at being alone with Jeremy.

But was she in a position to leave, even if he wanted her to? She knew she couldn't take the puppy back to her home. She had neither food nor bedding and no crate to transport him in her car. Plus they were going out for dinner in a couple of hours, and she couldn't leave Baxter alone.

With the pup held against her chest like a newborn, she searched the kitchen cupboards until she found a bowl that might work for water. She thought of Kristin's car, the dog bed, bowls and squeaky toys, which she knew had been in the boot for a fortnight. Gently, she filled the bowl with water and stooped to place it delicately on the floor. As she did, she felt her own phone vibrating in her pocket.

Standing over the puppy, she reached for her mobile and checked the message.

H, are you at ours? Petunia's just had a heart attack.

Omg is she OK? Are you OK?

Hailey's hand was trembling, her thumb sliding clumsily across the letters on the glass keyboard.

No. She's gone. It was awful. But I can't find Jez. I'm frantic. Has he been back to the house by any chance?

Hailey remembered his phone flashing with messages on the counter a minute ago. In a distant corner of the apartment, she heard water running. She couldn't believe it: Jeremy had actually gone to take a shower. How did Kristin put up with this childish, selfish behaviour from him?

Oh, darling. Is anyone with you? I am at yours. Jez just got here. Puppy definitely a surprise for him . . .

Jesus. He said he was just going for a walk. What am I going to do? Fred is still on his sleepover.

Hailey listened again for the noise of the shower, wondering how long she had before he came back into the kitchen. Her fingers felt like jelly, but she hurried, pressing the number at the top of her screen.

'Hailey?' came the voice. Kristin had clearly been crying.

'Are you okay, Krissie? What's happened?'

'I'm okay, just it's all a bit of a shock really.' She sniffed. 'Is Jez there? I still can't get hold of him.'

'He's jumped in the shower, I think. But I'm here, what can I do?'

'Oh, okay. Thank you, Hailes. I'm all over the place. I was only talking to Petunia twenty minutes ago. The doctors said she had a massive heart attack, and they couldn't get her back. I can't believe she's gone, Hailes.'

'I'm so sorry, Kristin. Don't panic. I can sort anything you need.'

'Thank you, thank you so much. I don't even know what I'm supposed to do now. I think there's some sort of paperwork, but Jeremy is down as next of kin, so I think he's going to have to deal with it. Do you think you could take the puppy with you, just until we can pick him up later?'

'Why don't I drop the puppy at Vee's? I'll call her right now—'

'She's away this week, she flew earlier today – I reassured her that everything was OK, that she should definitely go. I'm so sorry to ask, Hailey, but if you wouldn't mind holding onto him for a little longer, I'd be so grateful. There's no way Jeremy will be able to bring him to the hospital.'

'Of course, I'll take him. I'll give Bibi a call as I'm out for dinner tonight. I'm sure she'd love to have Baxter for a few hours. And, Krissie, I don't want to add to your stress, but I don't think Jez is mad keen on the idea of a puppy...'

'Oh, God... do you think he was just surprised? Was he really pissed off?'

'Well, erm, maybe. I guess he's got a lot going on at the moment.' She hoped that she was sugar-coating the situation enough not to freak her friend out even further.

There was a strange gulp as Kristin attempted to stem further tears, desperately trying to compose herself.

'I really didn't find the time to talk to him about it properly, it all started... happening with Petunia and he disappeared.'

'I'm sure it will all work out. It's an awful time. And Fred will need little Baxter more than ever now.'

'You're right. Jeremy's just so *weird* about dogs.' Her voice was tremulous again.

'I'm going to call Bibi right now, it will all be fine.'

'Thank you, thank you. You're the best. Oh, and one more thing...'

'Of course...'

'Do you think you could ask Jeremy to call me urgently or even tell him what's happened...?' she whispered. 'It's not fair that he doesn't find out as soon as possible but he's just not answering his phone, and he should have someone with him when he gets the news.'

Just as Kristin said his name, Jeremy appeared, scowling at the kitchen door. He had a towel round his waist, and not for the first time Hailey was struck by how out of shape he was without the flattery of wearing the club's performance enhancing sportswear. She felt very uncomfortable and unsure where to look, although a part of her suspected this was *exactly* what Jeremy wanted.

'Do you want me to just hand over the phone?'

'No!' Kristin's voice was almost a shriek. 'I'm so sorry, no, I just can't face it. I'll cry all over again and he shouldn't hear all that nonsense from me, not now.'

Kristin was sobbing, and all Hailey wanted to do was to reassure her that she should be allowed to cry within earshot of her husband. That she had a right to feel as sad as they all would at Petunia's death.

'Don't panic. I've got this.'

'Thank you, Hailey, I don't know what I'd do without you.'

'Take care of yourself, OK—'

But Kristin had already hung up.

'You've got what, may I ask?' Jeremy was glowering at her. Hailey's eyes darted to the corner of the room, where Baxter was still lapping at the water bowl. She took a breath, an attempt to centre herself before the incoming storm.

'That was Kristin—'

'Yeah, so I gathered.'

'She's still at the hospital.'

'Clearly.' He looked around the room as if checking she wasn't there. Sarcasm dripped from his voice.

'And I'm afraid it's not good news.'

Jeremy was still now, that impassive glaze was back.

'I'm so sorry to have to tell you this, but Kristin's been trying to get hold of you. In the last hour or so your mum has had a sudden cardiac arrest. She's dead, Jeremy. I'm so, so sorry.'

Hailey saw his knuckles whiten as he gripped the towel.

She didn't like the man, but she still felt empathy for anyone who'd just lost their mother. Even Jeremy Hale. 'Shall I get you some water?'

No response. Hailey picked up the water bottle he'd dumped in the sink earlier and refilled it. He didn't take it. As he stood there, water dripped from his wet hair down the side of his neck and onto his collarbone. Hailey tried to focus on it, rather than staring indiscreetly into his face, waiting for a response.

She extended a hand towards him, reaching to touch his shoulder in reassurance, a peace gesture after the earlier sharp words. But before she could make contact, he had stepped back, shrugging as if to avoid her hand at all costs. He looked up now.

His eyes were glassy, as if tears might come if only he'd let them. But he didn't. Instead, he looked down at her, almost imperious.

'I guess it's good news for dear old Justin then, isn't it?'

Hailey stared back at him, wondering what on earth he meant.

'With Mum gone, he can finally get back that fucking money he's always nagging me about.'

Now …

Chapter 23

ELEANOR

Before Eleanor had managed to reply to her, Bibi had stormed off to hunt for Kristin on the club grounds. Relieved to have been left alone, Eleanor nevertheless felt terrible that she hadn't been able to protect her boss better. She felt as if she were drowning, unsure how to get back to the surface, at a loss as to how to help, everything she'd prided herself on being able to do, seemed suddenly to be no longer of any value whatsoever.

She'd been standing at the front desk, trying to tidy what didn't need tidying, just shuffling bits around in an attempt to look busy, when a second car pulled into the car park. The sleek black Tesla was silent as it slid into a space; it only caught Eleanor's eye because reception – with its perfect view out onto the forecourt – was nowhere near as busy as it used to be. She knew who it was long before the thud of the door and the emergence of a slim leg in a neat capri pant from the driver's seat.

'Eleanor,' said Hailey as she stood up, smiling brightly, giving her a wave as she stood on the steps to the clubhouse.

Hailey ran a hand underneath her hair, lifting it up and over the stiff collar of her buttery beige leather jacket. Her curls bounced as they fell, reminding Eleanor of her marzipan replica on top of the cake. *The almondy yellow curls must have taken forever to create*, she thought, imagining someone in the patisserie carefully winding slivers of marzipan around a small crafting tool to create each individual curl. She was snapped out of her reverie by Bibi's voice, calling out from the path between the tennis courts. There she was, with Kristin. The two of them were holding hands like primary school kids. Kristin was wearing a pair of tracksuit bottoms, a cashmere hoodie and a pair of Birkenstock clogs. She looked as if she had sneaked out to take the dog for a wee. She also looked vulnerable, almost frail.

'Hailey, we've found you!' exclaimed Bibi, her arms thrown up theatrically. Kristin's hand went slack by her side as Bibi let go. She was staring in Hailey's direction, but her eyes were glazed. 'We've been so worried!' Bibi's voice was shrill, strained even.

But all Eleanor could think about was that conversation she had overheard a couple of weeks ago. Those two club members discussing the menace of Garrett O'Brien. She had dismissed it as nonsense, gossip, at the time – but now it had all her senses tingling. Why was Bibi so energised?

'Bibi was just telling me about … Justin,' said Kristin, her own voice slightly shaky. Hailey's face gave away nothing. Years of training meant she was a master of that.

'Oh, that,' said Hailey as the three women stared back at her. Was she going to explain what was going on? Bibi was blinking, perhaps a little faster than normal.

Hailey started to speak, just as Kristin's phone rang. Hailey immediately paused, while Kristin frowned at her screen. She shrugged.

'Unknown number. The last thing I need right now is to speak to someone who doesn't know what's, well, what's happened.' Bibi rubbed the top of her back gently and dipped her head a little to one side.

'Anyway, Hailey,' she said, her voice softer now. 'Is everything OK with you?'

Eleanor wanted to hear what was being said, but was aware that she felt increasingly conspicuous standing on the clubhouse steps. She wasn't sure she was invited to listen, but she definitely didn't deny herself hearing what was being said.

'Ladies, why don't you come in?' she offered. 'Mrs H, shall I put the coffee machine on and get you all some hot drinks? Won't take me five minutes ...'

'Oh, Eleanor, that would be wonderful – don't worry about coffee, but I'd love a fresh mint tea.'

Perfect. Eleanor stayed where she was and ushered them all into the clubhouse. As she did so, she noticed that Bibi's usually impeccable lipstick was slightly smudged on her teeth. There was something off, something askew about all of them. Eleanor felt as if she were watching these women being played by actresses who hadn't quite learned their lines properly. Pauses were off, eye contact not quite made. The whole thing was making her both long to disappear, yet unable to look away.

Reluctantly, she headed to the kitchen, making sure the door stayed ajar, slightly propped open by a mop that had been left in the wrong place by the police after they had finished their search of the area.

The three women sat on the leather sofas in the lounge area. Hailey was stiffly removing her jacket and placing it carefully on the arm of one of the chairs.

'Oh, the police have gone,' she said. 'The housekeeper had got herself into a frightful twist.'

'Oh, really?' replied Kristin, who sounded like she was speaking from the end of a very long tunnel.

'Well, Justin ordered the cake, of course he did.'

Eleanor turned the tap off, paused filling the kettle to cut out the noise of the water.

'...he was so proud of us. And he wanted to do something nice. So, he used his whizzy new typing thing on his wheelchair and got online, ordered the cake, the whole thing.'

Eleanor gasped. Justin. He'd killed Jeremy. Silently, she placed the kettle on the kitchen worktop and leaned towards the door.

'My God!' cried Bibi. 'What a mistake!'

There was complete silence from Kristin.

'Oh, Jesus, I'm so sorry. I haven't explained properly at all...'

Eleanor couldn't bear it and leaned ever further towards the door, trying to peer through the gap at its hinge, to see the women's faces.

'They did come round, and they chatted to Justin about the cake. They came at the crack of dawn, like they were going to catch him doing something dodgy. What did they think he was going to do, run away? And did they really think that if he was going to order some sort of murderous cake, he'd do it on his own system, used only by him?'

Eleanor noticed how strange and impassive Kristin's face was. Was she even listening?

'Sorry, Kristin, I don't mean to be facetious about it, but really ... if *these* are the finest minds His Majesty's Constabulary has to offer ... Anyway, they were there for hours – apparently while I was getting in a state and calling you, Bibi, and then they got a call. I'm not convinced that I was supposed to have heard any of this, but I'm sure they'll be right round to tell you – they had a call from the lab, and they don't think it was the cake at all.'

Bibi gasped. Eleanor only managed not to by clasping her hand to her mouth.

'He was poisoned. Arsenic. Of course, there are traces of it in almonds – as I well know from my own research for Justin. So, I imagine that's what confused the toxicology or whatnot in the labs.'

The relief all but made Eleanor's knees buckle. She was in the clear. A second later she chastised herself. The man was still dead, how dare she let that fact slip her mind, no matter how wonderful it felt to know it hadn't been *her* responsibility?

Bibi was once again rubbing the top of Kristin's shoulders.

'Oh, darling,' she said. 'What a horrible shock. At least we know it was an accident now, no one at fault!' Her laugh reminded Eleanor of the sound her car made when she struggled to change gears properly.

But Kristin was making no sound at all. She had stood up and was tugging at her top, as if trying to straighten herself out. And as Eleanor saw her boss standing there, shoulders stiff, awkward, for the first time the terrible thought crossed her mind.

What if this wasn't shock, but guilt?

One week before…

Chapter 24

BIBI

The velour of her dressing-table stool was soft against the backs of her thighs as she sat in her tennis skirt and looked at her own reflection. Her eyes were undeniably tired, despite the expensive gel mask patches she had placed underneath them for the past half-hour. She pulled them gently away from her face and patted the remaining serum into the delicate skin there. From the other room, she could hear Baxter tumbling around.

It was only a friendly game of tennis they had today, and with some of her best friends, but Beatriz desperately didn't want to look anything less than her usual glamorous self. She couldn't let them know about it, about how she had panicked. Not yet – not today. Not while Kristin was still so fragile.

She took a dark-brown pencil from the neat Perspex tray in her top drawer and drew tiny strokes, filling in the patches where she could see that she must have plucked out one too many of her brow hairs last night. God, she hadn't done that for years, maybe even a decade. The hours she used to spend perfecting those brows, making sure that the evidence of her nervous habit was hidden. It felt like a lifetime ago. Then again, so did the way that that same habit had just disappeared when she had met Garrett. Once they were together, and she'd felt that blanket of security for the first time, it had just faded away.

Her brows had grown back, as perfect as they'd ever been. In fact, she had forgotten all about this habit as she had eased into her new life in the UK, with not just a husband who she adored but solid friendships with women she trusted.

Now, she was back to doing this, papering over the cracks. Recent years were starting to feel like a dream, one from which she had been unwillingly wrenched, and dumped back into reality. Would these brows ever grow back again? Could Garrett's magic save her a second time?

She closed an eyelid to dab a taupe shadow across it, but as her vision darkened, an image of Jeremy shot across her mind. The leer he'd had. The grab he'd made. The panic she'd felt in that moment. How it had reminded her of who she used to be, how she used to feel, the ways she'd had to fight to survive.

She took a deep breath and dabbed the subtle shimmer across her lid with the tip of her ring finger. Normally, her face came to life with the smallest amount of make-up. But today it needed more than the smallest amount. She took a brush and swiped it across the top of her lipstick. Velvet Ribbon. She brushed the colour across her mouth, put the lipstick down, and smiled at herself. But it was undeniable: she found it hard to see the woman she had been a year ago in that reflection. The woman she had been before Jeremy. Before all of this.

When they had moved to England there was only one club Garrett was interested in joining. Nearby Cavendish Lane had a fantastic reputation, but Garrett wasn't fussed, instead making a beeline for the Royal Oaks. He said it was about the golf, but Bibi had never been entirely convinced. But why not go along with it? The club had all the facilities the couple wanted, it was almost on the doorstep, and the grounds were stunning, the sort of place that it wouldn't have been surprising to find as a film set for an episode of *The Crown* or *Bridgerton*.

These friendships had all started out so naturally. It had been just the sort of British companionship that Bibi could only have dreamed of back in her Miami days – even when she had lived in LA, she had longed for something as low key, as genteel as she'd found the tennis world in the south of England to be. Just as the weather proved to be less changeable, as gentle on the soul as it was gentle on the skin, so too had the people proven to be loyal, dependable and fun. Kristin's sweet, even temperament, Vanessa's warmth despite her more caustic tongue, and even Hailey's tender consideration for all of them regardless of how much she had on her plate. These qualities had made their friendships feel not just easy; they enabled her to be her best self among them.

Perhaps that was part of the problem: she had made it to England in the hope of leaving the fire in her behind. She wanted to put her past behind her, forget about the searing Miami sun as much as she wanted to forget the obvious choices she had made beneath it. But she couldn't run from herself. She was always going to be there, front and centre, causing problems for herself. Some of the harshest lessons she had learned about men early in her life were perhaps just too difficult to unlearn.

It was during one of the Friday night barbecues at the club that Garrett let slip that he'd known Jeremy 'back in the day'. Bibi had been intrigued. Perhaps the promise of meeting up with old friends had made him so super keen on joining Royal Oaks? But if so, why only say so now? Either way, she knew better than to start probing, especially when both of them were reluctant to respond to her initial questions. All she gleaned was that it was something to do with Jeremy's time as a rookie pro. 'What happens on tour stays on tour,' they both said. It was clearly some kind of secret pact and so Bibi had decided to let sleeping dogs lie.

She loved how relaxed Garrett seemed around their social group at the club. The wearying jealousy and one-upmanship that so often dominated group 'couple date nights' just didn't seem to exist when they were at Royal Oaks. Bibi didn't know why – maybe it was the people, or the fact that there was clearly an incredibly welcoming environment, or even just the sheer beauty of the place – but she revelled in it. She fitted in. She was free.

Until she wasn't.

At first, flirting with Jeremy had felt like a bit of silly, harmless fun. She didn't find him attractive, not really, with his flabby chest and his pasty face. He didn't even have the drama of Garrett's startling white skin and jet-black hair. Yes, he had gorgeous brown puppy dog eyes, but he was otherwise just, well, a charmingly average Brit. Maybe it was that which made him feel safe to her. Someone with whom she could flex that long-dormant flirting muscle, and remind herself of the old days when flirting was at first survival, then business, then a well-honed skill she deployed to persuade men to do whatever she wanted. Much as she enjoyed the peace and quiet of life in England, she had found that she enjoyed being reminded of her previous self. A self which, even if she hated to admit it, was when she'd been at her most powerful, most independent.

With Jeremy the consequences had always felt so lowball! She wasn't asking for favours, she just wanted to see if she could use him to keep Garrett on his toes. Really, it was only ever a quiet hour for him to look at her groundstroke after lunch, mid-week, at the house of course, or perhaps the steadying hand on her while she stretched out a hip flexor. He was a good coach, he really noticed things, worked her hard and always made time for her. She enjoyed the attention of his gaze following her around the court, watching her intently as she bent and stretched for the ball. He pushed her, made her sweat, then praised her effusively. It felt like being let out into the sunshine after a significant period in the shade.

Until it didn't.

Only now that she had the benefit of hindsight could she see how naive she'd been. She'd enjoyed the little trip of charming him, knowing it meant nothing. She wanted nothing. It was Garrett whose attention she'd been chasing; Jeremy was just a pawn. But she'd been a fool to assume that he would be a willing accomplice in that. She had never once considered how he might respond.

It had been late last summer when his hand had travelled those crucial few inches. A routine stretch after an hour's intense training on the private court at the O'Briens'. As she had leaned against him, eyes closed against the fading heat of the late-September sky, her hamstring slowly relaxing, she had felt it. The heat of his hand on her flesh. Moving up, and beyond the hem of her tennis skirt, his thumb moving back and forth against the seam of her Nike undershorts. At first, she hadn't realised. Not until she had felt the warmth of his breath on her ear.

She had stepped away. It was a lesson learned long ago that it was unwise to provoke men mere seconds after rejecting them. Better to pretend she hadn't noticed. She ran her hands through her hair briskly and thanked him for the session.

'You're welcome. Plenty more where that came from.' His smiled was crooked. He licked his lips as he wiped sweat from his brow with the sweatband on his wrist. His face didn't bear any hint of what had happened, and for an instant she wondered if it was she who had read the situation wrong. Had she imagined it? And had he even realised he'd been rejected?

As autumn drew in, it was easy to put a bit of distance between them. The end of the summer meant training indoors at the club, where there were inevitably more eyes on them than at her home court. She focused on her fitness, let her tennis slide a little over Christmas, even feigning injury in the new year. But once the league matches had started hotting up Jeremy just seemed to be everywhere. And whenever he could snatch an opportunity, there was a comment, a glance, *something*.

She had tried to be chill about it. She had stuck to Garrett as much as possible when Jez was around, but this had only made things worse. Her husband had seemed to sense the uncharacteristic clinginess in her, something she knew he would despise. Sure enough, she felt him withdraw within a week or two, almost palpably uneasy about her sudden need to be permanently attached. There was also an obvious edge between the two men, which she suspected had nothing to do with her. One evening in May, when she could see that Garrett had had a good few scotches, she had tried to ask him what the situation was with Jez and him. Testing the water, she gently queried what had gone on when they were younger men.

'I can barely remember it,' he'd said. 'But I know this much about the man, he didn't play fair then, and I'd wager he still doesn't now. If I were a betting man, that is.'

The mention of betting had made Bibi's skin prickle. She had heard the whispers that betting sites were the source of Garrett's original fortune. But had it been legit? Or was he involved in some sort of match fixing operation?

A quip to Jeremy the following weekend seemed to confirm her suspicions. She'd been having cocktails in the clubhouse with the girls when he had come over to say hi.

'We were just discussing whether the club members bet on the outcome of leagues,' Vanessa had said with a sly smile.

'Stop it, I can't take the pressure!' Kristin had replied, theatrically.

'Don't be daft, your game is dynamite this summer,' Hailey had reassured her.

Jeremy had said nothing, smiling broadly at the women and checking if anyone wanted a second mojito.

'I'm sure they do,' Bibi had ventured. 'I mean we could get really clever and start throwing matches, just for a laugh. Imagine old Major Humphrey's face if he was counting on us for a major return on his stake and we didn't produce the goods?'

Vanessa giggled into her salt-rimmed glass but Jeremy's face had unmistakeably darkened. He said nothing and walked off towards the pro shop, hands deep in the pockets of his shorts.

A week later at the pickleball tournament, she had made the mistake of trying to help out when Petunia had had her funny turn. She had followed Jeremy to his car to collect a bottle of Gatorade for his mother when he had tried his luck with a kiss, putting his hands on her hips and pulling her towards him as if his patience were wearing thin.

'I see you, looking at me at the club,' he had mumbled into her ear. 'And I hear you, making your little cheap jokes about throwing matches.' His hand was gripping against her hip tightly now, his thumb close to leaving a bruise. His head was tilted, looking up at her as he sat in the boot of the car and she stood over him, desperate to step back. His gaze was more of a leer. 'That was a long, long time ago, so don't think you and Garrett can hold it over me again now ...'

He'd leaned in to kiss her, but she had managed to move her mouth fast enough to miss his. Her teeth had clashed awkwardly with the side of his face though, and he hadn't managed to move his hand fast enough to remove the lipstick before Kristin appeared. Bibi's blood had run cold, unsure if her friend had seen the interaction, but Kristin had shown no sign of being perturbed, not then nor in the weeks that followed.

'Don't worry, babe,' Jeremy had said to her as his wife walked away. 'She's cool.'

Bibi was not so sure. Nor was she sure what the mention of 'a long time ago' had meant. But she was starting to piece it together.

Perhaps the sense of 'getting away with it' was what had given Jeremy his confidence as the weeks had passed. She had stopped taking his calls or replying to his Instagram DMs – despite their increasing frequency – but this seemed only to have convinced him that they were co-conspirators with some secret between them. Where she was trying to demonstrate a lack of interest or enthusiasm for his little jokes and sexual innuendo, he was interpreting her as 'being discreet' or 'keeping things on the down low'.

'There is no secret!' she had wanted to yell. But she hadn't. She knew her temper had got the better of her in the past, and she wanted to protect Kristin from whatever reality Jeremy had concocted for himself. But staying silent meant his pathetic jibes hadn't let up.

Bibi was all too familiar with Jeremy's knack of being given an inch and taking a mile. He could spin an excuse for his behaviour in an almost admirable way, and she was often surprised by how people so often fell for it. If only she hadn't been one of them, if only she had taken her own advice sooner.

Perhaps now it was too late.

In the moments before her party had begun, when she was alone, taking a moment to herself before she turned on the charm and went to greet her guests, Jeremy had known exactly where to find her. He must have crept round to the far side of the garden, avoiding Garrett on the patio steps, knowing that this secret enclave where she liked to sunbathe was where he might find her. And so he had, creeping up behind her, slinking his arms around her waist and leaning over her shoulder.

'Sooo good to see you again,' he'd muttered, his lips on her ear. 'You look sensational. This dress! It's so good to have you all to myself for a moment.'

'Well, not for long, my guests are about to arrive!' She had wriggled out of his arms, trying to keep her voice light, her ankle twisting in her heels as she tried to get away.

'We don't need long. I've waited long enough.' He grabbed her wrist as she moved past him, holding her against him in the shadows of the tree where he'd been hiding. For a moment, she felt as if she couldn't breathe, so tight were his lips against hers. Managing to wriggle her arms free, she pushed against his chest with both hands, releasing herself and gasping with relief.

'What are you doing?' she whispered.

'Chill, no one will see. Just quickly...' He moved towards her, and she stepped away fast, into the shadows of a privet hedge.

'Leave it,' she said, her voice a hoarse, but authoritative whisper. 'Just leave it, Jeremy, you've got the wrong idea.'

'Oh, really? Is *that* what Garrett will think?'

'What are you talking about? Think about what?'

'I don't know. I guess he'll only know what I tell him.'

'You aren't going to tell him anything, Jeremy, because there isn't anything to tell.'

'Sure.' His tone was sarcastic, teasing. Beatriz felt things unravelling inside of her. She shrugged, determined not to lose her cool.

'Listen, babe. I won't tell Big G about you messing around with me this last year or so, if you get him to quit nagging me about the cash.'

'We haven't been messing around! What are you talking about?'

'You can tell him what you like, Bibi, but the fact remains, you've asked me for an awful lot of private lessons while he's been away. I'm not stupid. I know what you've been up to, and I'm sure Garrett won't like it.'

Bibi threw her arms in the air in frustration. She could hear the voices of her guests over the distant strains of the band now. They were all so close. She couldn't tell if she wanted someone to come and disturb them or not – she was aware this didn't look good and she was still shaking from the way he had grabbed her.

'You're talking nonsense! And anyway – what cash?'

It was Jeremy who looked momentarily stunned now.

'Look, it's just an investment opportunity I put his way. He was slobbering all over the idea last year, but now he wants payout, and things are just going to take a little longer than initially planned. No biggie. But the man needs to get off my back. So you can tell him to, or I can tell him about what we've been up to.'

'For God's sake, Jeremy, I don't get involved in Garretti's business and I never have. He wouldn't listen to me anyway.'

Jeremy shrugged.

'And anyway – what the hell makes you think that if *you* told him there *was* something going on, that it's me he'd take it out on – not you.'

'You seem to forget that I've known the man a long time.' Jeremy's lip was curled. There was no doubt he believed in this threat. Beatriz had shivered despite the warmth of the evening.

She looked at him, gobsmacked. None of this made sense. Had she been played?

'It's not going to happen. There's nothing between us, there never has been. Leave it.'

'Is that I wonder what Kristin thinks, though? I mean, she's already seen me with your lipstick smeared on my face.'

She gasped. To handle an angry Garrett was one thing, but to lose the trust of a friend was another. She felt queasy, the noise of the party rising behind her, reminding her that there was no way to escape him tonight.

'This is madness, Jeremy. Leave me alone.'

He had reached for her again, but she recoiled sharply, the naked skin of her back beneath her pink silk dress catching on a twig. She yelped, putting her hand behind her to check if she was bleeding. There wasn't time to find out, she realised, and took to her not insignificant heels. At that, Jeremy chuckled, low and sneering. Then he turned around and sauntered back to the party. Bibi could feel her heart beat rapidly in her chest, the *thump, thump, thump* drowning everything out. She took a moment, trying to steady her breathing, then ran back to the crowd.

She managed to steady her walk and smooth a hand through her hair before she was back in view of the guests. But she had been full of anxiety ever since. It was only later, once all the guests had left and the house was quiet, that she saw — tucked in among the messages of thanks and photos of the night — a menacing text from Jeremy. She looked at the time on the screen: he must have sent it while he was still at the party.

Think about my little offer, BB. Don't disappoint me. See you soon xxx

She turned her face into her pillow. Her breath smelled of alcohol despite brushing her expensive veneers and even the lush fragrance of her favourite night cream could do little to hide it. Just because she'd indulged one final time in the temporary high of flirting with a younger man, everything was at risk. Her marriage, her finances, her friendships.

Now, as she tried to smile, convincing herself she was ready for those self-same friends to arrive, she was concerned to see the trace of a grimace in her lips and fear in her eyes. As there always was when she thought of Jeremy and the position he had put her in.

Chapter 25

KRISTIN

'Will Daddy be very angry?' came the small voice from the back seat.

Against the warm black leather of the steering wheel, Kristin's wedding ring glinted in the sunlight as they turned onto the main road towards the O'Briens'. Her eyes flicked up to the rear-view mirror where she saw him, clutching his favourite soft toy. Bunny hadn't come on a car journey for years. She remembered a time when Freddie was in that huge car seat, his legs sticking straight out in front of him, and no journey could even begin until Bunny was in place. That hadn't been the case for a very long time, but today was different, of course it was.

'Oh, darling, I'm sure he'll be very sad. We all are. But he won't be angry.'

Guilt clung to the back of her throat like sugar syrup after draining a fizzy drink in the sun. Was this really her son's first question after the death of his grandmother? A worry about anger? Since yesterday, Kristin had been living in what seemed like a different universe, one from which a filter had just been lifted. Having heard Petunia speak so plainly about her own son left her seeing Jeremy in a completely new light. She had long suspected that Petunia thought him a bit soft, a bit of a daddy's boy, a little more indulged than she would have liked.

But that she hadn't trusted him? That she would lie to him so comprehensively? How had Kristin been so blind to this?

Now it seemed that Freddie, too, was showing what he really thought of his father.

'I'll miss Granny.'

Kristin glanced up again. Freddie was staring out of the window, Bunny clasped between his hands, a tear smudged across his cheek. He looked as tired as she felt.

'It's horrible, sweetie. It really is. We are all going to be sad for quite a while, I'm sure. But we must support Daddy as much as we can. Because he's going to be the saddest of all.'

'Where is he?'

Oh, how Kristin wished she knew. He hadn't been at home last night when she had finally returned from the hospital, and after a fitful night she had woken to see her phone full of messages of condolence – but nothing at all from him. She knew he'd been home – Hailey had told her. But he seemed to have left, more distressed by the arrival of Baxter than the news of his mother – and no one had seen him since. Well, no one she had dared to call. Who knew where he had gone? The realisation that she had no idea what he might want or need to do in a moment of intense grief had left her sitting in bed at 3 a.m., hollow with sadness that her husband had become like a stranger to her. And not just a stranger, but an angry, volatile one.

It was only ten o'clock and the sun was already high in the sky, but she felt chilly, fragile, unsure of what she should be saying to anyone. Should she admit that Jeremy was missing to anyone beyond the four of them? Should she even confide in *them*? And what should she tell them about Petunia, about the money, about the growing pile of secrets and lies. She was even lying to Freddie, sweet innocent seven-year-old Freddie who didn't deserve any of this.

'He's gone for a walk. You know what he's like when he's got things in his mind,' she said, trying to give him an encouraging smile in the mirror.

Fred said nothing. *He shouldn't know what Daddy was like when he was stressed*, Kristin thought. He shouldn't even know what that word means. Kristin wriggled her fingers against the steering wheel again, an attempt to stem the clamminess against the seamed leather. Her entire body was in turmoil, her mind racing. She inhaled deeply and exhaled slowly. All those yoga classes had taught her to calm her inner self.

'But I have some good news...'

Still no reply from the back seat. What she'd give to know what was going on in that little head. 'There is someone at Bibi's who is very excited to meet you...'

'Who?' He was paying attention now.

'You'll see when you get there, but I think you're going to love him.' She could tell her voice was strangled, it's pitch higher than normal.

She hoped Freddie wouldn't notice how hard she was trying today. This game of doubles at the O'Briens' had been planned for weeks – a last big practice for the four of them before the final league match where a victory would make them champions for the first time. This year, they'd given it their all, training together, and competing all over the county, slowly climbing up the league table and keeping the Royal Oaks at the very top of the local tennis scene in its centenary year.

Of course, Jeremy had feigned disinterest. When prodded by Vanessa on why he hadn't been out there supporting them or why he hadn't brought Freddie to any of the away matches and why he seemed to change the subject when their winning streak was mentioned, he had simply told her that he 'knew they'd boss it' and that's why he wasn't giving it 'undue' attention. Kristin had seen the look of fury on her sister's face when he'd said it, but she hadn't interfered. The growing animosity between the two of them hadn't needed stoking.

Thank God she was about to see her friends today. And how lucky that they were able to play this final practice match on the O'Brien's pristine grass court, away from the distractions of the club. She wouldn't have to explain to anyone about Petunia, she wouldn't have to console anyone about her, and best of all, she wouldn't have to pretend that she knew where Jeremy was to anyone. To top it off, Freddie would be over the moon to be playing with Baxter, Garrett would be firing up the barbecue and keeping an eye on him, then there was the promise of a splash in the pool for all of them before lunch.

For a brief moment, Kristin started to look forward to the morning ahead. But then her mind jolted back to her worries. Not just Petunia, but the rest of it. Jeremy's hand on Beatriz's hips at the school. That smudge of lipstick on the side of his mouth. Vanessa sneaking up to her at the Memorial Day Party and asking casually 'what's the deal?' with Bibi and Jeremy. To her shame, Kristin had shrugged the query off and spent the rest of the event trying to avoid her sister's eye.

What had Vanessa even meant? At the time, Kristin had felt insulted, her privacy invaded. She didn't want others to be noticing things she was barely starting to admit to herself. But there, curdling deep in her gut – along with that image of Jeremy's smirk as his face had emerged from behind Bibi's hips – was the real question she was avoiding: what *was* going on with them? And what might that mean for her?

She had hoped to avoid confronting any of these questions for weeks yet. This summer just didn't seem to have let up

– event after event piling up at the club, school runs, play dates, admin, league matches, Freddie's activities ... She had hoped to put it all off at least until the puppy was settled, because if she was going to have a blow out with Jeremy, she was determined to get the dog into a routine first.

But Petunia's death had upended all of this. Now it wasn't just the general life-admin that seemed to be snowballing, but years of unspoken niggles were now coming to the surface, mixing with all the anxieties she had had about her marriage and picking up speed as they raced towards her.

The blast of a car horn pierced through the relentless churn of her thoughts, followed by the realisation that the screech of tyres was coming from her car.

'MUM!'

She grabbed the wheel, steadying the vehicle. 'I'm so sorry, sweetie, it's all OK, we're nearly there.'

So preoccupied, so exhausted was she that she had just run through a red light. *Get a grip*, she told herself, mortified. She pressed her fingers against the steering wheel, as if clinging to it could keep her aligned with reality, in control for today at least.

'I know, Mum. You frightened me, though.'

Moments later they turned into the O'Briens' driveway, the familiar crunch of gravel beneath them as they approached the house. Nerves swished in the pit of Kristin's stomach. She couldn't even remember when she had last eaten. Had Jeremy bought her a sandwich in the hospital or did she just have a memory of him saying he would? She certainly couldn't bring the thought of any sandwich to mind. *My breath must stink*, she thought, trying in vain to check. She leaned into the mirror one more time to check her face and immediately regretted it, then reached across into the glove box to grab a mint imperial.

When she looked up, Beatriz was on the steps to the house in a brand new white tennis dress, her monogrammed tennis shoes and a customary pair of huge gold hoops in her ears. Her skin was glowing, flawless. Even her long, tanned legs seemed to shimmer in the morning sunlight, as if she were wearing dancer's tights. She smiled, that broad red smile, and for a second, Kristin felt relaxed. This was her old friend, things would be resolved. Everything would be okay.

Then she spotted him: there in Bibi's arms was the black-and-brown bundle of fur that was Baxter. The knots in her stomach loosened and unfurled even further. *It is going to be OK*, she told herself. This was the *one* thing she knew she had got right lately. Screw Jeremy and his petty insecurities – look at that little thing!

Bibi waved at them, the dark red of her nails familiar, welcoming. Kristin thought how many times she'd seen them, those same rings she always wore, wrapped around tennis rackets, cocktail glasses, coffee cups.

Don't panic, she told herself and looked back at the puppy.

'Oh, wow,' said Freddie, his voice as wobbly as it had been when she had jumped that light. 'Is that...?'

Excitement temporarily replaced the anxiety and grief that was sloshing around Kristin's gut. She got out of the car and ran round to the back seat as fast as she could. She opened the door for Freddie, her heart full, brimming with emotion at the sight of his beaming face as the situation dawned on him.

'Mum...?' he looked at her quizzically, his eyes sparkling for the first time in weeks.

A few feet away, Bibi lifted one of Baxter's front paws and waved it at Freddie.

'Well hello there, big brother,' she said in a sing-song voice. 'I'm ve-wy excited to meet you...'

'Brother?! Is it...?' Freddie looked up at his mum again.

'Yes,' she said, a lump in her throat. He galloped up the steps and took the puppy, which Bibi was holding out to him, immediately bursting into overwhelmed tears. Undaunted, Baxter nuzzled into him, licking tears from his cheeks.

'Mummy, is he really mine? For real, for real?'

'He is,' said Beatriz at exactly the same time that Kristin said, 'Yes, darling. He's yours.'

As they turned to face each other against the full glare of the sunlight, their smiles looked not dissimilar to two women baring their teeth at each other.

Chapter 26

BIBI

The puppy had already left some scuff marks on the door frame to the living room, and Stella, Bibi's beautiful grey-and-white ragdoll cat, had been hiding upstairs all day, quivering. The makeshift crate that Garrett and one of the garden staff had made for the puppy looked a little forbidding, so Bibi had ended up removing him from it and letting him sleep on an old duvet at the end of her bed. She was quite sure this broke all the rules on house training, but this was a crisis, and it was only for the night. Garrett tried to pretend he was annoyed, but she suspected he loved the pup already too. Anyway, the pair of them were glad of the distraction as the silence between them was growing. Beatriz suspected that a night or two at the end of their bed wasn't going to be the biggest of the problems confronting this little dog might face, and Garrett was due to go away for business the following night, so the matter was settled.

Hailey's panicked phone call, and the sight of her troubled face when she had turned up with the puppy shortly afterwards had been unsettling to Bibi, who was not used to seeing her friend in anything but full control. That evening Hailey was flustered, dishevelled, even her curls seemed to have lost their bounce.

'God, I'm glad we got the poor little mite out of the flat,' she had said as she popped Baxter down in a corner of the kitchen, staying crouched to reassure him while he sniffed around. 'I honestly think Jeremy was on the verge of hurting him, and that was *before* he heard about his mother.'

'What do you mean?' Bibi turned, offering her friend an enormous glass of iced tea, stuffed full of mint leaves and lemon slices.

'Exactly what I say. Do you know, I think it might not be that he *dislikes* dogs, but that he's *frightened* of them. He all but kicked him, a real shove he gave him.'

'That man...' said Bibi, stopping herself from going any further.

Hailey said nothing, focusing on the dog. 'I didn't feel like I could say anything,' she eventually admitted. 'The man's mother was seriously ill. And then I had to tell him she had died. I felt terrible just leaving him with that news; honestly, it goes against everything I think one should do in such a situation. But we just had to get out of there. I know it sounds dramatic, and I know you know that that's not me – but it didn't feel safe. It just didn't.'

'You don't have to explain yourself, darling,' said Bibi, stroking her friend's arm. 'We can't control how we feel but, well, we can control how we react to things. It's awful about poor Petunia. It all seems so sudden. But Jeremy... well, an *explanation* for bad behaviour is not an *excuse* for bad behaviour.'

She had paused, remembering his grip on her upper arm last week at training. Why had she even turned up?

It had happened on Thursday evening. Her weekly individual lesson with Jeremy on Court One was usually one of the most anticipated events in her diary. Bibi had thought more than once about cancelling, but her desire to work on her approach to net shots in preparation for the last few matches of the league season trumped her continuing distrust and dislike of her coach.

She decided to take the lead from the outset and make it clear what she wanted to focus on. She was a paying customer after all. And more importantly, she wanted to avoid any small talk.

'My priority tonight is to improve my speed up to the short ball and my depth on the approach shot to help me get into a better position to play an aggressive volley.'

She had been rehearsing her wording on the drive to the club, something she had never done before and which clearly signified her concern at facing Jeremy in a one-to-one situation.

Jeremy had looked at her quizzically for a few seconds before sarcastically replying, 'Of course. You know best.'

He had begun the lesson by feeding a short ball cross court for Bibi to practise her speed off the mark from the baseline and had set out two yellow marker lines to indicate where she should aim her shot to and where she should then recover to after the hit.

Court One was the closest court to the clubhouse and directly in front of the bar and restaurant. Jeremy loved the fact that the members could watch him through the windows or from the terrace and he always played to his audience. Tonight was no different and he delighted in sending Bibi short balls with excessive backspin that forced her to lunge so much that she almost toppled over. 'Too slow!' he shouted. 'She's no FloJo, is she?' The elderly gents on the terrace guffawed and raised their wine glasses to him.

Each time Bibi reached the ball and struggled to control her shot towards the target, Jeremy growled, 'Too short,' and took enormous pleasure in ripping his next shot past her at the net or sliding a perfectly timed lob over her head. On one occasion he nailed an outrageous topspin backhand straight at her head, causing her to duck and then to fall backwards, her arms and racket flailing wildly. More laughter from the gallery and Bibi, picking herself up as gracefully as she could, walked up to the net, leaned forward and hissed, 'I'm finished. And I'm going to make sure that you are too. In more ways than one.'

Jeremy smirked and grabbed her upper arm. To the casual observer it may have looked like a friendly gesture but the red marks it left told their own story. At the sensation, Bibi found herself doing something she never thought she would. She didn't even realise she was doing it until after the fact. She raised her hand, and swung it across Jeremy's face, heat burning in her palm.

'Bibi?'

Hailey had been crouching, petting the puppy, while Beatriz had been staring into space. She had been about to speak, but thought better of it. Either way, she knew Hailey had noticed that she was distracted.

She ran her hands through her hair, shaking it out so that it fell behind her, bouncing as if freshly dried. She opened the fridge, pretending to look for something, but was aware that Hailey suspected she was just trying to hide behind its door. She'd have been right.

'Beebs?' Hailey had offered again, standing up now, tilting her head towards her. 'Is there something you want to tell me?'

'It's nothing. He's nothing.'

Now, a couple of days later, as Bibi was welcoming Kristin and her family into the house, she hoped that this was true. That grief would wash all this aside, and that Jeremy's focus would shift far away from her and Garrett and whatever lay unresolved between them. Perhaps, with her make-up perfect and that darling puppy to cause endless distraction, she could, like she'd had to so many times, find a way to wriggle out of trouble.

Chapter 27

VANESSA

Half an hour later all four of the women were on court, with the first set underway. The Chappell sisters were playing Bibi and Hailey while Freddie messed around with Baxter and a variety of specially selected toys nearby. He was under strict instructions to stay well away from the pool and was doing a very good job of keeping Baxter entertained with a handful of old tennis balls, some twining the gardener had found, and a bag of puppy treats that Beatriz had slipped into his pocket – after nervously asking permission from Kristin.

It was late morning, and the weather had been getting warmer all week. After nearly a month of unbroken sunshine, the court had hardened significantly and was playing fast – just how Vanessa liked it. She had only made it back from a conference in Edinburgh late the afternoon before, having cut the trip a little short when she had heard the news about Petunia.

Perhaps it was the heat that was preventing the women from reaching their usual high standard of play, but Vanessa felt sure it was something else. Hailey seemed fine, if a little more reserved than usual. And Vanessa had noticed her leaning into Bibi once or twice, and it wasn't to whisper tactics. It was as if she were trying to console or reassure her. Kristin was even more of a bag of nerves than when Vanessa had set off last week, but still seemed determined not to let on. Vanessa wanted to shake her, to remind her that they were sisters, and she could tell her anything. Kristin was avoiding her though – she was terrible at hiding it. The harder she tried the more obvious it became. She simply didn't seem to want to be there.

But they ploughed on, each of them trying to make it work, trying to keep that fun, conversational ball in the air. The atmosphere between the four of them was stilted though; there was clearly so much being left unsaid. This kind of faux-formal mood was putting Vanessa on edge. She wanted to throw her racket on the grass and scream. All four were missing easy shots, stumbling over their own feet, each seemingly preoccupied by something. In what seemed like every game, Vanessa asked her sister if she was OK, if she was happy to keep playing, or would she rather stop.

'I'm *fine*,' Kristin replied. But she wouldn't meet any of their eyes, focussing on fiddling with the band around her racket handle, picking at her strings, tightening her French braid, or brushing away a tiny speck of wood chip that had found its way onto the grass of the court.

They played on in silence, Hailey, Vanessa and Bibi all eventually catching each other's eyes, trying to communicate silently on whether Kristin really was fine. Sure, she was pale, tired. Of course she would be. But there seemed to be something else.

She lunged for a drop shot, falling as she did, almost grazing her face on the net.

'Seriously, Kristin, we're nearly at the end of this set…' began Hailey. 'We don't have to keep playing. It's just a practice. We can bag it anytime.'

'Honestly, guys,' replied Kristin. 'I need this, it's taking my mind off things.'

'I get it, let's keep playing,' said Bibi, unusually businesslike. 'We need to win.'

They played a few more points before the yelp of the puppy was heard over the hedge, causing Kristin to drop her racket and run round to where Freddie was. The others stared at each other in silence, trying to work out what had happened. Seconds later, Kristin returned.

'It's fine, it's fine. Teething problems ...' she said with a smile.

'Do you want to leave him here for another day or two?' asked Bibi. 'You know, if you don't want to deal with Jeremy just yet? Is he ... okay?'

Hailey and Vanessa shared a glance. This was the most anyone had dared to ask all day. Kristin wasn't answering. She was staring at her tennis shoes as if she'd never seen them before in her life. She looked up, glancing across at all three of them, then said quietly.

'I don't know. I don't know where he is.'

She was at the back of the court, waiting for Hailey to serve. But Hailey wasn't moving.

'What do you mean you don't know where is?' Vanessa turned to face her sister.

'He hasn't come home. I don't know if it's the puppy, or *me*, or his mother's death I just don't know. I'm worried about him, but also ...'

She paused now, taking a breath as if steeling herself. Beatriz and Hailey moved right up to the net, while Vanessa stood facing her sister, offering her arms for a hug.

'It's been easier without him the last day or two. I ... I ... well, I just haven't been handling things very well lately.'

At last, thought Vanessa. *The truth. Now, surely, we can sort things out.*

Kristin stepped towards her sister and started sobbing.

'I'm just so scared, Vee, I'm bloody terrified,' she sobbed into her sister's neck. 'I don't understand why she's done this to me...'

Hailey and Beatriz glanced at each other. Had Kristin just said '*she*', not 'he'?

Chapter 28

HAILEY

'Krissie, what are you saying? Come on, you can tell us.'

Hailey pulled at her tennis top. She had the horrible sensation of needing to open a window, even though they were all outside. Kristin looked up at her.

'It's Petunia. She told me she has left me everything. Money-wise. She's left it all to me. Which obviously should be a wonderful thing, but she told me outright: she did it because she doesn't trust Jeremy. Her own son!'

'Oh, darling, she was a wise woman. And look how she trusted you. What a wonderful thing to be trusted by someone like that. How could that be a bad thing?' said Bibi. 'Doesn't it mean a bit of—'

'Freedom?' chipped in Vanessa.

For a second, Hailey couldn't work out why her friend looked so genuinely stricken. Then she realised: Jeremy.

'Don't panic. I know what you're thinking.' She reached her hand out to Kristin's. The four of them were still standing at the net. This match was never going to finish. Someone had to call it. 'Bibi, can we go and sit in the shade or something. I think we need to talk about Jeremy.'

There. The bubble had been burst. They *did* need to talk about Jeremy.

Ten minutes later the four of them were sitting comfortably in the shady dell to the side of the O'Briens' house. While their main sweeping steps headed out of the glass doors at the back of the house and down to the lavish, immaculately maintained lawn where the party had been held, the barbecue area was a cosier spot altogether. Tucked round the side of the property, where the garden sloped a little more, it was an area lined with red brick and flint, the walls covered in climbing vines, and a huge barbecue station around which some benches and even sun loungers were arranged. Despite seeming to be overlooked by the large conservatory that was the back half of the kitchen, they were actually almost invisible from the house – sitting in the shade, rackets and tennis bags lined up against one of the flinty walls, loosening their tennis shoes and removing their visors, knowing that tennis practice was over for the day.

Staff had appeared from nowhere with fresh celery juice, as requested by Hailey with Bibi's eager approval. They had even found some protein powder and added it to the juice for Kristin who was clearly undernourished and hadn't had a decent night's sleep for weeks.

The minute she had declared the practice was done, Hailey had felt herself slide into professional mode, immediately assessing the legalities versus the very real human emotions and practicalities at hand. Kristin seemed numb, defeated, almost slumped over her glass of juice, holding it with two hands as she looked down at her laces. Bibi seemed skittish, desperate to please, clucking around everyone while clearly still scared of discussing the situation. As far as Hailey could tell, Vanessa was simply seething – furiously chewing the inside of her mouth, but largely taciturn.

'Look, you can't do anything about the money,' explained Hailey. 'Petunia was in her right mind when she made the changes to her will. It can't be contested, whether Jeremy wants to or not. I think we can all agree that the biggest issue is—'

'Your safety when he finds out,' said Vanessa plainly, placing her glass with a clank to the glass side table. Bibi's head whipped round.

'Really?' she gasped. 'I thought it was just—' She stopped herself.

What is going on with her? Hailey had had enough. If she was popping bubbles today, she may as well pop all of them.

'Bibi, I think we need to be realistic about Jeremy's state of mind now. He has just lost his mother. We have all got wind of the fact that he clearly owes a few people a lot of money. He is missing. And now he is on the precipice of finding out that he is not going to inherit what he clearly thought he once might.'

Kristin was nodding slowly.

'I'm worried about him,' she said. Her voice was barely more than a whisper. 'He's not as strong as he tries to make people think.'

Vanessa rolled her eyes at Hailey – neither of the two of them had fallen for *that* act . . .

'And we're worried about *you*,' said Vanessa. 'I'll come and stay till he's home. I can sleep on the sofa bed, help out with Freddie, liaise with Mum and Dad – and Eleanor – about all the club admin that needs sorting. Whatever it takes.'

Kristin looked up, tears already falling.

'Thank you.'

'I'm just glad we're at a point where we're talking about this,' continued Vanessa. 'Things have seemed bad for so long, and the other day Freddie—'

'What?!' Kristin looked anguished.

'Well, he said he saw you crying lots. The morning after Bibi's party. Krissie, he shouldn't be seeing that.'

'I know, but—'

'We're not blaming you,' Hailey interjected. 'We're saying that it's clear you've been suffering for a while. And now we can talk about it. I'm just sorry we didn't step up sooner.'

Vanessa was nodding frantically. 'We'll find him, and we'll sort this. However you choose.'

There was a moment's silence between the women. In the distance Freddie was giggling, an occasional yelp coming from Baxter on the lawn. Vanessa's last words seemed to be echoing between them. Even Hailey was impressed at her friend's courage in putting it out there: Kristin might yet choose to get Jeremy out of her life altogether.

'It's too much,' said Kristin, putting her head in her hands. 'I can't think straight. There's a funeral to plan now. There will be lawyers to deal with. There is the final league match coming up. Wherever I look there is someone I'm going to let down. God – you know I'll make sure the thing with Justin and the money is all sorted out, don't you?'

Hailey waved a hand dismissively. She wasn't sure that her friend had come even close to grasping the sums that were involved, the magnitude of the con Jeremy seemed to have pulled off on her poor husband. Either way, it wasn't Kristin's fault – and the emotional damage was done anyway.

'I say we call time on today's tennis, right?' said Hailey. 'We've trained all summer. What each of us probably needs more than anything is a decent meal and an early night. So shall we give ourselves the rest of day off?'

'Suits me,' said Vanessa with a grin. 'I could speak to Eleanor, have a discreet word and see if she knows about any suppliers meetings, or off-site coaching or anything Jez could be at? There might yet be a perfectly reasonable work excuse.'

Kristin smiled at her sister, but it was obvious that Vanessa was clutching at straws.

'OK, maybe not,' continued Vanessa. 'But I could get started on some calls anyway. Just in case there's something we're missing here.'

'Please stay ...' Kristin took Vanessa's hand in hers and looked up at her big sister.

'At least for lunch!' said Bibi with a flourish. 'I will go and find Garrett and tell him we're going to eat earlier. He'll be thrilled, he's been like a bear with a sore head his morning. Meat on fire will calm him down, the sooner the better...'

'Well, that sounds like a plan,' said Kristin with a pale smile. 'And thank you, my darling, darling friends. I know I could have confided in you sooner, and I'm sorry I didn't. You're amazing, all of you. Now, I'm just going to go and wash my face and get some water, if that's okay, Bibi.'

Bibi smiled and held her arm out to point the way. As Kristin walked towards the house, wiping at her eyes, her shoulders still shuddering a little, the three remaining women just looked at each other until she was safely out of earshot.

'Bloody hell, what a mess,' said Vanessa as soon as she could. 'Thank you both for being so amazing. Neither of you deserve to be dragged into this family hellscape.'

'You're our friends,' said Hailey, simply. 'Of course we want to do what we can to help. We can all see that none of this is her fault. In fact, I wish I had said more sooner.'

'Exactly, exactly,' said Bibi, whose eyes were now darting quickly around the area keeping an eye out for either the return of Kristin or the arrival of Garrett and his meat tongs.

'Did you guys notice the same thing I did though?' Vanessa was whispering, quickly now. 'That she said she should have confided in us earlier?'

Hailey had noticed the comment too. 'Exactly – he's only been missing a day. What does she think she has to confide in us about? Is there something else he has done, or is doing?'

'Of course there is!' The force of Bibi's words struck Hailey as quite different from her usual tone. She was usually the first to try to move any harsh words or moments of melancholy along, with promises of the next drink, the next massage, the next shopping trip never too far away. Today she had seemed unsettled from the get go. Hailey started to wonder if her mood was a result of worrying about Kristin ... or something Garrett had done to her.

'He's toxic,' said Vanessa. 'Absolutely toxic.'

'The man is a pig. She deserves better. We have to protect her.' Bibi's face was still scowling, a vitriol Hailey had never witnessed before now unleashed.

'Bibi, are you OK?' she asked, trying to keep her own tone as delicate as possible. 'He hasn't ...?'

'Shsh!' said Bibi. She raised her index finger to her lips, the red of her manicure glinting in the sunlight. 'I don't want Krissie to know. Or Garrett.'

Hailey shot a look at Vanessa. What was Bibi talking about? She leaned in, put a hand on Bibi's arm to let her know she was safe, and said nothing at all. If she was going to share a confidence, she'd have to be quick.

'Oh, for God's sake, I can't tell you now. Not properly. One of them will hear.' Her face was beaded with sweat now, even in the shade. She ran the back of her hand across the top of her lip. Her breathing was shallow, anxious.

'Bibi, what on earth are you on about? Has Jeremy done something to you too? Has he hurt you?' Vanessa was leaning in now as well, just as concerned as Hailey.

'Enough!' Flecks of spit came from Bibi's mouth as she tried to hush them. 'I will tell you, not now, but I will. But, my God, the trouble that man has caused. It would be better if he stayed disappeared, wherever he is. I'd be happy never to see him again.'

Now ...

Chapter 29

ELEANOR

The kitchen suddenly flashed with blue lights, the steel counter-tops and large white catering fridges strobing with light, on and off as Eleanor looked up in shock. She dropped the kettle she had been holding while she had leaned at the door, desperately trying to keep up with the three women's conversation. The kettle lid flew open and the small amount of water she'd started to fill it with immediately trickled onto the linoleum floor.

The lights had now stopped, and she could hear the slamming of car doors and the murmur of a man's voice. Closer, there was Vanessa's voice too.

'Hello? Aaah, here you are! Did you know the front door is open? And no one's on reception. I was going to go round to the flat but...'

There was a whisper of hellos from the other women before Vanessa spoke again, her voice quieter now as she read the mood in the clubhouse. Eleanor was dabbing at the wet floor with a roll of blue catering paper, hoping no one came in to check on her.

The male voice was closer now. Eleanor held her breath as she stopped, crouched on the floor still holding her blue paper towel. It was the police, looking for Kristin. So that's what the blue lights had been. They hadn't done that before – was there some fresh emergency now? Eleanor stood as slowly as she could, desperate not to make a sound, hoping they had forgotten she was there at all.

'Yes, so we have a bit of an update for you. Not quite what we were expecting this morning,' the older of the policemen was saying.

'Well, I should hope so.' Hailey's voice was icy, her usual gentle southern accent sounding almost threatening.

'So, if we could come in and speak to Mrs Hale, as next of kin?'

'Yes, yes, I'm here. God, where's that cup of tea. Eleanor!'

Eleanor peered round from the door.

'Yes, Mrs H?'

'Inspector…' – Kristin waved her hand to indicate she had forgotten the policeman's name – '…and a colleague are here with some news about the case. Could you put on a large pot of tea, please? And see if there are any biscuits in there? I know we've not had a delivery this week but if you could just have a quick check.'

Eleanor nodded frantically, before almost running back to the kitchen to get the kettle on properly this time. She didn't want to miss a thing, so moved as quietly as she could, the door still propped a little open.

'Mrs Hale, we have an important update on the case. Are you sure you are happy to talk with such a… crowd?' The older of the two policemen glanced up at the four women, sitting huddled together across two sofas.

'Yes, of course I am. Anything you want to say, you can say in front of us all. Nothing will surprise them.'

'Well, if you're sure…'

'Of course I am sure. I trust these women with more than the truth. I trust them with my life. But let's start with the truth, shall we? What happened to my husband?'

As she said this, Eleanor wondered if it was her imagination or if she saw the shoulders of Kristin's friends and sister stiffen.

A few days before ...

Chapter 30

KRISTIN

It took several minutes of scrabbling around at the back of her cupboard, pushing aside multiple pairs of toppling trainers, to find the black heels she was looking for. Kristin remembered joking with Bibi not too long ago about whether she should get rid of those suede court shoes or not. It had only been last summer, and Bibi had come round to give her some advice on outfits for the school's cocktail evening. When she looked back now, Kristin could see that even then she had been trying to catch her husband's full attention, sensing it waning already. There was no way she could have admitted it to herself, let alone anyone else, back then, but this morning it seemed all too obvious.

She and Bibi had pulled out all of the shoes she had, lined them up against the edge of the bed and hurled all her frocks, skirts and blouses across the quilt, trying to see what still fitted and what went with what. Kristin had found this honest appraisal of her limited wardrobe and increasingly mumsy style agonising at the time, especially the way it involved constantly comparing herself with Bibi – who was always immaculately turned out. Kristin had wanted to crawl into a hole when Jeremy came into the room and found them mid-session trying things on, and asked if Bibi was giving her a 'tutorial in hotness.' Back then, Kristin had thought that was one of the most mortifying moments of her life: if only she had known how much worse things were going to get.

Bibi had been on form though, waving Jeremy away like she was swatting a fly, then staying focused, determined to get Kristin feeling good about herself – and equally determined to get her to enjoy wearing heels again.

'It's not that they're painful, just awkward!' Kristin had protested. 'They make me feel as if I'm playing "dressing up" – they're just not *me*.'

She had begged Bibi to suggest somewhere to buy chic flats to wear with evening dresses and had been told that it was out of the question.

'Chic flats and evening dresses do not co-exist, chica. And name me a man who doesn't love a woman in heels. I'll wait...'

'Can I at least get rid of *some*?' she had asked. 'There must be a few pairs here that make you despair. Go on, Bee, tell me...'

'Well, now that you mention it...' Beatriz had replied, from her position on the small sofa under the window in the bedroom. 'But don't get rid of those.'

She had pointed to the conservative black heels that Kristin now had in her left hand.

'They are perfect for a funeral. And no one ever feels like going shopping just before one of *those*. So, stick them back in the closet, forget about them, and hope that it's a very long time before you have to wear them.'

How right she had been. And Kristin really had forgotten about them. But how surreal that a funeral had come around so fast. Kristin swallowed hard, doing her very best to hold back a fresh flood of tears. It had been an overwhelming week or so since Petunia had died partly due to the grief and anxiety over her will, but, largely because of Jeremy's absence for the last few days.

At first she had been consumed by sleeplessness, frantic with worry for over forty-eight hours. Then Hailey stepped in with some sort of home-made tincture – about which she'd asked no questions – and she'd had not just a blissful night's sleep but a nap the following afternoon. Only to be woken by the trill of her phone. He had been found, and her number had shown up on his phone under 'Missed Calls (47).' The manager of a betting shop now had him, locked in her office.

'I don't like getting the police involved, and he swears you can be here within half an hour,' came the woman's world-weary voice down the line.

'My God, where are you?' Kristin had gasped, reeling that her husband had come close to being arrested. It turned out that it was the gambling den in the next town over – where so many of their club members lived! He had spent two consecutive nights at the casino in Southampton, and might have made it home had it not been for one last punt at the bookies. And it was after this had failed that he'd started mouthing off at the rest of the customers, threatening violence towards one, which had got him locked in the office, his phone confiscated.

Her utter humiliation at finding her husband this way had left her feeling as if her insides had been scraped away by an ice-cream scoop. The intensity of the shock at so much bad news – and a missing husband – had kept her on autopilot for a few days, her face aching from smiling to members whenever she left the flat to brief the staff or take Freddie for yet another playdate. She had simply survived as if frozen in aspic, coping at the expense of all else, determined not to crack.

Then the call had come, and she had had to make the grim journey to pick him up. She'd flicked past station after station on the car radio, no tune appropriate for a journey like this. Eventually, she had surrendered, driving in silence but quite sure the hammering of her heart could be heard by the surrounding traffic at every set of lights.

Once Jeremy had been collected, his hair greasy, his skin pale and lined, the reality of her situation had truly found its way in, a virus that couldn't be ignored. His clothes filthy, after several consecutive days of wear, with noticeable stains where he'd spilled food while focusing on God knows what bet he'd had in hand. The stench of sweat and adrenaline filled the car as she drummed her fingers on the steering wheel, making the reality of what was becoming of him impossible to deny. She had acknowledged the vanity of the worst fear she'd had about him – that he had a mistress – just as she had acknowledged that it had probably never been true. Instead, he'd had something worse. Gambling. He had been addicted to risk for as long as she'd known him, and she had for so long banked on him growing out of it, realising the stakes weren't worth it, or maybe even just preferring to spend time with her and Freddie.

Now, as he sat, his face turned away from hers – perhaps to look out of the window, but probably to avoid her gaze, she had accepted that this would never happen. If he couldn't stomach being present to plan his own mother's funeral, when would he be? She had had to organise the entire funeral service alone, making choices based on vague memories of Petunia's favourite music and readings. Hailey had of course been amazing, stepping in with a Mary Oliver poem and a gorgeous version of 'Let It Be'.

But she shouldn't have had to ask! The end of season tennis finale was only days away as well and she felt like she was being pulled in a million directions. It had been torture enough to have to get on with everything while Jeremy was missing, but now she had to carry the panic about whether he was even up to the job of delivering the eulogy he had promised he would. She shuddered at the recent memory of having to cover for him, saying he wasn't well enough to see people; she would blush forever at the moment she had had to explain to the chaplain that her husband was too stricken with grief to have much input in the funeral plan. But these minor humiliations paled into insignificance next to her terror about what might yet happen in Petunia's village church.

The prospect of social annihilation was not the worst of her fears. Because there was also the ugly truth that Jeremy had long assumed that his inheritance would save him. This left Kristin exposed, harbouring a secret that rendered her financially secure, yet more at risk than ever. Who knew how he would react when this all came out?

Jeremy had stayed silent on the drive home, and they had managed to get into the flat without being disturbed. Kristin had sat on the bed and begged him to take a shower and get some sleep, so that they could talk later. But Jeremy had been on edge, pacing the room, opening and rifling through drawers as if looking for God knows what, a set of keys, anything that might mean not looking her in the eye.

'Stop trying to fucking micromanage me,' he snarled.

'I'm not,' she had replied, more calmly than she felt, using what she suspected were the very last dregs of her self-respect. 'I am trying to talk to you. We need to get you help. You're grieving. It's been a terrible shock. Let's deal with this together.'

'And how exactly do you propose to deal with the situation? Bring her back from the dead?'

'No, darling, but you can't go on as you are. *We* can't go on as we are.' With this, she had stood, stepping forward to reach and touch his shoulder. But as she'd done it, he had swung his arm, swiping her hard in the face with the back of his hand.

Kristin had screamed, stumbling away from him and hitting the door frame with the side of her head. Her shock as she made contact with the wood had been as bad as the impact itself. A sharp, searing flash of white-hot pain raced through her from ear to eyebrow. But her hand flew to her mouth, desperate to keep the noise as she cried out to a minimum.

He promised it wouldn't happen again, she thought. *He promised.* Within seconds Jeremy was leaning over her, apologising, saying 'sorry' over and over again, he cupped her face in his rough hands. His nails were filthy and she could smell tobacco on his fingertips.

He ran to the kitchen, wrapping ice in a tea towel before tenderly holding it against her brow bone. For a minute or two, she felt hope swell in her like a wave gathering speed. He still loved her; they could do this. She could find a way to make it OK, couldn't she? She'd done it before. No one had ever known.

'Sorry, darling, that was so clumsy of me. Jeez, we don't want you having a shiner in the chapel,' he chuckled as he left a whisper-like kiss on her forehead. That wave of hope crashed as the penny dropped: he wasn't sorry he had hit her and caused her injury; he was sorry it might be visible at his mother's funeral.

As it turned out, his swift action with the ice pack had done its job and the swelling had gone down relatively quickly. Under a thick layer of foundation, the bruising was barely visible. But, as Kristin got ready for the funeral that morning, she knew that something inside her had irretrievably broken.

What she had been telling herself was a one-off, an exception, was no longer that. It was the start of a pattern of behaviour that could only be described as domestic abuse.

She slid her feet into the black court shoes and stepped towards her bedroom mirror. She smoothed the skirt of her shift dress, then made a snarling face that allowed her to check her teeth for lipstick. There was none, so she smiled at her reflection, as if rehearsing for the rest of the day. The concealer around her eyes had done as good a job of masking her exhaustion and the rosy red lip gloss had brought some much-needed colour to her face.

Blinking, she hoped her body wouldn't betray her with any more external signs of her internal turmoil. The eczema patches at her temples were bad enough and she prayed that the autopilot that had carried her this far would last just a little longer. She couldn't bear to sob in front of everyone, in case she never stopped. All she really wanted was to shut the bedroom door, run herself a bath full of bubbles, light some scented candles, and lie there, dreaming of being somewhere sunny and safe with Freddie.

Sweet, sweet Freddie. She had to make sure that not only did he never know about this, but that he never had to feel the sting of his father's hands either. If only Petunia could see what her act of enormous kindness had done. She thought she had been gifting them security, a future, freedom from Jeremy's whims. Instead, she had placed them in a well-appointed trap. God, how she longed to be anywhere but here, this morning, a sitting target for Jeremy's rage and envy – and the blows that might ensue.

But where could they go? They couldn't just up and leave like other families. Jeremy would always know where they were, their lives and livelihoods were so inextricably tied to the club. For a split second, she imagined the shame of getting him barred from the property just to feel safe. It would only be switching one version of trapped for another. There must be a way through this. Kristin closed her eyes and imagined herself on a beach at the other end of the country. Freddie might have an ice cream, a new fishing net and bucket. They would be heading home to a little cottage somewhere. Remote. Safe.

Then, just as easily as that beach image would dance across her mind, calming her for seconds, the reality of her situation would slide into sharper focus. To escape wasn't just to leave Jeremy behind, but everyone. Because for as long as he knew she had that money, he would want to control her. A discreet word with anyone would put them in danger too. And the one person she most wanted to pour her heart out to was the person she least wanted to expose to harm: her sister. She knew that if Vanessa found out even a whisper more than she already knew about the situation, there would be no going back. But what Vanessa didn't appreciate was that that might work both ways: Kristin felt dizzy with terror knowing that her sister would spring into action like a tiger ready to pounce, an avenging angel but equally filled with horror at how much danger this might put her own sweet sister in.

The situation had to be contained, but all avenues presented unimaginable risk. She knew she had to do something. But what? And when?

Chapter 31

VANESSA

The sun seemed inescapable already, moving round the room as if taunting her. She had woken up sweating, a stripe of light from the side of the blinds across her face. Now, as she sat at her dressing table, she could feel its heat hitting the side of her face. Vanessa grabbed a tissue and dabbed at her top lip, praying she wouldn't sweat through her blouse before she got to the church. It was so rare that she dressed this formally, she felt as if people would point and stare in disbelief at the sight of her in nude tights, carrying a proper handbag.

Who cares? she told herself. *Let's just get everyone through the service with as little collateral damage as possible.* Frankly, she'd be beyond proud of herself if she could keep her temper with Jeremy all day. Grieving or not, the man had been spiralling out of control for too long now, and she was fast losing her patience with trying to be diplomatic for her sister's sake.

It was Hailey who had let slip about the shady investments Jeremy had squirrelled out of Justin, and, she suspected, Garrett. Some discreet questioning had reassured Vanessa that this was, though despicable, probably not illegal. Sure, he had made promises about property investments and 'innovative sporting technologies' – classic pie-in-the-sky schemes, which were clearly about to tank.

But it had now become clear that wasn't the extent of it.

She had long been aware of the gossip that swirled around Jeremy on the Tour – how he threw games to win favours and repay loans and how it had ultimately cost him his career. How could he not have realised what a shortsighted plan that was? Sure, it was easy cash up front, but of course if he was prepared to lose for the money, how could he ever become a real winner? Maybe he had always known he wouldn't get to the top, so the thrown matches had been an elaborate way of shifting the blame onto external forces. Perhaps telling himself he'd *had* to lose had been the perfect way out when his form and fitness had started to dip. Easier to be a cheat than a man who couldn't win. Easier to take the bung than put in the hours, days, weeks of endless grind in the gym or on the court? But had he been up to something similar recently? Knowing that he was about to fail, was he looking for a quick fix and therefore raising the stakes as a smokescreen? Taking out bets in the hope that he could win big and fast: risk piled upon risk, in an attempt to create enough chaos not to get caught? Vanessa had shuddered at the thought of how obvious it now seemed. What she didn't know was how far things had gone.

Which of the company accounts for Royal Oaks had he had access to? Earlier in the week she had tried to look at how the pro shop accounting was done: how he was paying for stock, how many of his lessons went through the till, if the outgoing invoices were being paid on time, whether the business was functioning at all. She hadn't been convinced that the finances were entirely safe. But how could she speak to Kristin about this? The woman was planning a funeral; her stress levels were at breaking point. So, she had kept quiet, kept snooping, kept trying figure it all out.

Because as well as the financial side of things, there was Jeremy's increasing menace towards her sister: the way that his mood had curdled, even in grief, into something far more aggressive than her worst fears had imagined. How long did they have before he found out the truth about Petunia's inheritance, and how great a threat would that put her sister under? Vanessa's blood ran cold. She could see that there was a clear and present danger and Kristin seemed to be running on borrowed time.

Finding out about the will might drive him to do something irrational, and it was obvious he would find out before long. He'd be itching to put Petunia's property on the market, and he'd be in for a nasty shock when he discovered that it wasn't going to be up to him to do so. Vanessa could no longer see a future for her sister where her husband was not either a danger towards the club, and therefore the entire family's livelihoods or to Kristin herself. It would be too risky to open up about the money right now. She must try and keep it a secret for as long as possible in order to protect it for Freddie, and that meant that she'd be living on eggshells.

Just thinking about it created a fresh sheen of sweat on her top lip. She fanned herself with her clutch bag and headed for the door, ready to meet her parents and drive them to the church. Her father was all set to be a pall bearer, in fact he had insisted on it, despite both sisters worrying about the strain it could put on him. So, Vanessa had made sure she drove them, so he wouldn't have to get into one of his characteristic frets about parking.

She nodded at herself in the mirror, as if she were her own coach, and they were headed into battle together. Then she shoved two packs of travel tissues, a hip flask of scotch and some sweets for Freddie into her clutch bag before taking a breath and reminding herself that today was for Petunia.

Chapter 32

BIBI

Beatriz put the back of her hand to her lips and wiped hard. What had she been thinking, to wear lipstick that red to a funeral? Only now she had smeared it onto her hand in frustration, she had to run to the bathroom to wash it off. The red stained her skin, leaving her rubbing at it in frustration. She grabbed a flannel, staring at herself hard in the mirror, and wiped every trace from her face. Back at her dressing table she told herself not to panic.

There is a way through this, she repeated to herself as she applied a thin stick of nude gloss. *There must be.*

But she couldn't think, no matter which way she turned things over in her mind, what this way through might actually be. She looked down at her arm and marvelled that no one had yet noticed it. There was only so long she could get away with covering it in this weather.

There was part of her that was longing for Garrett to notice the purple bruise. To ask her what had happened, if someone had hurt her. She had even tried to talk to him, fishing about Jeremy, trying to test the ground. His focus was business though. Something was rumbling, she had seen it before. A high-risk deal, a bad investment, a gamble that he'd taken a little too far – something was pumping him with adrenaline the way that she used to. God, this was how it had started, her pathetic bid for Jeremy's attention when Garrett was busy with work. And how she wished she could wind back the clock now – no amount of flirtatious behaviour was worth the turn this had taken.

Bibi knew that no matter how intense the depth of Garrett's fury with Jeremy might be, it wasn't worth the risk. She couldn't tell him. Jeremy was such an adept liar that once she admitted to something, absolutely anything might be believed. And now that she had struck back, slapping his face as she'd felt the excessive pressure of his hand on her arm that day, Jeremy was acting like a wounded lion, hell-bent on revenge.

Why hadn't she remembered that she was still wearing the ring that Garrett had given her last Christmas? She had taken to wearing it every day, a symbol of how good things had been not so very long ago. And when she'd got to training that day she had been too preoccupied to remove it and place it in her bag. Instead, she had twisted it inwards, and that was how the sharp emerald edge had scraped his cheek as her hand had made contact.

In that moment, his eyes had gone black and her stomach had lurched in realisation: she now feared Jeremy more than Garrett. More than she had ever feared Garrett. Now, everything was at stake. He could ruin everything for her, if she didn't play her next move to perfection.

She parted her lips and gave a full-wattage smile. Perfect. Exactly what today needed. No one should know that she was facing losing everything she'd fought all of her life for. She must not let her friends down, nor her friendships explode – which she was sure they would if the sisters and Hailey came to believe (as well they might) that she had been making a move on Jeremy. Or worse still, that she had been having an affair with him.

The memory of Jeremy's face as he'd threatened telling them this flashed across her mind. He had been stretching out his hamstring, leaning forward over an extended leg as he looked up. His eyes were dark as they peered out from under his cap.

'You've got way more to lose than me,' he had told her, barely audible. 'Kristin's at the point where she'd just be grateful I'm "opening up", as she calls it. She would believe anything I tell her.'

His laugh was arrogant. He knew he was right. And so did she.

Beatriz's hand shook as she removed her rings, smoothing hand cream across them, checking for any last traces of lipstick. She didn't have time to think about how her marriage might be on the line too, not now. She picked up her perfume bottle and went to spray at her throat, only for the glass bottle to slip out of her hand, clanking on the mirrored glass of her chest of drawers. She screamed, grabbing for the bottle, desperate to avoid glass shattering across the bedroom.

Get a grip, woman, she told herself. *Breathe.*

There had to be a way to de-escalate this situation, she tried to persuade herself. The stakes are high, but she had faced higher, hadn't she? But wherever she let her thoughts turn, there seemed to be carnage, all of it created by Jeremy.

She was better than this. She had to get hold of herself. The glint of her Christmas emerald caught the sun as her hand reached for the pale pink bottle of perfume, before wiping it against the downy softness of a fresh face cloth from her drawer. She placed the bottle gently on the dressing table, her own face staring back up at her from the mirrored glass. She pouted at herself. She would smile and front it out today. It would be her greatest performance yet, keeping the peace for as long as she could – for Petunia and Kristin's sake, if nothing else.

Chapter 33

HAILEY

As she knelt in front of Justin, helping him to knot the scratchy fabric of his woollen tie, Hailey wanted instead to put her head onto his lap and weep forever. The weight of carrying her sadness, not just about Petunia's death but about the slow ebbing away of her beloved husband, was starting to feel unbearably heavy. Watching what Jeremy had done to Justin's confidence was threatening to be the final straw. So much of Justin's self-esteem had already been compromised by the cruelty of his illness, but Jeremy had pushed him far further. He felt he had become what he had once been scornful of: a man who could be taken for a fool. A man who needed help. A man who was no longer a sound judge of character.

Of all people, Hailey knew how much this hurt him. Because they were birds of a feather: high achievers from good families who had worked hard and made the most of what blessings they had been given. They weren't wasteful people. But they weren't soft touches either. It gave them a buzz to know that others were professionally intimidated by them, it gifted them the little in-jokes they'd chuckle about in bed.

Yet somehow Jeremy slipped through the net. They had let him in because they thought he was a friend. His sheer gall had bamboozled Justin, but they weren't a couple used to being treated so carelessly, so Hailey didn't even feel she could console her husband, as mentioning what had happened would feel like rubbing salt in the wound.

So she didn't; she had ploughed on, trying to be there for Kristin, and trying desperately to buoy Justin's spirits. She stroked his neat tie, then held his palm in hers for a moment, hoping with all she had that the cool weakness of his hand was not an indication that he was giving up the fight. He had survived this long because of her incredible devotion to getting him the very best treatment, and his refusal to back down in the face of disease. Now, he seemed depressed, irritable, and the possibility of trouble from the police on top of this would surely do irreparable damage. His spirit seemed to be fading by the day.

But Hailey hadn't lost her own spirit. In fact, even as she held his hand in hers, she forced those years of suppressed grief to alchemise into something stronger, more useful: a rage she could barely contain. As if Jeremy's threats to speak to the police about her medical garden weren't enough, the only part of the funeral planning that he had engaged with was to veto her from reading at it. Kristin had protested, pointing out how supportive Hailey had been, how it was she who had suggested the Mary Oliver poem that Petunia had loved so much, but that had only made things worse. Of course it had.

Jeremy had simply announced that Hailey 'was never a proper friend', and had asked a neighbour who Kristin had immediately said was clearly startled to be asked but presumably too polite to say no. Hailey knew that Petunia despised the woman and had long suspected she had had an affair with the late Mr Hale. This had been a petty power move too far. A final act of spite from her son.

She felt her cortisol rocketing, transforming that dull thud of sadness into something almost electric. *There wasn't enough of any kind of herb in her garden to contain this fury*, she thought as she squeezed Justin's hand and stood to take the handles of his wheelchair. She felt as if her blood was boiling, so much so that she was not even sure if she should be attending this funeral. That man had wreaked havoc with her life recently and she barely trusted herself to be anywhere near him now. But hell hath no fury like a woman scorned and Hailey was ready to unleash it all on Jeremy. In her own time.

Chapter 34

KRISTIN

She arrived alone, one of the very first, knowing that she needed to be safe inside the church where no ugly confrontations could occur. Freddie's hand felt so small in hers as they walked up the aisle together, him holding Bunny, her hoping the rattle of the tranquillisers in her bag couldn't be heard as she walked.

Each time she turned to see the congregation, another of her friends had arrived. There was Bibi, looking discreetly elegant next to Garrett whose face was dark, his wild, wavy hair refusing to comply with any appropriately funereal style, despite the copious amount of wax he'd clearly applied to it. On the other side was Hailey, her head bowed down, Justin next to her in his wheelchair, on the far side of the pew.

Minutes later, Vanessa arrived with their mother, making their way straight to the front of the church. Her sister sat down on the other side of Freddie, giving his hand a little squeeze as she did. His eyes were wide, taking in every detail of what was a new experience for him. He had been just about old enough to remember when the queen died, but beyond that they had barely discussed anything to do with death, or even grief. Now, here he was, no doubt about to ask endless difficult to answer question about the coffin and heaven.

Kristin chewed the inside of her mouth, wincing as she bit a little too hard. She thought that her son should be next to his dad for this, not his auntie. But none of them knew where Jeremy was, only that he had promised he would be there, and insisted that he would be a pallbearer. He had left 'for a run' at dawn and replied to no calls since. Each of the four women's trust in him had well and truly vanished, and there was no way that Justin or Garrett were going to be asked to step in, so Kristin had been running on her last remaining shreds of hope all morning.

'How much can you nag a man on the day he buries his mum?' she had said to Vanessa with a shrug. 'I can't keep calling, I just can't. Not because I'm not desperate to know if he's coming, but because I can't take any more of him simply blanking me.'

She was refusing to call any more. His behaviour was unforgiveable and it still seemed unbelievable to her that she had left for her mother-in-law's funeral with no idea when or if he might turn up. *Would he even be in a fit state to give a eulogy?* she wondered.

The organist started to play, the congregation hushing accordingly. Kristin looked down at her son, running the back of her forefinger across his plump cheek.

'Be brave,' she mouthed at him, while inwardly telling herself the same thing.

She heard shuffling at the back of the church and turned to see if the funeral cortège had arrived. Instead, she saw Hailey, her face ashen, standing and almost running out of the church. Justin was still there, looking straight ahead, but Hailey had left. There was no way Kristin could find out where she had gone and if she was all right, because the funeral the procession had appeared at the doorway.

It suddenly felt as if there wasn't a breath of air in the church. Kristin longed to be outside, even if only as far as the churchyard. On a bench, anonymous. Alone. But here it was: the coffin, and with it Jeremy, looking immaculate on the front left corner of it, his face cleanly shaven, his shoes gleaming, his face impassive. As the six men carried Petunia to the front of the church, and laid the coffin on its trestle table, Edward came to sit in the pew behind, his wife patting his knee reassuringly, and handing him an Order of Service.

Jeremy, too, turned away from the coffin and came to sit next to her – as if it were the most normal thing in the world. His eyes looked straight ahead, not even acknowledging hers. His hands sat clasped in his lap. Kristin didn't dare turn her face to his, to check for a sign, any sign. Was he furious? Was he distraught? Was he drunk? Or had he just decided to freeze her out as punishment for the calls this morning?

She felt as if she were underwater, floating, no longer sure where solid ground might be. She couldn't have imagined the state he had been in for most of the last week, could she? She didn't imagine Bibi's lipstick on his mouth? Or the tragedy of Petunia turning out to not even trust her own son? Was it only this morning that she had been standing in her dressing gown, frantically calling him as he had scurried off to wherever he had gone to clear his head?

To her shame there was an old, hardwired part of her that wanted to reach out her hand, to stroke his knee in a gesture of affection, solidarity. She almost felt the side of her hand bristle as it fought the instinct to move, then didn't. Meanwhile, Jeremy sat there like granite. Kristin's eyes darted to Vanessa's.

She pulled her sleeve down instinctively, covering her wrist, remembering the thumb marks circling it. One, purple. The other, already yellowing. An imprint on her body that would show her sister in an instant that this was no longer a one-off.

Not today, she prayed. *Just don't notice today, Vee.*

A single bead of sweat dripped from Jeremy's hairline, silently making its way down his temple. Kristin resisted the urge to dab at it with a tissue. She noticed that he was wearing the aftershave that he used when they had first got together. Clean sandalwood and something grassy. It made her yearn for the man she had fallen in love with. The man who bore so little resemblance to the one who she was sitting beside her today, in front of all their friends and family. Again, her hand longed to move. But her heart, which had withstood so much, said no.

Chapter 35

VANESSA

It took biting hard on her own lip to stop Vanessa from snapping at Jeremy. How dare he just vanish, leaving all the organisation to others for the entire morning, putting her sister through yet more anguish, only to turn up like this, as if nothing had happened?

She glanced across at her sister, for whom this little gas-lighter's dance was presumably being performed. *Don't fall for it*, she longed to whisper to her. *You're not imagining things.* We can all see it. Kristin's breathing was shallow and her eyes glassy as Jeremy sat down next to her.

It's a game. It's all a game. He's taunting you, making you question yourself instead of him. Acting irrationally and irresponsibly and making you anxious and ill. Wake up and see him for who he really is.

For a second, Vanessa imagined herself up by the coffin, shouting to the whole congregation about the disingenuous behaviour, the bullying, the pain that Jeremy had been putting her – and them – all through. She wanted to explain to each and every one of them that for him this was a dare, to see if Kristin would stand up to his unacceptable behaviour or allow herself to be played by a bigger, stronger, more calculating opponent.

She shifted in her seat, trying to keep her composure. As she did, she felt the cards in the pocket of her neat suit jacket: the spare speech that she and Hailey had written in case he failed to turn up or if he arrived in no fit state to enter the church, let alone stand at the front of it.

But no, it wasn't needed. Ten minutes later Jeremy stood up when invited to by the priest and gave the performance of a lifetime: a pitch-perfect eulogy, which brought most of the con-gregation — including her own parents — to tears. He had even taken the time to dab the corner of his eye dramatically with a freshly pressed hankie, and to pause a little, his voice almost breaking. Moments later, it was all over, and as he returned to his seat his eye caught Vanessa's. If you hadn't been looking you might not have noticed it, but there it was. A smirk and a quick wink. It wasn't just Kristin he was taunting.

Chapter 36

BIBI

It seemed safest to keep her head down for most of the service. Bibi knew that if she started crying, she might struggle to stop – and she didn't want to pull focus from Petunia's family, nor attract any undue attention from Jeremy. Garrett, sitting beside her, was still, silent, unreadable.

She had been dreading this moment. Seeing him again, feeling the shudder in her flesh. She had been prepared for him to arrive in a state – but not this. She was braced for a man who was erratic, sleazy or dishevelled. Someone out of control, displaying his now-dangerous temper. But here was an immaculately dressed grieving son, with a fresh haircut and a clean shave. For a moment she felt a stab of pity for him, seeing what looked like the man she thought she knew. Before she remembered what he'd done.

It was barely the blink of an eye that she allowed herself, raising her head an inch and stealing a glance at Kristin. Was she OK? What did she know? Was she safe? Even in that instant, the briefest of looks, she could see that her friend was a shell of herself. Sure, most of the rest of the congregation wouldn't see a thing – just the same dutiful and kind wife and mother they were used to – but Bibi could see that a light had gone out.

If only she knew why. If only she could think of a way to

find out if her friend was safe without worrying her more or implicating herself. Or indeed Jeremy. Because who knew what he would become once this charade was over?

Chapter 37

HAILEY

Sitting on a wooden bench at the edge of the graveyard, Hailey had been doing her trusty box breathing when the funeral cortège arrived. She didn't know what had come over her – she had felt fine all morning. Well, 'fine' within the context of getting ready for a dear friend's funeral while being desperately worried about another friend. But then, as she had sat there in the hushed tones of the church, the panic had risen in her like bile after a bad oyster. Uncontainable. The injustice of it all, the way that they were all so tightly coiled, waiting for Jeremy's next move, how everything seemed to be dependent on him and his erratic behaviour, even though all he had ever done was to lie to them and use them to line his own pockets. It was the lying that was the worst of it, the damage spreading like a fungus. No, she rather liked fungi. He was a toxin, a horrible silent gas, seeping into everything without people realising.

The breathing was just about working its magic: in for four, hold for four, out for four, hold for four. She had almost calmed herself when she saw Jeremy arrive, as smart as if he'd spent the morning at home being spruced up and comforted by his loving wife. How much longer could they live like this, never knowing which Jeremy was going to show up for any given event? She watched him standing there, accepting condolences from the other pall bearers, dabbing at his eyes and talking about his treasured relationship with his mother.

The ease with which he was able to put on this performance was breathtaking. She knew that he had left her, the Chappell sisters and Bibi feeling physically threatened lately, but as she saw him there with his shiny shoes and his suit, she knew that not a soul in that church would believe them if she stood up and said so now. Where would this end?

Chapter 38

KRISTIN

All day it had felt as if the ground beneath her was unstable, moving too fast, as if her legs might be swept away by the fast-moving tide of betrayals. The future seemed unimaginable. But once she was back at Royal Oaks, Kristin let herself relax a little. She was home. She would find a way to be safe here. After all, she and her parents had been here first, hadn't they?

The funeral had gone without a single hitch. Even Freddie had been perfectly behaved – supportive of her and Jeremy even. And now, as she took her heels off one by one and felt the hard polished parquet of the clubhouse floor, solid beneath the thin fabric of her tights, she felt her shoulders dip a little. She shoved her shoes back on as people started to flow into the clubhouse for the wake and enjoyed speaking to a few of Petunia's old friends and a handful of club members who had known her well (even if no one seemed to have played tennis with her any time in the last decade, despite her protestations that she still loved the game). As Kristin raised her first glass of champagne to her lips she actually felt pretty proud of herself, and dared to believe that Petunia might even have felt the same.

Vanessa looked at her across the room and raised her glass at her with a wink.

'Thanks, sis,' said Kristin, crossing to her for a hug. 'I actually cannot believe that today passed without incident and is oh so nearly over.'

'I bet,' replied her sister. 'Where is he anyway?'

Kristin shrugged, glancing quickly around. She had told herself she would neither care nor look until Freddie was in bed and things were calmer. But she was desperately hoping that Vanessa would offer to stay a while, possibly even overnight. She couldn't bear to be with him alone tonight. But how could she ask without worrying her sister?

'I've no idea,' she finally said. 'He must be here somewhere.'

Vanessa scanned the room, before uttering an 'Urgh' at the sight of him heading in from the grounds, striding cockily through the French windows as he swigged from his water bottle. Freddie was tottering behind him, and made his way towards the sisters.

'Hello, darling,' said Kristin, ruffling his hair.

'Hey, you,' said Vanessa, giving him a high five. Then, to her sister, 'You going to be OK tonight?'

'I mean, I will, but...'

'Don't let's talk any more. I'll stay.' Instead, she glanced at Kristin's wrist, then back up at her, before saying, 'I know what he's done. I know what he's *been* doing. I wish he was dead.'

Kristin reached so quickly to cover Freddie's ears that she was worried she'd hurt him. She wanted to glare at her sister, to tell her son that she didn't mean it, to tell him it was all going to be OK. Instead, she stood, paralysed, unsure what her next move would be.

'Well done, darling,' said her mother, approaching in a purple shirt dress from the table of immaculate vol-au-vents where she had been chatting to guests. Her dad was next to her, trying to sneak as many pastries as he could before his wife told him off. 'You've done a wonderful job. It was a marvellous send off. Petunia was very lucky indeed to have a daughter-in-law in you.'

'Thanks, Mum,' replied Kristin. 'I think it actually went OK.'

'And Jeremy, how's he doing? That was a smashing eulogy. So moving.'

Kristin bit down on her teeth, her jaw flexing. She had enjoyed not thinking about him for the last half-hour or so. Where had he got to anyway? He'd disappeared again.

'He's OK,' replied Kristin. 'Well, he's as well as he could be. It's been a real shock.'

'Of course, and we're here to support all of you.'

As she said this, Edward Chappell leaned in to give his daughter an enormous hug. While Kristin's face was peeking over his shoulder, she saw Jeremy enter the function room. His hair was erratic, the top few buttons of his shirt undone. His tie and jacket were nowhere to be seen. He scanned the room quickly, then walked towards her – slowly, but with the purposeful stealth of a shark.

'Oh, here he is now!' said Kristin. She had tried to keep her voice bright, cheery, but it left her throat shrill and strained. 'How are you doing, darling?'

Jeremy smiled at her parents, then looked back at her.

'I'm fine, long day. Can I have a word?' As he said it he grabbed her arm just above the elbow, his thumb pressing hard against the bone, and steered her to the far side of the room – towards the office, where he had just come from. Kristin looked up at him, smiling; anything to keep the peace in front of everyone. No such luck.

'May I ask when you were planning to tell me?' His eyes were wide, glowering. His mouth almost frothing at the corners. Had he been drinking or was this all anger? Kristin felt ice water running through her veins. How had he found out?

'Tell you what, darling?'

'Don't you "darling" me. When, exactly, were you planning to tell me that my *mother*...' His voice was getting louder now. 'That *you* had persuaded my mother to leave her entire estate, *my inheritance*, to you?'

Kristin was speechless, frozen, just praying that no one had noticed this confrontation in the corner of the room. Then, a sudden wailing in the doorway. There was Freddie, in a cosy onesie, his face streaming with tears.

'Mummy, Baxter's gone.'

Now...

Chapter 39

ELEANOR

By the time Eleanor had made the pot of tea and arranged the cups on a tray to bring through, she had resigned herself to the fact that she would have missed whatever news the police had come to tell Kristin. So she was surprised to find that they had barely got started.

'...so the good news is that we are now satisfied that the death was accidental.'

'Oh, that's a ... a ...' Kristin seemed lost for words.

'An *enormous* relief,' said Vanessa, chipping in. 'So what do you think happened?'

'Well, the toxicology was never going to be cut and dried. There is no definitive answer. Arsenic poisoning is not as unusual as many assume – it is a relatively common cause of death – accidental or otherwise. And of course, there is a small amount of arsenic in almonds, which is why we and the team back at the lab were initially distracted by the cake, and the allergy situation.'

'I see,' said Kristin softly.

'But thanks to your help, and that of everyone we spoke to ...' The policeman gestured towards the four women as Eleanor carefully placed cups and saucers in front of each of them. They were all immobile, looking blankly at the officers. 'We have found no case to answer. Jeremy was a popular man with a young and loving family.'

The sisters were nodding furiously. Eleanor thought back to Jeremy's eyes the evening of his mother's funeral. Black with rage as he ranted at his wife about Petunia's will – how he assumed she had been keeping some secret for months. It had seemed fairly clear to Eleanor that this wasn't true, and she wished she hadn't heard a word of it. But he'd been livid, accusing her of all sorts.

'We've have found no evidence of enemies, no motive for anyone to kill him,' continued the policeman.

'Oh, quite right,' said Hailey. 'As Justin and I explained earlier, everyone *loved* him. He was a huge part of the Royal Oaks community.'

Bibi, who had been chewing her nails, said quickly. 'Yes, yes, such a very special man.'

'As such, the investigation into the death of Jeremy Hale will now be closed. This will be the last you hear from us!'

Kristin was nodding gravely as the police spoke of Jeremy's lack of enemies. *Did she really think this?* wondered Eleanor. The more she thought about it, the more it seemed as if confrontations had been racking up. It had only really been the distraction of Baxter going missing that had disrupted those angry words the night of Petunia's wake. She placed the milk jug down very carefully – as slowly as she could – while wondering if it was true that dear Mr Hale had really been as loved as they were all professing.

The police got up to leave, their teacups still empty. As they did so, Eleanor watched the colour flooding back into Kristin's face and wondered if it was relief on behalf of her friends, who she was so worried would become embroiled in a complicated murder case. That could undoubtedly wreck friendships and destroy the reputation of Royal Oaks. Or was the relief her own?

Hailey looked entirely impassive as Eleanor walked past her to show the police out of the front door to the club, but when she came back, she was weeping – most uncharacteristically. No one seemed to be paying any attention to Eleanor, so she stayed close by, just outside the door. She told herself that no one had, no one had they? She was there just in case anyone needed her. Yes, that's what she'd say if anyone did ask.

Bibi sat down again, clearly shaken by the fact that this was now all over. Vanessa gave a huge noisy exhale, and looked up at the ceiling, as if to thank the Lord.

'Well, we're safe. We're all safe. Breathe … After all, the man had no enemies…' There was a definite hint of sarcasm in her voice and was that a smile forming at the edge of her mouth?

'I can't believe I have to plan another funeral now,' said Kristin, as lightly as she dared. 'Just as well I kept those shoes Beebs.' The ice was broken. The friends giggled nervously. 'I'm at a total loss as to what to do,' continued Kristin. 'But people will want to say goodbye.'

'Will they really though?' Hailey hadn't looked up as she said this. But she had said it. Eleanor could barely believe her ears, raising a hand to her mouth to stop herself from gasping.

'Well, it has transpired that tributes to Jeremy have been strangely thin on the ground,' said Vanessa. 'People have been so kind to Krissie, club members and whatnot expressing their condolences – but very few have passed comment on Jeremy himself.'

Kristin started sobbing.

'I loved him, of course I did,' she cried while Vanessa rubbed her back, 'but it's only since he's been gone that I have realised how deceitful and manipulative he was. He *did* have enemies;

we all know it. Oh, God, what shall I do about this funeral? You will all be there, won't you? You can even wear all the same outfits as you did to Petunia's...'

'There is no way that I would be there – not for him – if it wasn't for you,' said Bibi. 'But for you I would do anything. Let's get it done. As fast as possible. How can we help?'

'Do you really mean that? That you wouldn't go to his funeral?'

'Kristin, I was no fan of that man. No fan at all.'

'I know he was difficult, and I know there was some murkiness to do with Garrett and the business.'

'It wasn't that,' said Bibi. Her face was like stone now. Quite the opposite of the Bibi Eleanor had known up until this moment. 'It was the flirting, the bribes, the assault – sexual and physical.'

Bibi's voice, which had started out quiet, almost breathy, was now hoarse as the tears seemed to come and she rasped to try to hold them back.

'I never cared about the money. And I don't think Garrett would do either. But until the day he died, Jeremy was threatening me – that he'd tell you, or Garrett or whoever that we'd been having an affair. Which we hadn't. Of course we hadn't. But he made me feel like I was going mad, like I had done something wrong. The gaslighting, the menace, the little comments at every opportunity. It wore me down.'

What was she saying? wondered Eleanor. If she hadn't just heard the police confirm that there was no case to answer, she might have heard this as a confession. No one else seemed to think so though. Hailey reached out and put an arm in the small of her friend's back, rubbing it gently as she tried to quell her sobs.

288

'My God,' whispered Kristin. 'I knew there was something going on with the money, but this – I had no idea.' There was a pause. The police car revved outside and pulled out of the car park.

'Really? Did you really have no idea?' said Vanessa quietly. 'I think you're doing yourself a disservice.'

'What do you mean?'

'Even I saw the credit card bills stuffed into random kitchen drawers, him jumping to get to the mail first, paperwork not quite adding up in the pro shop. I don't believe you didn't know.'

'It's not that I didn't know, I suppose. It's just that it was all too much to accept. I didn't know how much to fix it and I couldn't see a way out. I couldn't believe that there might be a way out... until...'

'Did you tell the police about any of this?' asked Vanessa softly, her hand now resting on her sister's hand.

'I didn't, I never said a thing,' said Bibi, urgently. 'I wanted to protect you. I wanted you to be free of him!'

Vanessa slowly looked from Bibi to her sister. 'I meant you, Krissie. Did you tell the police about any of this?' She shook her head. 'So there really is no case to answer.'

Had Vanessa said that to herself? wondered Eleanor.

'Look, it's a real tragedy that this poisoning – however it happened – dodgy pipe work in the shower block or arsenic in his water bottle – got him. But, Krissie, you mustn't feel guilty about having worried about the financial side of things. You mustn't feel that you betrayed him in any way by being terrified. His behaviour was out of control.'

Vanessa was walking now, pacing between the sofas, back and forth. None of the other three women seemed to have flinched but all Eleanor could think of was the specificity of that water bottle comment. He always had that bottle with him. *Always*.

'And look at Bibi.' Vanessa was in her flow now. 'It wasn't just you that he was hurting. And it wasn't that this was new behaviour even. The rumours about him back in the day were ghastly – impulsive tantrums, reckless spending, match fixing. I thought maybe it was jealousy and didn't pay much attention. It's only recently that I realised that they were more than rumours. It wasn't on you to change him: he had always been who he was. And it was never going to end, not unless…'

'…someone stepped in,' Hailey interjected. She had been silent for so long that Eleanor had almost forgotten she was there. But the implication that someone had 'stepped in' seemed as stark as Vanessa's comments.

'Someone needed to,' she now said. 'He came so close to destroying Justin's spirit – and at a time when his mind and his body were was so frail, when he has so little time left. He manipulated Justin, pretended to be a friend and conned him out of a small fortune. And he did it all while threatening to ruin me by exposing my medicinal cannabis remedies to the police.'

The others were staring at her aghast, Hailey's generally reserved nature giving greater gravity to the clear disgust in her voice.

'I'm so sorry, Krissie – I know it must be hard to hear, and I do know it's not your fault. We've all seen the way he has gaslit you too. But I'm with Bibi: if not for you, I wouldn't be attending the funeral. And I'm glad someone – no – something happened.'

'I had no idea, Hailey, I'm so sorry,' said Bibi. 'I wish we could have talked more. And I bet Justin wishes he *had* ordered a bloody poisoned cake now!'

Hailey shot her a glance. Eleanor was unsure how to interpret it.

'Look, we all know it wasn't that cake now anyway. I guess he had been ingesting small amounts of arsenic from somewhere for a while. And in the end his body couldn't take it any more.' Kristin's eyes were glazed now. Eleanor wasn't sure if she'd cope with any more revelations.

'I don't think we need to dwell on his death,' said Vanessa, interrupting her. 'He was on a dangerous path, with us in his way, and now that's all over. Let's plan a funeral that will work for you, and for Freddie, and of course we'll all be there. To celebrate your freedom, even if we're dressed to grieve.'

Bibi was nodding vociferously. Hailey smiled at them all.

Eleanor thought of all the times she had seen Vanessa by the side of the court while Jeremy was coaching, sitting by the water bottles. She thought of Jeremy swigging, and what might have been in the water – in this case that the police had decided to leave well alone because they thought there was no motive.

'Thank you, my darlings,' said Kristin. 'You're so right. We mustn't dwell on how he died. We must plan a funeral, and find a way to help Freddie remember the best in his father.'

'Yes,' said Hailey. 'I am sure we can find a way to do that.'

'Agreed,' said Bibi. 'You have a future now, and you must enjoy it.'

'Exactly,' said Vanessa. 'You and Freddie are safe now. And you're always going to be able to tell him that his death wasn't foul play. It was just an accident.'

'Yes, his death was just an accident,' repeated Kristin. 'Wasn't it?'

The four women looked at each other. And just for a second, Eleanor saw the slightest flash of a secret understanding pass between them. And she realised that there had been nothing accidental about Jeremy's death at all.

But what she also knew, with complete conviction, was that she would never tell a soul – their secret was safe with her.

Author's Note

If, like me, you enjoy a good 'who dunnit?' I hope you enjoy reading *Game, Set & Murder*. Set in the tennis world – of course – in a fairly prestigious club in the South of England, it focuses on the championship-winning ladies' team. And talking of a winning team, I would never have got this to publication without the expertise and guidance of a number of special people.

To my friend Alexandra Heminsley, and Charlotte Mursell, deputy publisher at Orion, for their incredible support in developing the storyline and dealing with all of my unforced errors (pun intended). To Elizabeth Allen, my publicist at Orion, for masterminding the promotional activity, to Dan Mogford for his wonderful cover design and to Lucy Cameron, the marketing guru who has created so many fun opportunities to showcase the novel.

And, lastly, to my literary agent, Kerr MacRae, for gently but efficiently weaving everyone and everything together with the Orion team.

Credits

Judy Murray and Orion Fiction would like to thank everyone at Orion who worked on the publication of *Game, Set & Murder* in the UK.

Editorial
Charlotte Mursell

Copy editor
Francine Brody

Proofreader
Holly Kyte

Audio
Paul Stark
Louise Richardson

Editorial Management
Anshuman Yadav
Snigdha Koirala
Charlie Panayiotou
Jane Hughes
Bartley Shaw

Contracts
Dan Herron
Ellie Bowker
Oliver Chacón

Design
Charlotte Abrams-Simpson

Finance
Jasdip Nandra
Nick Gibson
Sue Baker

Marketing
Lucy Cameron

Publicity
Elizabeth Allen

Production
Katie Horrocks
Ameenah Khan

Rights
Rebecca Folland
Tara Hiatt
Ben Fowler
Alice Cottrell
Ruth Blakemore
Marie Henckel

Sales
Catherine Worsley
Esther Waters
Victoria Laws
Rachael Hum
Ellie Kyrke-Smith
Frances Doyle
Georgina Cutler

Operations
Group Sales Operations team